The Wild Birds

The Wild Birds

Emily Strelow

A Genuine Rare Bird Book
Los Angeles, Calif.

A Genuine Rare Bird Book

A Rare Bird Book | Rare Bird Books
453 South Spring Street, Suite 302
Los Angeles, CA 90013
rarebirdbooks.com

Trade Paperback Edition

A Rare Bird Book | Rare Bird Books Subsidiary Rights Department,
453 South Spring Street, Suite 302,
Los Angeles, CA 90013.

Set in Minion
Printed in the United States

PAPERBACK ISBN: 9781644282007

10 9 8 7 6 5 4 3 2 1

Publisher's Cataloging-in-Publication data
Names: Strelow, Emily, author.
Title: The Wild birds / Emily Strelow.
Description: First Hardcover Edition | A Genuine Rare Bird Book | New York,
NY; Los Angeles, CA: Rare Bird Books, 2018.
Identifiers: ISBN 9781945572753
Subjects: LCSH Families—Northwest, Pacific—Fiction. | Northwest, Pacific—
Fiction. | Family—Fiction. | Coming of age—Fiction. | BISAC FICTION /
General
Classification: LCC PS3619.T74558 W55 2018 | DDC 813.6—dc23

For Andrew, Lewis, and Zephyr,
my stars and my map.

The trees and the muscled mountains are the world—but not the world apart from man—the world and man—the one inseparable unit man and his environment. Why they should ever have been understood as being separate I do not know.

—John Steinbeck (from his notebook
while writing *East of Eden*)

I like to define biology as the history of the earth and all its life—past, present, and future.

—Rachel Carson, Humane Biology Projects

Trees, trees, beautiful trees.

—Brown Creeper (*Certhia americana*)

Concatenation

Burning Woods, Oregon, 1994

THE NORTHERN HARRIER FLEW higher than usual above the fence line, catching an updraft off the hillside and letting the warm air loft her into the sky. Below, in the Willamette Valley, an orchard-bordered grassland gave way to the foothills of a small mixed conifer forest. From the great height where the tawny bird hung as though paused, a thin patchwork of forest extended below in a jagged line westward toward the ocean—the slimmest of remnant green corridors for the songbirds, insects, or hard-pressed large mammals to travel from the valley all the way to the Pacific. The bird let her senses take in the immensity, as it is not just humans who find pleasure in regarding the expanse of water at the edge of land. Beating hearts are mapped by this longing for the infinite. She let the wind carry her as high as it could and then slowly glided back toward the earth. Her ears picked up the rustle of life below, and she was hungry.

At the back of their filbert orchard, Alice and her teenage daughter, Lily, played a game to pass the time as they crouched in the messy, expansive garden pulling weeds. The game was called Mary-for-Jesus and the rules were simple: swap out the name of a male protagonist for a female in a notorious work of literature and imagine how the plot would change. Mary-for-Jesus. Humila-for-Humbert-Humbert. These moments discussing books, reimagining the canon, marked increasingly rare peace between the two.

"Okay. How about *Nineteen Eighty-Four*?" Alice started.

"Let's see…Winston. Winston." Lily stabbed her trowel deep into the earth to get at a dandelion taproot. "Winnie."

"Nice!" Alice threw a handful of rush weed onto the pile. "And how do you think Winnie would rewrite history?"

"Less party line, more panty line?" Lily inspected the dirt under her nails, the dark brown loam filling in the gaps where her black nail polish had chipped off.

"That's the spirit," Alice said. "One point for you. Maybe not a Camille Paglia–approved answer, but I'll take it."

"Whatever, feminazi." Lily ducked a flung dirt clod and cut some arugula with scissors, starting a pile to take into the house later. She turned to her mother. "How about *Lord of the Flies*? If those boys' mothers had anything to say about it, that conch shell would totally be intact at the end of the book."

"Exactly," Alice laughed. "Rogerina-for-Roger." One point for Alice—not that anyone was really keeping score. "And if London's protagonist in *To Build a Fire* were female, she could probably will that fire into existence with her mind, then convince the fire it was its own idea to start in the first place."

Lily paused, trying to recall the name of the character. "No-name-dude-for-no-name-lady," she offered. Another point for Lily. She turned the scissors on a slug and snipped it in half without remorse, leaving the carcass in the garden as if to warn off others, then gathered the rocket and stuffed the spicy greens into her overalls pocket. Alice threw a handful of weeds in the general direction of the wheelbarrow and said, "How about…"

"How about we are done with this game?" In the way teenagers are like wolves, Lily cut her off, turning suddenly impatient. "I have to go meet people. Plus, I'm ahead." She smiled a canine grin she liked to call the "grim reaper."

Alice blew a fluff of dandelion seeds in her direction.

"Mom. We're just going to have to pull more weeds if you do that."

"How else would I get to spend time with my beautiful and gracious daughter anymore?"

The barely warm rays of spring sunshine bore down on the soggy valley, lifting steam off every green surface as Lily and Alice gathered up armloads of the uprooted weeds and piled them into an ancient, rusted wheelbarrow. The wheelbarrow could have been any color once, but no one who might remember was still alive to name it. Some thirty feet away, on the property line of their hazelnut orchard where the razed and tilled land gave way to a stand of smallish Douglas fir, one of their barn cats leapt from behind the corner of the old, peeling blue storage shed, chasing a mouse. There was a splash of blood from the pursued rodent on Fickle Cat's front paw and the flayed mouse tumbled over itself in the dirt and grass ahead of the predator. Just before going in for the deathblow, Fickle made her singular mewl—a honk like a groggy drunk—then bolted off into the long grass, abandoning her prey. Busy watching the cat and mouse, mother and daughter failed to see the harrier flying low on the left, just grazing the sedge with the tips of her wings. The striking raptor looked disheveled and half plucked in her worn winter plumage. She rose and circled the ground a few feet above the mouse before dropping with precision. Alice set down her trowel and drew closer, compelled, her long, strawberry blonde braid sliding over her back and off her shoulder as she crouched.

"Lil," she whispered. "Come look."

The harrier consumed the finally, truly dead mouse, taking strips from the flesh with her long, hooked beak. As they approached within twenty feet of the bird, something strange became apparent. Where there should have been golden, knowing raptor eyeballs were two empty, healed-over sockets.

"She's blind," Alice whispered. "Hunting blind. Unbelievable."

At the sound of Alice's whisper, the bird held her head at attention and rustled her large wings, the smallest of small intestines dangling from her beak, then returned to her meal and let the two watch her briefly before swallowing the rest whole and flying off, her crop bulging. She skimmed the grass and disappeared behind the pressboard skeletons of future tract housing on the adjacent acreage, stealthy as a serpent's retreat.

After dumping the weeds in the compost, Alice and Lily walked the quarter mile back to the house through their hazelnut groves. Alice was alive with speculation. She thought that maybe the harrier was able to hunt blind because she had facial disks like owls that allowed her to hear her prey more easily than other raptors. She thought that maybe Fickle Cat, never a particularly adept huntress, had been inadvertently helping the harrier survive by providing prewounded prey. She thought that maybe—and for this she raised her eyebrows and turned to look into her daughter's eyes—they had on their hands some sort of *divine* creature. The manic intensity in her mother's voice made Lily brace for a fall. She knew this phase well.

The word "divine" was secularly defined in their house but used often. Wine was divine, film was divine, books and music were divine. These moments received the heavenly, swirling crescendo of her mother's contagious enthusiasm. Lily's outfit from her first day of high school of ripped jeans and an old Pendleton wool shirt, or her black nail polish and matching lipstick and attitude—not so divine, according to Alice. Lily's sass about her mother's opinion on such matters, also less than divine. This decrescendo could be steep. For Alice, divinity was really a matter of opinion, and people should understand that on her farm, in her world, her opinion was the only one that counted. The orchestra of whim and wonderment was not to be conducted by anyone other than herself.

At the suggestion of a divine creature, Lily simply nodded with a clenched jaw and said, "Divinity is really in the eye of the beholder. Isn't that what you always say?"

Alice smiled and put her arm around her much smaller daughter as they walked back toward the house. Something caught Alice's eye and she stopped to check out a small oval-shaped black sore on the trunk of one of the hazelnut trees, her mood shifting further out of orbit.

"God*damn* it. Damn fucking dammit." She turned to her daughter with her finger still on the sore. "This fungus is going to kill my trees and then me, I swear."

"Yes, you do swear. That will be a dollar twenty-five since noon," Lily said. "Leave it. Come inside and eat something." The turn in her mother's voice released a familiar turn in Lily's stomach. The pitch up in tone indicated she would soon be swinging wildly down from her happy place, and the mere thought of it made Lily's shoulders tense up.

"*Dam*mit all." Alice sighed as they approached the old two-story white house, listing on its foundation a little more every year. She waved her daughter into the house without really looking at her. "I just want to put out some oranges for the tanagers, then I'll be right in."

"Bird nerd your heart out," Lily said, letting the screen door slam behind her.

Alice picked up the oranges she'd set on the deck railing and sliced them with a deer-dressing knife she produced from her pocket, the blade flicking open with dangerous grace. She pulled the flat of the blade across her arm, the risk of the blade pushing into her skin a familiar, comforting thrill. She then halved the oranges and speared them on prominent nails sticking out from the side of the deck. The stabbing of fruit flesh released some of the pressure building in her brain.

"I saw the first western tanager of the season yesterday," Alice offered to no one in particular, as though idle chitchat could stave off the inevitable storm churning in her neurons. She punctured another orange half hard, then glanced around, as if the brightly colored migratory birds were waiting in the trees to rush the oranges.

"You feed the birds, Mom, but forget to feed yourself. It's messed up!" Lily yelled through the screened-in kitchen window.

"Whaaat? Can't hear you!" Alice lied, splitting the last orange.

Fickle Cat slunk up from underneath the deck through a broken, rotting slat and rubbed herself on the doorframe, still hungry. Because barn cats are regularly taken by coyotes in the night, Alice decided they should always name the creatures _____ Cat, as if the "Cat" suffix were some sort of acknowledgement that these animals were one paw in this world, one paw in the next. She let her daughter name them all, and in Lily's fifteen years of life they had gone through Moo Cat, White Cat, Fatface Cat, Stinky Cat, Chicken Cat, Zombie Cat, and now finally Fickle Cat and Concatenation Cat (named after the kitten found its way to their door during one of Lily's PSAT study sessions). Though, Alice always let Lily choose the name, the attached "Cat" was not up for debate. "A cat is a cat is a cat," Alice's mother used to say when a barn cat went missing.

It used to be that no one in the family was allowed to name them. Animals were not bound for the kingdom of heaven, so why should they be christened with names? But after Alice's parents died in quick succession, leaving a young Alice and even younger Lily alone on the farm to fend for themselves, the changing names acted as a sort of abacus ticking off Lily's awkward progress toward adulthood—from Moo to Fickle and everything in between.

In the kitchen, Lily made sure her mother couldn't see her, took four dollars' worth of quarters from a jar on the shelf, and pocketed the change to buy cigarettes later. The small thievery always elicited a thrill, a shudder, in Lily's core.

Lily cut up their early spring harvest, the arugula she'd collected from the garden, and wilted it in a pan with leftover roasted potatoes in some fresh sage and butter, then cracked a duck egg over the top, adding a little hard cheese at the end. The plate was steaming on the table when Alice came in.

"Eat," Lily ordered. Both girls were a little surprised to hear the forceful intonation in the way Lily said this. In some moments she could sound just like Alice, but with a *force majeure*.

"Yes, ma'am, your highness." Alice took a seat. "But come eat with me."

"Already did. The food's salted and peppered, but there's more if you want it. I'm going out. You owe me a dollar twenty-five, no, dollar fifty. Don't forget." Lily glanced toward the large glass jar full of quarters on the wall among the preserved beets and beans with a sign reading *I SWEAR I didn't mean it*. The price was one quarter per transgression. More than once Lily had imagined lugging a red wagon full of jarred quarters into the financial aid office at the university. At that point she might have enough for, maybe, a half semester of classes. Or if life continued on status quo, she could just keep smoking cigs for a year or two.

"Stay." Alice bordered on pleading.

"Can't," Lily said, dabbing her black lipstick on a napkin and checking her reflection in the hallway mirror.

"Please?"

"Don't, Mom." Lily looked annoyed. "I. Have. Plans."

Alice sat in front of the plate and whispered an almost inaudible "fine" after her daughter had already left the house.

The still-young Alice, at thirty-one, looked like a child in some ways and acted like one in several others. Her long, strawberry blonde braid and thin frame led people to regularly mistake the duo for sisters, or cousins. Lily was even lighter in coloring than her mother, her pigment-poor skin almost that of an apparition. Her curly, fine hair bordered on white, her veins a visible blue underneath the surface of thin, pale skin. It bothered Lily that anyone on the street had a window to her inner workings, that map of blue pumping blood intended to be understood only by doctors and deities. But her natural patina paired with her requisite black lipstick left Lily resembling the walking dead, and that's just the way she liked it. She respected all things zombie.

Alice sat alone thinking about the fungus that had killed off half her hazelnut crop last year, leaving them almost destitute, facing off with the food prepared by her increasingly surly teenage daughter. She sat and tried to forget about the black spots on her trees, the rotting floorboards and sagging foundation of her house, her daughter's growing disdain, and the dark pit inside her that felt like it was trying to turn her inside out. She got up and poured herself a large mason jar of cheap wine, then, finally, once the wine hit her blood, she ate.

That evening, Lily woke in the middle of the night to the sound of glass breaking against metal and her mother's howl trailing off into the quiet night. The drawn out, "Fuuuuuck yooooooooou, asshooooooole," echoed faintly on the hills by far away neighbor hounds. From the second-story window, Lily recognized Alice's on-and-off boyfriend

Randy's old Ford truck hauling up the dirt driveway with one taillight newly busted out. His part-wolf mutt Party Dog turned quick circles in the bed of the pickup before settling in a corner just as the one red light disappeared behind a bend of alders. Down on the front porch, Lily saw her mother sitting on the steps with her head in her hands, her reddish mane a tangled mess, glass shards littering the driveway, catching light like a flattened disco ball in the moonlight. Lily decided not to go downstairs. She was familiar with this scene and there was really nothing she could do. Instead, she lay in bed with the spotlight moon fixed on her face, listening to her mother's soft sobs drift up. She didn't even close the drapes to block the light. If she concentrated hard enough, maybe her flesh would actually turn to stone.

"That'll be fifty cents," she whispered. "But who's counting."

∾

IN THE MORNING, LILY walked into the kitchen to find her mother vacuuming a hole in the wall with one hand, a large jar of white wine in the other. Alice wore a diaphanous nightgown that, with the strong morning light pouring in behind her, left little to the imagination. Alice was thin but strong, her muscles taut from a lifetime of harvests and other manual labor, her limbs and core perhaps a little too lean from malnutrition, resulting more from absentmindedness than vanity. Tufts of fine hair glowed from between her legs, under her arms, and tapered to fuzz on her long legs. Her eyes were rimmed in pink as she vacuumed the wall, her irises an urgent seafoam color they turned only when she'd been swimming in chlorine or crying.

"Breakfast of champions," Lily yelled over the sound of the vacuum, nodding at the almost empty magnum of wine on the table.

"I'm glad you found the Vonnegut I left out for you, honey." She flashed her daughter an exaggerated thumbs-up before returning to vacuuming the wall. "These damn ladybugs hatched in the walls. They were everywhere this morning. Literally covering the table."

"Can't hardly blame the ladybugs, now can you?" Lily said, quieter than before.

"Whaaat?"

"Nothing."

Alice turned off the vacuum and the last few ladybugs left in the long black tube clacked against the plastic, two flying out from the end of the hose and circling her head like a halo. She swatted at the bugs, knocking herself off balance for a moment before removing the vacuum bag. The bag pulsed, alive with the hundreds of bugs ticking inside. She placed it on top of the garbage under the sink and changed to a new bag, taking the opportunity to refill her wine jar and address her daughter before she could slink out the back door.

"So, I have some news for you," she sighed dramatically. "Randy and I broke up."

"Shocker," Lily said as she cracked two duck eggs into a hot pan.

"That damn wolf-mutt Party Dog attacked Donnie Jr."

"What?!" Lily looked up, wrested from complacency by concern for her pet duck. "Is she okay?"

"She'll be fine. It's just a little scratch on her neck. We pulled the dog off in time and I dressed the scratch and put the cone the vet gave us on her to prevent her picking at it with her bill. So, anyhow, just thought you should know. She might not be laying for a while if she's too stressed out. We'll have to trade for eggs with the Wilkes or something."

"I always hated that dog."

Randy owned a bar in town called the Re-Bar that filled nightly with farmhands and construction workers. When he started dating Alice, he let her start a monthly poetry reading that baffled many members of the community and delighted a handful of others. He even bought a little beret for Party Dog and everything. Back when Party Dog was just a puppy, he taught her to shotgun a beer as a sort of perverse parlor trick. The stunt was a big hit with customers until Party Dog developed a problem and started turning surly, nipping more than one customer's heels when they wouldn't share their libation. Randy stopped letting her drink and kept her behind the bar to limit his liability as a business owner, but really she just turned into a dry drunk—nasty and without an ounce of humor to her disposition. She would sulk behind the bar looking daggers at anyone who addressed her by name. Party Dog, as it turned out, was not such a party after all.

"Dogs are a direct reflection their owners, you know," Alice said.

"True story," Lily sighed.

"So anyhow, after that mutt went after Donnie Jr., all hell broke loose and Randy and I started going at it, too. But it wasn't just the dog, of course. It was a looong time coming."

"No kidding." Lily returned to her egg frying, feeling herself about as social as Party Dog.

"That's one particular mistake I won't be making again," Alice said, her voice rising louder and higher as she flipped on the switch to the vacuum and continued to suck the little red, freshly hatched ladybugs from their brand-new world to an even newer and blacker one.

"Déjà vu," Lily said quietly to the egg pan. She pulled some toast and buttered it, put one of the eggs on the table, and nodded at her mother.

"Eat. Join me, honey." Alice wasn't asking.

"Can't. I'm meeting Sarah."

And with that, Lily grabbed her own egg sandwich and left the kitchen with its lingering aroma of alcohol and eggs mixed with the pungent funk of thousands of newly hatched ladybugs. If Lily were to bottle the scent and name it, like they do in fancy department stores, she would call it "Despair" and use the torso of a thin, hairy, naked woman as its vessel.

"Be home by dinner!" Alice yelled, but her daughter had already slipped through the door and off the back porch.

As Lily crossed the field toward the small housing development, she saw the blind harrier skimming low over the grass. The raptor kited for a moment, then landed hard into the grass, rising with empty talons before flying off into the distance. To Lily, the bird looked fatigued. She wondered how long a blind bird that size could possibly live. At the fence dividing their property from the new development, she rustled at the base of the fence post and retrieved an old rusty tin from under a patch of loose, wild grass. From it, she took out a packet of cigarettes from a ziplock and slipped one from the package, pocketing the rest. Alice would kill her if she knew. Crossing into the taupe wasteland, she ducked under some construction tape to enter the largest of the unfinished pressboard palaces, a cigarette dangling from her lips like Gloria in *The Lost Weekend,* Lily and Sarah's favorite movie.

"Don't be ridic," Lily said seductively into the dark room of their usual meeting place, the cigarette stuck to her lip.

"Don't be ridic," Sarah squealed from a dark interior corner of the house, jumping out to greet her friend.

"I mean, for cereal." Lily hugged Sarah and sighed. "Mom's on a total bender again."

"Dang. What happened?" Sarah accepted a cigarette from her friend and lit it with a pink, unicorn-stickered lighter. She blotted her matching black lipstick on the filter.

"Randy happened, I guess. But how many times can she freak out on different dudes before she notices, maybe, some sort of pattern?"

"Yeah, for real. Adults are so asinine sometimes. My parents totally hate each other but pretend they don't for our sake. As if we can't tell as they stab, stab, stab that salad that they'd rather be stabbing each another."

From the shadows, a figure stepped out into the light.

"Fuck! You scared the shit out of me," Lily said to the figure as Sarah giggled.

"That's some ugly talk for a pretty lady," the figure said, moving closer.

"You know Max," Sarah said. "You chicken shit."

At the realization that it was their classmate, Max, who had called her a pretty lady, who moved his being closer to her being, Lily's neck reddened, waves of pink moving up her translucent skin. She felt like an octopus standing there, emoting waves and colors for all the world to see. Thankfully the light in the bare-beamed construction site was dim.

"Well, if it isn't the entirety of the Philomath High science club in one place," Max said with mock surprise. "Meeting in secret to plan our world domination through the fabulous world of fusion?"

Max was the most handsome nerd Lily had ever met. Half Siletz Indian with a long, perfect nose and dark hazel eyes, he understood molecular science like it was Disney. Lily was more into ecology, and Sarah was smart but mostly just kind of a punk. Sarah, at sixteen, already had five tattoos she said she'd sweet-talked her way into receiving for free from various admirers in Eugene. Lily suspected she had done more than sweet-talk to get them. While science didn't really get Sarah going as much as standard forms of teenage deviancy, Lily was her best friend, and she thought Max was hot, so she attended science club on Wednesdays after school to be with them.

Max had always been kind of a nobody until one of the football jocks called him a "Redskin Redneck" early in the school year. After saying nothing to the jock in the moment, that afternoon Max donned full native regalia with an eagle-feather-and-fur headpiece, a brightly colored beaded shawl, and little moccasins. As the team prepared for an important homecoming game, they laughed at him as they did drills and called him an "asshole," an "injun," and a "half-breed." They flung whatever insults they could get their dirty hands on as they paused between running lines. Max ignored them as he padded in the dry fall grass around the football field doing a rain dance, singing low and looking up at the skies. That night in the fourth quarter, with the game tied, the sky threaded gray, then black, and poured down on the field in sheets of rain. Lightning struck one of the goal posts and a cheerleader who had been high-kicking a little too close to the pole got knocked unconscious. The game ended early, a draw. After that, no one made fun of Max—in fact, there was a whiff of fear among those in the student body. Jocks offered him seats and patted him on the back for no real reason. Lily suspected that Max's revenge was sweetest not only because he had called on ancient gods to do his bidding but because he had secretly called to check the weather graphs at NOAA. Max had white privilege and bias dialed and was an ardent believer in the power of both science and spirits.

As the trio walked around the half-built houses, they speculated on what would go where.

"This is where they'll keep their Jet Skis and other superfluous shit," Max offered.

"That's where the Jacuzzi bath will go," Lily said.

"For the wild orgies," Sarah added. Sarah was always full of life lessons.

After half a pack of cigarettes and a few hours of aimless wandering, Sarah announced she had to go.

"Sunday dinner," she said with a fake smile. "Everybody sit around looking miserable *together* now."

"See you at school," Max said. "Stay strong." Sarah gave him a lingering peck on the cheek and Lily felt something like bile, or jealousy, rise in her throat. When she and Max were alone, they sat on the front steps of the house looking out over the sea of tan pressboard. The effect was that of a giant, poorly placed, wrinkled Band-Aid laid out over an otherwise wild field.

"You ever wonder why we, I mean man, generally feel the need to dominate the landscape instead of just live with it?" Max asked after a moment.

"Yeah. I get you. Other species seem to have it all figured out. I mean, look at foxholes, beaver dams, bird's nests," Lily said.

"Exactly. They say it has something to do with thumbs, but I reckon it's more about hair."

"How's that now?" Lily did her best Randy impression in a deep backwoods accent.

"Like, because we don't have hair on most of our bodies, we're always trying to find ways to cover up. Our outfits have just gotten more and more elaborate until they look like factories and train tracks and skyscrapers."

"How very scientific of you, friend." Lily squinted her eyes at him and wrinkled her brow into a farm of furrows.

Max laughed and put his warm arm around Lily and she thought maybe she would like to wear *him* as an outfit, the blood rising again in her neck and down to her fingers and toes.

"Hey," he said, "I'm sorry to hear about your mom's bender. She seems like a cool lady from what I can tell. She has that old aqua Chevy truck with the bumper sticker that says, *A Woman Needs a Man Like...*" he trailed off.

"*...a Fish Needs a Bicycle*, yeah. Brilliant, isn't it?"

"Is she a lesbian or something?"

"Nah. She's kind of a slut, to be honest."

"Lesbians can be sluts," Max offered. "Just not in Burning Woods." They sat there for a moment to ponder this important idea.

"Well, I'll see you tomorrow in physics, right?" Max asked, peeling himself off Lily's arm, giving her a little pat on the shoulder.

"You bet your quarks, buddy."

Did I really just say that? Lily wondered as she made her way home through the grass. *You bet your quarks, buddy?* She stopped to put the cigarettes back in their tin at the base of the fence and rubbed some rose essential oil on her wrists, fingers, and neck to cover the smell of cigarettes. It wasn't even seven but it was already getting dark. She checked in on Donnie Jr., who looked miserable and ashamed of her little neck cone, sitting morosely in a corner of her pen by the kiddie pool, which was growing a significant layer of green slime on it. Lily reminded herself to clean the pool that week as she clicked her tongue gently at her bummed-out duck.

Inside the house, she heard the ladybugs ticking away inside their vacuum bag prisons. She looked around for her mom before taking all three bags outside, slipping the deer-dressing knife lying on the table into her pocket. She hauled the bags out to the tree with the pockmarks of spreading fungus. She switched the knife open, drawing the flat end along her forearm to clean it first like she always did, then slit the bags lengthwise with the precision of a surgeon. The sleepy bugs emerged, lining the slit with their red, tentative bodies before the first one took flight. It was as if the moonlight reanimated their bodies. They followed the leader in a perfect line and trailed off like little soldiers of fortune into the sky, out into the unknown with carnal appetites for aphid blood. To Lily's eyes they formed a perfect circle in the sky, like synchronized swimmers, then moved into a hypnotist's swirl before finally dispersing. A truck rumbled out on the highway in an unusually loud way as the bugs disappeared to far corners of the orchard. After the last ladybug had disappeared into the night, everything was quiet. Lily put the knife away. She must have smoked too many cigarettes or something because her eyes were playing tricks on her. She felt pretty sure there was no such thing as a ladybug hoedown.

Back inside, Lily found her mother passed out drunk in a fetal ball on the living room couch. She found the patchwork blanket her grandma made when she was born, the one with various animals and plants and patterns living in harmony. "Your own little Eden," Grandma liked to say when Lily was little, "where the lions lie next to the lambs." Alice would pull her aside after such comments and whisper, "You know that in real life the lion would eat the lamb, right? No denying that fact." It all left a young Lily a tad confused as to what was fact and what was fiction.

Lily pulled the blanket over her mother and briefly inspected the paisley skies above a giraffe and bluebird duo before sitting in the chair facing the fireplace that once upon a time had belonged to her grandfather. The only light on in the room was the accent light her mother had installed to highlight her most prized possession: an antique wrought silver box engraved with vines and flowers, with thick beveled glass and sun-bleached pink velvet inside, the threadbare velvet holding up an almost full collection of emptied bird eggs. The antique was over a hundred years old, and as Lily stood in the dark, fixed on the glowing speckled orbs, she wondered how a thing so fragile could last as long as it had. Glancing at her sotted mom shifting under the blanket of Eden, she wondered how anyone or anything could stand the pressure of merely existing any longer than fifteen years.

Devil's Teeth

C LOUDS OF SEABIRDS ROSE and fell back to the steep barren rock cliffs, disturbed as Olive set out on the narrow footpath from Beacon Rock, the highest point on the island where the lighthouse stood, to the rabbit traps a half mile away. As she passed by the birds, they squawked and clung to the rocky ledge, settling dark pear-shaped bodies back into the smooth granite divots that housed their green-and-brown speckled eggs. They reminded her of miniature penguins, these birds, with their slick black backs, white bellies, and long black beaks. They stretched themselves up on two feet and extended their long necks to check for potential predators before returning to their eggs, nudging the light green mottled shells deeper into their down to keep them warm. Gulls screamed above, waiting to plunder the smaller birds' nests next time they should be roused. The ruffling of black feathers and careful bird parenting were peaceful enough on the outside, but as Olive eyed the circling gulls, she was reminded that life was difficult to create and all too easy to erase.

The wicker basket, with its thick canvas strap slung low on Olive's hip, dug into her small shoulder. She held a brisk pace walking along in her boys' trousers, her legs skimming the short halophytic weeds growing along the path and gathering salted dew at the ankles. She had purchased the thick woolen trousers in San Francisco after arriving by train a month ago and couldn't quite get over the freedom of movement she felt wearing them. She did a little skip and skidded to a stop on the narrow path, surveying the land around her. The tallest plant she noted growing on the island was only a couple feet high or so. Mostly the islands loomed brown and rocky, with crags dotted by short succulents, weeds, and birds. Olive had never experienced a place so wet and treeless in her life. The whole island was laved in seawater and seemed to her as salted as a pile of mutton on holy day. She saw some small rabbits nibbling the weeds and took a breath in anticipation of what she would find in the traps around the bend. Death, that scythe-bearing barbarian, was ever present of late.

A month earlier, Olive had become an orphan at sixteen when her mother passed. After the modest funeral, she had gathered up her small bag of belongings, and, in accordance with her mother's final wishes, traveled west from Colorado to live with her aunt in San Francisco. But the aunt never appeared at the train station, nor could she be reached by telegraph or post. There was, in fact, no one to be found who had so much as *heard* of a Persephone Ellis. So, after two weeks of sleeping abreast three women in a cheap boarding house and roaming the streets entreating authorities to locate her aunt to no avail, Olive spent the last of her small inheritance money on fine boys' clothing and sought employment as a male.

What brought Olive to this decision was a convergence of events involving a daylong stroll around San Francisco's Market District. There were fishmongers, produce sellers with piles of mysterious fruits, the jingling trappings of horses, superb carriages thronging the streets, and hardworking people with an air of perseverance and success. They seemed a fast folk, these San Franciscans, most everyone walking, talking, and doing business with greater haste than back on the planked sidewalks of Boulder. As Olive stood on a corner taking it all in, a tall, thin woman with bright makeup approached her.

"Are you lost, ducky?"

Startled, Olive met the woman's gaze.

"No. Just watching."

"You waiting for someone?"

"Of a sort," Olive said, lowering her eyes.

"Well, why don't you come with me on my errands, tell me your story." The tall woman tucked Olive directly under her arm and walked toward The Emporium, a store known for selling everything "from needles to anchors." The woman smelled dank, her personal earthy scent covered over by an almost sickly sweet aroma of rose. There was the tender interest of a predator in the way the woman held Olive's gaze.

The woman's name was Hazel and she was a prostitute. It came out naturally in conversation, as though it were between items on her sundries list: *Oats, soap, thread, by the by, I work in a brothel. Oh! Ducky, let's go see about those new citrus fruits just come to market from down south.* Olive stood frozen, tucked under Hazel's arm as she handled the strange grapefruits, stroking them with long fingers as she might a lover's back. Knowing the common plight of orphans, Olive's mother had held Olive's hand one night as she lay ailing and begged her to avoid the profession at all costs. So later in the day, as the fog rolled in over the harbor and the streetlamps were lit by the longest candleholder Olive had ever seen, when in the darkening street Hazel held Olive's chin and complimented her young skin and light eyes, telling her she could fetch a nice price with such assets and youth, Olive averted her gaze and quickly excused herself back to the boarding house. "Don't run, little rabbit!" Hazel had shouted after her.

Lying that night close among the snoring scullery maids and other lost souls, Olive felt a strong pull to find Hazel again and give in. After all, any kind of friend was better than none at all. But as she finally drifted off, she heard her mother again, who entreated, pleaded, and begged that she resist. *Be my strong and resourceful fawn. Make your mother proud.*

The next day, Olive emerged from the boarding house in the afternoon to go check the train platform one last time for her absent, and at this point verging on mythical, aunt. As she passed by the stand where Hazel had stroked the grapefruits so seductively, Olive saw a tall woman with long brown hair like Hazel's tuck into a small doorway on the arm of a much smaller and much fatter man. The man slapped the woman's rear end hard just before they disappeared from view into the exotically tiled hallway. Olive followed and slipped into the dark passage after them by a few paces, watching as they knocked on a carved wooden doorway. They slid through a curtain made of glass beads, the sound of the beads clinking against one another setting Olive's neck hair at attention. A strange smell hung heavy in the hallway, like burning herbs mixed with horse sweat. Peeking through the still-swaying beaded threshold, Olive saw Hazel from the front, reclined on a long velvet couch next to the portly man, also reclined. The man grabbed at Hazel's breast and Olive saw the briefest glimpse of her swaying flesh and exposed nipple before Hazel tucked it back into her dress and playfully slapped the man on his wrist. They were handed long, carved wooden pipes by a Chinese man with the longest braid Olive had ever seen on any human. She coughed at the thick smoke filling the air, and the Chinese man turned quickly and shouted something at her in a foreign tongue, and she met Hazel's lidded gaze only briefly before darting back down the hallway. She thought she heard "Ducky" faintly echo through the hall as she ran out into the confusing sun, dashing through the market and knocking a pyramid of oranges down as she turned a corner. She careened through the streets and right back to the boarding house, where, by some miracle, she was completely alone in the bedroom to catch her breath.

Staring herself down in the mirror, Olive staved off tears as she unbuttoned her mother's vanity case and extracted a large, sharp pair of engraved silver scissors. Desperation welled up in her, underpinned by all the love she had for her mother and the anger she felt toward a world that had taken her away too soon. She pulled her braids over her eyes and in the cool dark remembered her mother's hands pulling the pieces of hair tight into formation, but never so tight that the pain was unbearable. After Olive's braids were sorted, her mother always put her hands on her shoulders, squeezed gently, and said, "Now you can face the day proud, my love." The reverie ended as Olive let the braids fall and the harsh sunlight flooded her eyes with the reality of another calendar day. She could see the days ticking into the future like a line of motherless girls, walking into the unknown. *How many of those girls would be condemned to a life like Hazel's?* She looked hard at herself before letting the scissor blades slice through one of her braids, pausing in a liminal, lopsided state to observe herself as she might another. She cut off her other precious brown braid and tucked them both into her suitcase. She shook her head back and forth. There was a lightness in the shearing—like she had shed her mother's, Hazel's, and society's expectations. *This is a man's world*, she could hear her mother sigh, and Olive let out a little laugh at the thought. *So be it.* She would avoid the social pitfalls of being a young and destitute girl; she would henceforth be *Oliver.* As Oliver, she would face the day proud.

The next day, she bound her small breasts with the softest cloth she could afford and finished cropping her dark hair close to the scalp but for the front, which she smoothed with bear-fat pomade. Down at the tailor, she spent the last of her paltry inheritance on high-quality boys' wool trousers, a vest, and a cotton shirt before winding her way to the employment office. Outside, a gruff-looking man with wild salt-and-pepper hair was just posting a sign on the board: *Farallones Lighthouse Assistant needed. Hard work, low pay, on an isolated and barren island west of San Francisco.* Olive turned to the man posting the sign and said, "Sir, I'm your man," in her most confident voice.

A man of vanity and letters who believed himself above his post, Amos Richardson found himself strangely taken with this delicate boy's formal demeanor and fine suit, as well as his confidence and the fact he could read. Amos decided to employ him on a trial basis. He said, "You are a touch small, boy. But if you can work hard, you may do." Amos's last young assistant had fallen from the cliffs and broken both his legs.

They left for the Farallones the next morning before dawn on an old and mottled tugboat called the SS *Atticus* that marked their wake with a trail of black coal smoke. The deep devilish scent seemed to engulf Olive's entire past with its plumes. Standing on the bow, she let the strong breeze and the spray of the ocean renew her, her short past retreating with the smoke lingering above the city skyline as they passed through the wide, unobstructed bay.

"Oliver," Amos said, looming two heads taller than she on the deck of the ship as it heaved and fell on the open ocean. "Change becomes rest to the weary. Ready yourself for the greatest change you can fathom in the Farallones."

"Yes, sir," she said, thinking, *Change, indeed.*

It took the tug almost all day to travel the twenty-seven miles off the coast of San Francisco and reach the Farallones, with their jagged cliffs of granite stone rising from the sea like teeth from some mythic, sunken monster. "Some call them the Devil's Teeth," Richardson offered as the islands drew nearer, as though this might ease her anxiety. Olive felt a shiver up and down her back and her skin goose-pimpled from top to tail as the pointed rocks came into focus. As they approached the northwestward side, the tug seemed to recoil from nearing the cliff and the bow swung suddenly away from the islands as a horse might rear from fire, the captain and deckhands cranking and swearing to right the course. She heard one of the sailors yell something about the selkies at it again with their tricks as hundreds of sea lions that had been camouflaged by the rocks dove into the ocean all at once. This collection of asperous cliffs did not seem like the kind of place humans should dwell.

Olive, Richardson, and a deckhand from the *Atticus* transferred into a dinghy that listed back and forth in the waves like a toy and headed toward what Richardson called the "North Landing." They closed in on a sloped edge with what appeared to be a miniscule, flat landing. She almost expected Mr. Richardson to say, "Ladies first," and offer her a hand as they docked, but instead received a short and gruff, "Stay here. Watch how I jump and then do the same. Stay in the center of the boat for ballast. Use your back foot when you jump. Don't you dare tip over my boat." Richardson paused with one foot on the edge of the crosswise plank used as a seat in the dinghy, frozen in a running position and waiting until the boat rocked back toward the shore, before leaping over the three-foot gap between the dinghy and the rocks onto the small, six-foot-squared landing area. He held the rope in his hands to steady the boat and tied it off around an iron cleat camouflaged among the dark rock. Richardson asked the deckhand and Olive to toss him the ten large burlap packages tied with string. Each one felt as though it weighed at least half her own body weight, and she had to put all her strength into each throw so that their precious supplies might clear the gap and not end up sinking down into the dark blue-black water as shark food.

By the time the last package had been flung, she found herself winded, her muscles stinging, exhausted before she even made it onto land. Her time had come. She would have to leap the gap and summon all her courage to do it. A "leap of faith," her mother would have called it. She mimicked Richardson's running pose, one foot on the edge of the boat seat, weight in the center, one on the boat lip. The boat rocked back and forth, and back and forth again, and back and forth a third and fourth time, before Richardson finally screamed, "Now, boy!" and something in her body responded with uncanny strength as she flung herself up over the dark blue chasm and all the way to the back of the landing pad, palms flat against the sharp rocks. She pulled away from the rock wall and stood up, inspecting her new ragged stigmata, two bleeding palms, as Richardson erupted into laughter.

"Well you jump like a gazelle, boy. Next time try half speed."

They waved at the deckhand who untied the dinghy and was gone in a splash back to the tug. They gathered what they could carry and headed up the path. A ways up the steep path, they found a very old donkey tied to a rock, staring off into space like a poet.

"Good. Charles remembered to bring the burro down. He's another lighthouse assistant. It takes a team, here, to keep the great light shining brighter than the moon." Richardson took a deep breath of pride. "I wasn't sure if the ass would be here, as the eggers have been known to untie them just for sport."

"The who?"

"There are good eggers and bad eggers, Oliver. But mostly they are all rapscallions and layabouts. Remember that." Richardson looked up into the descending fog, as though there were more words of wisdom to be gleaned from the mists.

"Eggers?" Olive inquired, clarifying her question.

"Ah. You are green, aren't you? The eggers are the men who collect seabird eggs to sell back at market in San Francisco. There have been wars and shots fired over those eggs, I tell you, Oliver. I just leave them be for the most part and you should do the same."

"I see."

"Let's load this ass up and bring our supplies to the lighthouse quarters before the evening winds rise up."

They clambered up the steep cliff trail toward the lighthouse. The lighthouse appeared through the fog as an apparition at first, its giant beam of light cutting a rhythmic path in circles, lighting up a tunnel through the fog about once a minute. The winds picked up significantly as the sun set. They stood on the stoop and Richardson regarded the lighthouse and sighed. They had not even stepped foot inside before he pointed down a path and sent Olive out on an errand to retrieve rabbits from the traps a quarter mile away. He handed her a basket from inside the doorway and sent her on her way. There was to be no welcome rest, no cup of tea to cut the journey's aches. Straight to work.

"I'll unload the supplies. You go down that path there about a quarter mile and check the rabbit traps so we will have something to eat for dinner. We'll be staying in those barracks with the lights on down there at the bottom of the hill. I take it you can find your way without plunging off the cliff and breaking both legs?"

Richardson's tone suggested the question was not so much that as an accusation. After an all-day voyage, Olive's bladder was so full the errand was welcome, as in order not to be found out when relieving herself, she would have to ensure she was alone. She walked far out on the cliff trail, gathering the evening dew with each step. Just before arriving at the rabbit traps, she scaled over a small bare rock peak to find a secluded spot out of the lighthouse sightline. She sighed with relief. With her pants still around her ankles, squatting behind a small outcropping, the voices of men below startled her. She pulled up her pants and lay as flat as she could, peering down. Three men in odd-looking, lumpy canvas vests made their way away from her some seventy feet below, scrambling along the rock toward a small, sandy beach where a soiled tarpaulin tent listed in the wind. Their canvas vests bulged with hundreds of seabird eggs, some clearly having ruptured as marked by wet yellow stains on the front and back. In the weakening light she could just make out that the men were tanned, hirsute, and rough-looking. They reminded her of loggers back in Colorado who'd come into town after weeks in the forest with their beards unruly and hair long in wild curls. Her mother always warned her to steer clear of such company, to stick to the planked sidewalks of Boulder and never deviate from her path. But there she was, clinging to a cliff, sans mother, from Olive to Oliver, with hardly a path to speak of.

Once the men disappeared back into the tent, she clambered back up and over the rock back to the wicker basket and made her way along the narrow path with slow, careful steps toward the rabbit traps. A dense fog rolled in, making visibility almost naught, each footstep risking a potential plunge to her death. At the rabbit traps, Olive bent down to find all three gin traps tripped, their snares sprung. A small coagulating pool of blood seeped out from underneath three lifeless tawny forms. She extracted them with some difficulty, pulling the metal jaws from the rabbits' necks, the blood seeping up her hands and onto the cuffs of her new, and only, shirt. One of the animals still had a slow pulse and was slightly warm. It twitched when she released the trap, a final, indelicate dance toward the beyond. She put the two dead rabbits in the basket and held a rock above the head of the third before delivering a blow. With the rock raised above her head, the sound of thousands of seabirds converged as a banshee wail on the winds, furnished, it seemed, for her ears only. She willed her arms down and the animal shuddered and became still. She was alone. Olive put the final rabbit in the basket and felt the night settling in as she walked back to the lighthouse, her basket heavy with dinner. *Survival*, she thought, *is cruel*.

Back on the stoop of the lighthouse, Richardson inspected the rabbits and said, "One fresh kill. These other two are too far dead," as he tossed the two rabbits high into the air and over a hill out of sight.

"The last five days were the shortest mainland trip I've ever had, but I couldn't trust Charles with the lighthouse for any longer than that." He sighed.

"But he's a lighthouse man?" Olive asked.

"Yes. But he used to be one of the Egg Company folk. Bastards and cheats, all of them."

"Yes, sir." Olive decided not to mention her one-way encounter with the eggers.

"Do you know how to skin a rabbit, Oliver?" Richardson asked from the small stone-countered barracks kitchen as he pulled the first animal inside out. The skin seemed to slide off easily, like it was merely a costume.

"No, sir."

"Well, never mind. You'll learn soon enough. And enough of the 'sirs,' thank you. Go change your shirt for supper." He looked at Olive's bloodstained cuffs.

"This is my only shirt."

"Then you best wash it. The last keeper's assistant was an ignorant man, and fiscally irresponsible. And as you are aware, at such a remote location one might quickly fall into a hurly-burly and rugged countenance. But I will not let that happen under my watch, Oliver. Use cold water for blood. Always use cold for blood."

Olive went to her room in the back of the stone house and unpacked a wool sweater to wear while she rinsed the blood from the sleeves in the tin washtub. Without an undershirt, the sweater raked against her skin. The soap flakes smelled of her old life in Boulder as she rubbed them into the cuffs and pulled the linen cloth over the washboard, a scent that was just part of the full aroma of the tiny kitchen where her mother had made venison pasties and huckleberry jam before she fell ill.

Olive took out the last gift her mother had given her, a silver collection box with thick, beveled crystal and deep red velvet lining. In it laid one single egg, that of a Broad-tailed hummingbird that had nested in a tree outside their home. Her mother helped her collect the egg, no larger than a pinky fingernail, from a nest smaller than a half-dollar coin. Olive tucked the treasure away underneath her bed, laying a cloth over it to disguise it from prying eyes, and hung the shirt up to dry. The smell of the rabbit stewing wound its way around the small barrack rooms as a spirit, beckoning her back to the kitchen where Richardson was singing at full volume a song about sailors and their one true love, the whiskeyed sea.

"How old are you, Oliver?" Richardson asked over dinner, dipping his hard bread into the under-salted stew. "Fourteen? Younger?"

"Yes, sir. Fourteen," she lied.

"Manhood has not yet found you," he said, rubbing his own stubbled chin. "Your skin is as a fawn's."

It didn't seem as though Richardson required an answer to such a statement. Noting the blush combing Olive's neck, Richardson took off his thick glasses and rubbed his eyes, changing the subject. She decided not to tell him that "fawn" was one of her mother's nicknames for her.

"I am inclined to believe this soreness in my eyes is caused by some impurity of blood," Richardson rubbed harder with the heel of his hand at his eyes. "But perhaps if I were to catch the occasional glimpse of the female form divine," he chuckled, "perhaps then the swelling might be alleviated."

Olive tried to force the blood back down her neck by sheer will, eating the rest of her bland stew in silence.

"Tomorrow I will introduce you to the other lighthouse assistants and the small community that calls this island home."

"Oh! There are more people?" Olive asked.

"There are. But be warned. The people living here have a slender hold on mankind."

Olive wondered what that might mean back in her room after dinner. The continual roar of the surf on the rock edged her closer to sleep on her small cot. She pulled the insufficient wool blanket closer, wrapping and tucking it into every crevice. She wondered where Richardson hailed from. He spoke the words of an educated man and seemed knowledgeable in many fields. On this strange West Coast, one never knew where anyone came from, it seemed. It was hard to imagine that the hardened folk were once their mothers' children. Her mind darted to her own mother, then to the collection case under the bed, and images from Martha Maxwell's Denver curio shop filled up the space just before dreams.

Despite her ailing spirit, the month before her mother died, she took Olive on an outing to Martha Maxwell's famous and controversial taxidermy shop. Her mother had wanted to take Olive to visit the shop as a gesture of encouragement, of what exactly Olive wasn't sure at the time. Though it was difficult for her mother to walk the ten-block journey there and back, they made their way slowly, arm in arm. Once inside the small, unassuming storefront, the rooms opened up into magnificent galleries of taxidermied animals. Mrs. Maxwell had two large rooms with catamounts and owls and pheasants, all shot and stuffed by her own womanly hand. She even had a perfectly stuffed terrier curled on a rag rug that Olive swore she could see breathing. As she greeted the two women, Mrs. Maxwell stood beside a deer with her hand gently resting on the haunch. The creature was so lifelike that Olive expected it to snort and quiver at any moment. A sea of pictures on the wall showed Mrs. Maxwell out in the forest, at work in her studio, and standing above her kill. One photo in particular caught Olive's eye—a picture where Martha stood up to her ankles in a duck pond, in men's pants, with a rifle slung over her shoulder. Olive stared at the photograph a long time as her mother and Martha engaged in polite chatter about the shop.

Once outside the shop, her mother stood clutching the railing, coughing with the death rattle as Olive wanted nothing more than to stop time, to stop each second from moving forward and to split the moments like a log. She would keep splitting them until tomorrow never came. But time, the cruel adventurer, continued on, and that night, as her daughter made a dinner of mutton stew, Olive's mother lay quiet, better for the moment, contentedly clutching a present—a silver box with a velvet lining from Maxwell's shop. She knew her daughter would be pleased to receive the gift. It was a place for new memories to be made, collected, and esteemed long after she was gone.

Unbaking the Cake

Burning Woods, Oregon, 1994

O N HER WAY OUT of the house in the early morning, Lily stopped by her mom still splayed on the couch, mouth open and drooling on a needlepoint pillow of dogs wrestling. Lily felt for breath under Alice's nose with the back of her hand, confirmed, then slipped out quietly and started the long walk up the driveway to wait for the school bus by the highway. There were barred owls out in the early dawn, hooting at her with some urgent message she felt too sleepy, or too human, to understand. *Whoo-hoo-hoo-hoooo.* Her science teacher mentioned that there was a pneumonic phrase for this call. *Who-cooks-for-you? Who-cooks-for-you?* Who did cook for Lily? Not Alice, certainly. As she waited for the bus to come rumbling up the highway, she leaned against a milepost marker, sighed, and wondered how her mother came to be the way she was. She shuffled her feet to keep warm, thinking about it. It seemed to Lily that Alice had a sort of perverse, destructive nature like a volcano or virus— she couldn't exist without destroying something else in the process.

In third period science class, Lily sat next to Max at the raised lab desk, slowly stirring a hot bowl of pineapple mush. On the board, their teacher Mr. Janowicz drew a denatured enzyme, its once tightly curled form unfurled across the chalkboard like a garden snake, or a sperm, as Sarah pointed out through a crude, concealed hand gesture from across the row. Mr. Janowicz lectured on the effects of heat on the enzyme, how once it became denatured there was no way to wind it back into its previous form.

"Think about it this way," Mr. Janowicz said. "You can't unbake a cake, or unfry an egg. That's because once heat is applied, the molecular structure is changed forever."

Max doodled a picture in the margin of his notes of a decidedly unscientific scene—a dragon and a warlock doing battle with similar-looking denatured enzymes flying through the air all around them like lasers—not paying much attention to Mr. Janowicz's lecture. *At least some of it was getting through,* Lily thought, looking at the little enzymes flying out of the wizard's fingers. Or were they lightning bolts? Lily knew that no matter what, Max would still ace the test.

"Max? Care to join us?" Janowicz asked, peering over their desk at Max's drawing before returning to the front of the classroom.

"Ooh. Caught red-handed," Lily whispered.

"That's totally racist," Max said, cocking his head, deadpan. "Like saying thieving red Indians."

"Really?" Lily asked, heat rising yet again in her neck. "Dude. Sorry."

"Nah. Just fucking with you," he said, poking her in the rib, ignoring the narrow-eyed gaze from Janowicz. He scribbled a note in the margin below the dragon and warlock.

> *It's actually Scottish in origin. It means to have blood on your hands after the hunt.*

Blood. After the hunt. Lily became acutely aware of his presence not inches from her right thigh, her side and waist, the curve of her ribcage and cheek. She could still feel the point where his finger met her rib. She saw him with his nose in an etymological dictionary. She saw him after the hunt with bloodied hands, straddling a slain animal. She felt how close their own bloods were to one another. It was a matter of inches. Eleven, maybe. She stirred her puree and added a little more hot water. She told herself, *Denature those enzymes. Focus!* Her cheek burned, her fruit steamed, and she could smell Mr. Janowicz's garlic breath from just outside her field of vision. The combination overwhelmed her, leading her down a familiar dark tunnel, releasing a spreading blackness in her brain. The tunnel led her into a new and different form. Sound wound in on itself and disappeared like someone abruptly turning down the radio dial. She was unfurled—she was the snake—as she slid down and out of her seat. The world faded away into complete darkness and she heard Sarah's somewhat blasé voice, as if from a valley away:

"Mr. Janowicz. Lily fainted again."

When she woke, she lay prone on the floor. Her vision returned slowly. Mr. Janowicz and his strong garlic odor bent over her, his white dome of backlit hair glowing in the fluorescent lights. He snapped two fingers in front of her face, holding her head and neck with the other.

"Welcome back," he said. With her head in his hand and his glowing white, frizzy hair luminous under the fluorescence, Lily thought they almost looked related. Maybe he could be her father? She closed her eyes a moment and pretended he was, which felt kind of nice, the knowing.

"Nothing broken?"

"Nah. Not that I know of."

"You have a ride home?"

"No," she said, closing her eyes again.

"I'll take her." Max peeked out from behind him. "She lives on the way to my uncle Boomer's."

Lily felt the blood returning to her heart and limbs, faster and faster. She cursed Max a little for his control over her blood flow. Any self-possessed girl should be able to take care of her own oxygenation needs. Any feminist daughter knew that.

After school, Lily gazed out the passenger's side of Max's old Ford truck as they waited to turn out of the parking lot onto the street. Two of the Dickerson boys, junior Todd and fifth-year senior Dempsey, walked in front of the truck and went down into football hike positions and growled like they were going to charge the truck. They found their own antics extremely funny as they walked off up the street kicking inanimate objects.

"The accent's really on the first syllable of those boys' last name, isn't it?" Max said, shaking his head.

"Absolutely."

"You know why I did that rain dance last fall?"

"Because they're total douchebags?"

"Yes, but also because those boys actually took the time to save up their feces and leave them on the hood of my truck. I mean, do you know what kind of planning and foresight that must have taken? They probably busted the one working neural pathway between the two of them."

"Man. I'm sorry. People are shitty."

Max laughed. "Pun intended?"

"Absolutely." Lily gazed in bashful self-satisfaction into the blurring trees as the truck picked up speed heading toward the highway. She enjoyed seeing everyone disperse after school, as though the density of so many youths in one place were unnatural, dangerous. There was relief in the untangling of souls back to their wooded nooks. Max revved the engine as they headed away from the school, and as though he had read her mind, yelled out the window:

"Run, rabbits!"

Kids bussed in from teensy towns like Burning Woods or Logsden that dotted the patchwork Siuslaw Forest and Willamette Valley to come to high school in Philomath. Some of the "towns" were no more than an intersection with a fruit stand or a market selling beer, fishing supplies, and candy. Every day after school, said rabbits scattered back to their corners of the musty, wet woods. They fell back to their logging, milling, or farming families. They retreated to their back-to-the-landers or skittered back to the commune. The green squares of the checkerboard forest somehow managed to pad the enormous gaps between people and their politics. The freaks nestled in nicely next to the rednecks, the trees acting as silent wardens of the peace.

Some twelve miles away from school, Max turned off the highway onto the forested two-lane highway out to Lily's house. The gray sky hung threateningly low and the dark green leaves quivered in the overcast light, waving a manic plea for sunshine as the Pacific squalls shook them up. When they dropped down from the blacktop onto the gravel of Lily's driveway, something big in the bed of the truck made a loud thud.

"What's back there?" Lily asked, eyeing a blue tarp covering something large in the bed.

"Elk."

"Seriously? Dude, that's totally out of season," she pointed out, puffing up a little, self-righteous as a dandelion bloom. "It's spring."

"I know, I know," Max said. "Relax, kitten." He made a tiger-scratch motion with one hand while he cranked the manual steering hard to go around a curve. "Someone poached him out on my uncle's cabin on the rez, probably for the velvet antlers. There's some big market for velvet. Supposedly cures cancer. Helps with the sex drive, or some shit."

"Really?"

"Who knows. But people apparently take the ground-up horn in capsules or teas. Some ancient Chinese hoo-ha. People will do anything for a boner. Anyway, my uncle chased off the poacher and gave me this little elk here to process."

"Well, ashes to ashes," Lily said, hearing her grandmother's words caught in her throat, feeling just about as prissy as her grandmother would have at the mere mention of a boner.

"More like elk to jerky," he said. "We don't exactly get down with the King James in my family."

"Right. I mean, neither do we. Not really. Not since my grandparents died, anyway."

They rode the remainder of the long gravel driveway in silence. *So he will be straddling a slain animal, after all,* Lily thought. As her dilapidated white farmhouse came into view, Lily felt a little embarrassed by the dirty set of Tibetan prayer flags flapping in the wind, and by the prominent scrap-metal Gaia sculpture out front. Moreover, she was washed by a weird sense of shame at the giant carved Native American wooden salmon in the side yard, leaping, forever leaping, into the air. As if seeing herself for the first time through Max's eyes, it became clear to Lily that her mother's world was one of appropriation. She tried on beliefs like they were costumes in a dress-up chest; hers was a sort of spiritual tea party.

"How's Donnie Jr. doing?" Max asked.

"Aw, she hates wearing the cone. But I have to say, it's kind of hilarious."

"Well, take care of that sweet little duck of yours," he said, knocking her gently on the jaw with a slow-motion punch as she stretched to get down from the tall truck cab.

She watched him as he backed up and turned around, rumbling fast up the gravel driveway, the blue-tarp lump in the back of the truck slumping to one side. *Did Max just wink at me?* She felt a bloom of warmth where he had gently grazed her chin with his knuckles and had to sit down on scrap Gaia's knee for a minute to let the dizziness pass. She was curled up, sharing Gaia's lap with a sculpted version of the earth as constructed from old tires, fenders, radiator tubes, springs, and tractor parts, when it started to rain. The drops came slowly at first, then poured cool and fast down her face. She closed her eyes and let the water roll over her, each drop pinging loud on the metal goddess, and tried to melt back into some sort of state she could understand.

Inside the house was empty and cold. It felt as if no one had been in there since the morning hours. The patchwork quilt was crumpled on the floor next to the couch and the previous afternoon's dishes remained in the sink. Ladybugs clung to the hole in the wall, but in significantly smaller numbers. One of her mom's books on feminism was propped open on the kitchen table next to an empty magnum of wine. It read:

> *The sort of flaw that is often excused in men—the precipitous fall from grace—is commonly perceived as "ruin" when observed in females.*

After reading the passage, Lily went to the library and leafed through the dictionary on its little podium to look up the word "precipitous." The second definition was "very high and steep" and she thought of the quote again, picturing naked women falling off mountain peaks like pink flightless birds flapping their arms, a pile of them squirming below, ruined. She closed the book and put some kindling in the wood stove and started it with a match. Two days before it had been sunny and warm, and here she was again, the air in the house cold as winter. *Oregon spring is like that,* Lily thought. It would love and leave you with the passing of a cloud over the sun.

Rubbing her hands together for warmth, Lily could see the partially fogged window to her mom's sculpture studio, the back of her mom's friend Darla's head taking up most of the space with her giant black bouffant, the two of them presumably imbibing and talking shit about recent ex-boyfriends. Darla went through at least as many boyfriends as Alice, almost as though it were some competition. The two tried not to overlap, but in their town that was an almost statistical impossibility. Smoke curled from the chimney in the studio and Darla's old Dodge Dart waited patiently in the drive.

Lily walked outside and circled the small studio like a coyote. The one window was cracked open to let in air but was almost completely obscured by condensation. Lily heard the two friends' voices drifting out the space and paused to eavesdrop. They slurred their words a little.

"You know, that fucker Randy wasn't even good in bed," Alice said. Darla cackled and they both started laughing. "Like two minutes, tops. I swear."

"Good riddance. He was also not father material, if you ask me."

"You really think I need a father for Lily? Naaaah," Alice said. "That girl is better off without one. She's a genius, you know."

"She's very bright, for sure," Darla said. Lily peeked up and saw them pouring some more wine into handled mason jars—the "fancy" glasses, her mom would joke to friends.

"It's almost scary sometimes. Like I don't really know if she could be an evil genius or just a genius. Did I ever tell you why I named her Lily?"

"No. Why?"

Alice threw back her wine, paused for a long moment with her face pointed skyward, as if to reconsider telling the story, then finally said, "Because when I found out I was pregnant at fifteen, I tried to get rid of the baby by drinking a whole bottle of Lillet I stole from my parents' cupboard. I was almost two months along. My parents found me passed out in the pasture with cuts on my body, and when I woke up they were force-feeding me ipecac to make me throw up. I guess I must have spilled the news in my drunken state. They carried me inside into bed where they bandaged my cuts. Then they tied my arms and legs in place with belts."

"That's horrible," Darla said, sounding a bit sobered.

"That's just how they were. Well, my mom, anyway. My dad said so little I feel like I hardly even knew him, you know? He certainly never stood up to my mother. She turned me over in the field that day and must have thought, 'You're not going to die? Good. Now go stay in your cell.'" Alice poured herself more wine. "After a few days they took off the belts. But they locked me in my room for most of the first trimester and kept me under supervision for the entire pregnancy. When I had to throw up from morning sickness, they gave me a bowl. I peed in a bedpan."

"Alice, I'm so sorry."

"Well, you know, my mother believed it was a child of God they were protecting. But that little girl, she was meant to be here, child of God or Gaia or whomever. She just grew and grew into the most intelligent thing. She changed my whole life, that little one. I'd never really known love until I met her."

"I bet your mom tried to own that victory."

"Oh, absolutely. But I refuse to give her credit for that one. Things would have worked out as they were meant to without her 'meddling.'" From her place below the window, Lily could just see her mother's long fingers perform dramatic air quotes.

"No kidding," Darla said, the sound of her chair screeching on the concrete floor as she rose to embrace her friend. "I'm so sorry you had to go through that."

Lily slumped under the window as it started to rain again, her back picking up little splinters from the cedar shingles as she slid down to the ground. She could care less about a few splinters. This was the first she'd heard of her mother's in-utero attempt to off her, but somehow she was not completely surprised. She could hear quiet sniffles from her mom and Darla as they embraced inside. *And here you are the one crying?* she thought as she listened to the sobs. *Because everything is about you, isn't it?* The rain from the roof dripped off on her in a line on her shoulders, her skin like ice. She decided she didn't want to hear any more and slunk away from the window to curl up into a ball at the back corner of the building, out of earshot. She held tight to her legs as she rocked and looked out over the misty field.

The harrier was back, rising in the distance. Lily wanted badly to cry, to feel something. But her whole body felt numb. The harrier dropped, missed, dropped, and missed again. *Shit,* she thought. *I'm not even supposed to be here. I guess every damn one of us hunts blind.* The closest her body could get to crying was a strange itching behind her eyeballs. She rubbed at her dry eyes with her flannel as the harrier landed in the distance under a tree. The great bird adjusted her soggy wings and something dark and acrid settled in Lily's center. She felt pure rage, digging her already black fingernails into the dirt. *Well, at least I feel something,* she thought. But as far as feelings go, it was not the welcome kind.

Lily went up to her room, put on a CD of the band Veruca Salt as loud as she could, and stayed there. Every lyric seemed to mock her newfound sense of shame. *Can't fight the seether—I try to ram her into the ground.* After a while, she moved to The Breeders, but they spoke the same kind of truth. *Spitting in the wishing well for sure.* An hour or so later, she heard Darla drive away and the sound of the kitchen door squeal as her mother came inside. The album ended and in the abrupt absence of the bass line she heard the clank of dishes being stacked and rinsed in the sink drift up. She knew this probably meant her mother would be on an upcycle. She could almost smell the remorse wafting up on the air. There would be folded sheets and limited drinking in the house for at least a few days, possibly a week or even two. Her mother would make breakfast and send her to school with a complete and balanced lunch. They would go through all this again—pretending they were a normal, functional family.

But there was no point in holding her breath during this phase. It would fall all apart like petals from the tulip. It's the flower that ends before it's done beginning, she'd heard someone say. Day by day the petals would fall and there they would be again two naked stems of women. A ruined pile. After overhearing Alice's confession about trying to abort her, something had shifted in the way Lily perceived her mother. There was a new chasm between them that was too wide to leap over. No reconciliatory hugs or gifts bought out of guilt could close the gap. Lily found herself on her own, the tie that binds a young girl to her mother severed. She still loved her, but from a distance.

Feeling a bit freed by the recent untethering, Lily decided that while her mother was consumed with her brief redemption, she would have to take action of her own. She put in another CD—Nirvana's *In Utero*. She scoffed. *In utero*, she thought. *What if she had succeeded?* As Kurt Cobain's thoughts on nothingness and pain seemed more acute than they ever had before, she told herself, *Fuck it*. She decided to seduce Max by the light of the upcoming lunar eclipse. There would have to be a picnic and booze involved. If it was how she'd come into the world, she thought, she might as well own the forces that had shaped her and harness them for her own. She knew she was not watertight. The cold from outside had seeped deep into her bones and she could almost feel something dark and moldy growing there. Her new independence felt intoxicating. The idea that she could have been killed before she ever lived made her want to live faster, harder, before someone took it all away.

Strawberries and Beer

Burning Woods, Oregon, 1977

As summer took hold of the Siuslaw, the populace freed their mildewed souls in prostration to the sun. Layers came off and people flopped their soft, over-wintered bodies onto towels by the river. It was the time of year when people became amnesiacs about the preceding nine months of rain, gushing to one another, "Why would we live anywhere else?" For the kids, summer break from school meant bike rides, swimming in clear crisp lakes, and picnicking relatively mosquito free. The brief reprieve from the eternal drizzle allowed for hikes and the harvesting of sweet, sun-shined fruits, as the grass crinkled like paper at the ankles and people explored their territory anew. But stark sunshine creates stark shadow, and in the darkest shade of peaceful moments can lurk the most vicious of things.

Alice and Sal, or "Sally" as she was known only on her birth certificate and to Alice's parents, laid their pasty bodies out on their towels under the sun on a slim, gray strip of beach lining the local swimming hole. Sal wore board shorts and a running bra that kept her almost nonexistent breasts firmly in place. Alice, always up for a little attention, wore a crochet bikini she'd made herself, the loose weave revealing flashes of pink nipple and hinting at the mound of soft blonde fur as she flipped onto her back and arched up toward the sun. Boys watched them from above where everyone parked their cars on the gravel shoulder, watching them flip back and forth like skewers in the hot sun. The guys whistled, but the two girls didn't deign to acknowledge them. They only had eyes for one another.

Sal clocked the way Alice arched her back and watched as a trickle of sweat formed between her breasts. She wondered what it would taste like were she to test her tongue against Alice's soft, glowing skin. When Alice lifted her sunglasses and found Sal looking at her in that particular way, her heart raced and she made sure to arch a little higher, to let her legs fall apart and sway back and forth, catching the sun on her long, smooth slopes. Both girls wondered the same thing but felt different kinds of guilt about their attraction to one another. Sal's guilt was rooted in the feeling that growing up on a commune, with hippies, had sculpted her into some kind of perversion of nature. She wondered if the feelings she had for Alice had gurgled up from the wellspring of free love she had been forced to drink from and whether that well was better off capped and boarded up forever. Alice, on the other hand, had been assured by her Catholic upbringing that with no uncertain doubt the feelings for Sal she let roll through her body and shiver her skin to attention were the work of the devil himself. To act on her feelings would be the most sinful transgression of her fifteen years, and one she feared might bring fire and brimstone to her doorstep.

"How can you be cold?" Sal asked, putting her hand on Alice's goose-bumped forearm. "I'm sweating like a pig."

"Not cold. Just got the shivers, I guess." Alice flipped her glasses back down to hide the obvious tenderness in her eyes and rolled over onto her stomach again.

A lifted truck started up on the road above and a male voice shouted something unintelligible as the giant tires peeled out from the gravel. Gravel tumbled down the hill, sifting into the enormous ferns, and a fine mist of gray dust lifted up over the girls and settled flat on the air, shading them with a veil of uncertainty.

Later in the week, Alice walked alone along the highway toward Sal's house on the commune. All summer, Alice had been waiting for yet dreading Sal's going-away party. A year ahead in school, Sal was leaving town to study biology at Northern Arizona University, and Alice would miss her terribly when she went away. Under the impending deadline imposed by Sal's plane ticket and packed bags,

Alice finally decided she needed to tell her something she'd never mustered the courage to tell anyone in her sixteen years. She had to admit she was *in love* with her. The act would take courage from somewhere deep within the pale well Alice called a self. The risk and potential outcome of such a confession horrified her into a state of nausea and sweaty-palmed nervousness. As she walked the two miles from her parents' orchard to the commune driveway, she wiped her hands on her blue cotton dress and nervously plucked hairs from her eyebrows, the pricks of pain keeping her steadied.

Sal greeted her with a double-armed wave as Alice walked the last hundred feet up the driveway toward the main house, past jaunty signs painted with flowers and spirals that said, "BREATHE" or "The LIGHT is Within YOU" stuck in the ground as a sort of empirical greeting for any and all venturing onto the communally owned land. Sal grew bigger and more real with each graveled step Alice took toward her, until she loomed large as an oak or an oncoming train. As the two embraced, Alice was not sure the light was within her, or that she was capable of breathing, but she did her damnedest to fake that she was breezing through the day like a samara on the wind.

In preparation for the party, Alice and Sal helped hang strings of lights outside, dragging feet upon feet of extension cords from the big house in order to hang a chandelier from the largest oak tree above the enormous reclaimed wood tables. The commune may only have been two miles from Alice's parents' house, but culturally it was light-years away. People wore corduroy and suede fringe, jewelry that jangled, bangs or long hair parted in the middle. There was no Sunday dress code except dirtied knees on coveralls from helping the garden. Worship involved not the Lord and Savior and His Son but the Sun in the Sky or a many-armed blue female elephant. They discussed commune business in a "forum" and danced regularly to exotic stringed instrumental music, winding their arms through the air like they were braiding the invisible. Sometimes they did a dance where they all held hands and wound the entire group from a loose and limbering spiral into a tight knot, their bodies crushed up against one another in a spiraled lump. Alice wasn't really sure of the point of the exercise, but always played along because she loved the people who lived there, the way they laughed from their diaphragms and not their throats and hugged strangers for far longer than she had ever seen her own parents touch anyone. But most of all, she loved that these were the people who had helped create her Sal.

Sal's chin-length, curly brown hair and dark skin seemed to suck the sun to it. Her almond eyes betrayed a strong mix of cultures in her blood. There was a particular reticence among commune children to pinpoint who *exactly* begat them, as often these facts were as fluid as a storyteller's tales, shifting and moving like sand under the wind's guile. Alice knew Sal's father well, as he was a prominent figure on the commune, but whenever Alice asked her about her absentee mother, Sal said with a smirk, "I am a daughter of the earth, remember?" And that summer, it seemed to Alice that the dusty earth of the southwestern deserts were all Sal wanted to talk about. Alice began to be jealous of the dust itself. It seemed to her that a place with things called Gila monsters, little pink-and-black dragons that once they bit you were almost impossible to unlatch from your leg, was more science fiction than a region of her own country. Sal talked about shrikes and thrashers, Mojave greens and kangaroo rats. She described the life cycle of saguaros and the skeletons of cholla. She spoke in reverent tones of a collection of plants and animals that more resembled a Dr. Seuss landscape than anything Alice had ever known stalking the coast range Sitka of the low-lying Cascade range or the oak savannah of the Willamette Valley. As they hung the last of the white lights, weaving the wires around the trunk of the oak, Alice promised she would come visit first chance she got, as long as Sal kept her safe from monsters. Sal laughed, the deep kind she liked to call the "hippie guffaw," and put her arm around Alice's much taller, bony shoulders. Sal's head rested there. She promised she would do her damnedest.

That evening at the party, the girls started a huge fire in the pit and mingled with the other guests. They were given beers with a wink by the eldest member of the commune and told to "be responsible."

Busses, Westfalias, and Volkswagen vans in candy colors rolled up the driveway and parked on the grass pell-mell, the loud doors releasing vaporous clouds that smelled like some kitchen experiment burning on the stove.

"A party here is really just an excuse for people to smoke way too much grass and participate in the doctrine of free love," Sal whispered to Alice.

"I didn't know regular love cost anything," Alice said.

"They say all love comes at a cost."

"Now that's not very bohemian thinking."

With the bonfire lit, the strawberries from the garden picked and still warm from the sunshine, the girls sat down with the rest of the party and Sal handed Alice another beer concealed in a red plastic cup, letting her hand linger a little while on Alice's as she transferred the beverage.

"Try it with the fresh strawberries. It's amaaazing," Sal said.

Alice was in a sort of ecstasy with the sweet, warm strawberries and bubbles dancing on her tongue. Emboldened by the alcohol, she gazed seductively into the fire, thinking of how to get Sal alone to reveal her feelings. She was lost in a scenario involving Sal, some tall grass, and moonlight by the frog pond, when she noticed a small, balding, blond man watching her from across the fire. He wore a tan suede jacket with fringe and beaded Native American moccasins, though clearly he himself was not. His thinning hair glowed almost white despite a fair amount of natural grease smoothing it back around his ears. Around his neck hung a bundle of necklaces including what appeared to be a shark or dinosaur tooth and a very tiny spoon. His eyes were wide, rimmed in pink, and a little crazed. Alice wondered how long he'd been staring at her like he wanted to eat her. She set down the bowl of strawberries and wiped her mouth, suddenly feeling self-conscious.

Next thing Alice knew, as though he had moved with the shifting of the smoke from the fire, the man was sitting on the bench next to her sidling closer and closer.

"You sure were enjoying those berries," he said, leaning in.

"Ah, yes," Alice said politely, waving the bonfire smoke from her eyes. "They're from the communal garden."

"Of Eden?" The man said, laughing far too loudly at his own proto-joke. Up close, Alice could see the broken capillaries in the whites of his eyes and could smell an unfamiliar acrid odor on his breath. She looked around the fire to see if anyone was watching them, if anyone knew this man. Sal had been called away to help with something in the barn, leaving Alice to contend with the man alone. He didn't introduce himself, but instead just stared at the bowl of fruit in her lap.

"Would you like one?" Alice said, again defaulting to a politeness her Christian upbringing had drilled into her, unsure what else to say or do.

"Indeed," the man said, plucking the largest one, letting his hand linger too long in the bowl sitting in her lap, then eating it with little grunts. Alice looked around for Sal to see if she'd returned, but she couldn't locate her among the crowd. Alice wasn't really sure what was going on, but she felt a flight instinct kick in.

"Excuse me a moment," she said, getting up.

"Don't go," the man grabbed her arm. She pulled it out of his grasp, hard, almost knocking herself over.

She walked away from the firelight and lit-up trees toward the big farmhouse, the beer feeling less ecstatic now in her body, more like the rocking of a ship in a storm back and forth in her veins. She stumbled through the dark and toward the porch light, twisting her ankle in a hole in the ground. She walked the rest of the way more slowly, the pain in her ankle growing warm and sharp.

Inside the farmhouse, she walked slowly through the living room while touching all the exotic items on display. There were large Turkish silver stars embossed with intricate patterns or with cutout patterns of flowers and vines. There was one extremely large sketch hanging over the fireplace of a man and woman lying down, entwined and naked. You couldn't see their faces, but you could tell by the intimate and gentle way they held each other that they were in love. On the couches there were throws and pillows in bright hues and mismatched patterns, vases filled with dried flowers on the end tables, and tapestries on the wall from unknown countries. There was nary a cross with Jesus crucified as could be found in every room of her parents' house. The closest this place came to a representation of Jesus was perhaps Kenneth, the longhaired bearded fellow who lived in the addition off the kitchen and made driftwood sculptures. She walked upstairs to the bathroom, the pain in her ankle biting with each step.

She was sitting on the toilet spacing out, trying to regain her wits and stop the rocking, when a loud rap on the door startled her.

"Occupied," she said quietly.

"Is that you, strawberry?" a male voice asked.

"Who?" she said, pulling up her underwear and smoothing her dress down. She flushed the toilet and turned on the faucet, washing her hands for a long time. "There's another bathroom downstairs," she finally yelled. She paused for a long time, looking through the cabinet and inspecting the bottles and tubes one by one—face cream, hemorrhoid cream, Tylenol, nettle tincture, arnica. She sorted and resorted the many toothbrushes before finally unlocking the door. Her hand paused on the handle before she opened it, but she had to go out at some point, and it had been quiet outside in the hallway for some time. But when she opened the door, the moccasined man was right there, quietly waiting.

"I thought you left me," he said, leaning up against the wall. "You offered me your fruit then ran away."

"Um," Alice said, attempting to sidle around him in the narrow hallway. "I didn't offer you anything."

"You were seducing me from across the fire all night," he said. "Don't think I didn't notice."

"I was just spacing out," Alice said, for some reason still bound by the tight boundaries of a politeness that had been disciplined into her with each lesson in Sunday school, each prayer before a meal. She felt roped by the confines of graciousness and courtesy when all she wanted to do was run.

"What you need is to loosen up," the man said, offering her white powder from a teeny round jar, heaping the powder into the spoon hanging from his neck.

"No, thank you."

He snorted the powder himself, then pinned her to the wall and kissed her in a sort of vicious way. She squirmed, but he held her by the shoulders, thrusting himself against her, holding her captive against the wall. She had never felt or seen an actual penis, but an image of what was grinding against her flew into her head like some toothy, demonic creature escaped from a black hole.

"No." She managed to get her mouth away from his for a moment. "No, no, no."

"Yes, yes, yes," the man said, pulling her by the shoulders into the bedroom with a pile of coats on the bed. "Don't be so disagreeable, honey." He threw her down into the coats and closed the door behind him. She felt her ankle twist again in pain.

"I have to go," she said trying to get up out of the coats. "I don't want to." To her own ears she sounded like a toddler.

Then, as if she were moving three times slower than the man, he was on her, his pants were down and her skirt up, and a new pain was ripping through her middle, far stronger than the throbbing in her ankle. The man was inside her and grunting like he had been while eating the strawberries, pinning her shoulders down but with his head turned up toward the heavens, as if to close his eyes against his own sin. She tried to make a noise, but only a little hiss of an exhale like a deflating tire came out. The man put his hand over her mouth, his other forearm across her throat pressing down. Still he refused to look at her and her wide, horrified eyes. Her mouth covered, Alice looked for something to focus on beyond what was happening. Her eyes settled on a large spider in the corner of the room, making its way from one wall to another, pausing briefly in the corner as if to watch.

He got up quickly, pulled his pants back up, and said, "Thanks, doll." As though she had given him something willingly.

He left the room and Alice buried herself in the coats, burrowing deeper like an unweaned kitten trying to hide, to find the smallest, darkest place she could. She wanted to cry huge, loud tears into the fibers of the partygoers', coats, but nothing came out. She rolled and punched the coats with quiet fists. *Fuck, fuck, fuck.* She looked again for the spider, as though its witness mattered somehow, but it was gone. She stamped each and every coat with her fist. What had she done wrong? Clearly she had done *something* wrong. She wished she could rewind the evening and change every moment. She needed to restitch, to sow time into neat, orderly, understandable rows.

After what might have been minutes or hours lying there, Alice extracted herself from the coats and pulled up her underwear. Outside in a tree on the dark side of the house, a western screech owl made its call like a bouncing ball. It sounded to Alice like the creature was mocking her with its laugh. *Ha-ha-haha-hahahaha.* There were two bright streaks of red on her thighs like someone had rubbed strawberries on them. She felt sick and ran downstairs and out into the darkness where she threw up all the delicious fruit, the beer, everything she could, into the grass. She vowed she would never touch a beer or a strawberry again, as long as she lived, and walked back toward the light of the fire, trying not to limp.

Back at the fir, Sal asked her if she was okay, putting her arm around Alice's broad, but somehow very fragile, shoulders.

"You were limping," Sal said.

"I just twisted my ankle is all," Alice lied.

"Can I help you?"

"No."

She stared into the fire feeling emptied and knew that she would never be able to tell Sal any of it, that she loved her too much, that the blond man in moccasins had raped her. She felt simply empty. The man with the tiny spoon was nowhere in sight and Alice understood somewhere deep inside that she would probably never see him again. And then, as quickly as a rain cloud covers the sky, the atmosphere of the party turned chaotic. There was a sort of running around of headless chickens, as it were. Everyone was looking for answers to a question they didn't understand.

"Where'd Donnie go?" Alice heard an unfamiliar man say from across the fire. "Son of a bitch owed me a pound of grass," he mumbled, getting up to refill his cup.

"Don't invite that dealer junkie over here again," Sal's dad Charles said from across the fire. "He's not welcome here, and you know it, John."

"He owed me a pound of grass, *man*. Relax, Mao."

"Calling a Korean man Mao is not funny in any way, *man*. And your tone is not conducive to open communication, John."

"And your tone sounds like an old dictator," John said, slurring his words and tossing a spray beer from his cup. "King Charles the communisss dictator is not happy?"

"Somebody take John to lie down?" Charles asked the crowd of onlookers.

Drunken John was escorted to the house by Kenneth-the-Jesus substitute to sleep off his drink. The rest of the party continued, feebly trying to shake off the chaos. A woman came over and comforted Sal by putting her arm around her.

"John didn't mean it," she whispered. "Your dad is no *dictator*." She whispered the word like it was the worst swear word in existence. "He'll apologize tomorrow."

"We can't fix all the unkind men of the world, as much as we may try," Charles said, settling in beside them, unsmiling. "And tomorrow doesn't always fix what's broken today."

Alice suddenly understood this to be true. There were some universal truths about breaking. Plans break, bones break, and spirits break. She knew then that some people break whatever they want. Across the fire pit, Sal smiled and waved her hands in the air in conversation with an older woman, probably describing some beautiful desert creature she would be abandoning Alice for in a few days. Sal looked so innocent and in love with life. Like gravity pulling water to flow downward, all the affection she felt for Sal drained into resentment, pooling at her feet in the shadows of the flickering fire. Sal remained unbroken and was probably unbreakable, at that. She sat and watched the fire in a decidedly unsultry way. The way the fire moved and flickered on the wood pleased her. The destruction felt deliciously final. She looked around at all the people laughing, saying nothing about something, and all she wanted to do was to burn it all down, piece by piece.

Russian Blue

The Farallones, California, 1874

O LIVE MADE HER WAY along the path to the rabbit traps, but when she got there they were empty. *Strange*, she thought. There were so many rabbits around she could hardly empty and set the traps back up before another little brown creature had jumped in and snapped its neck. She looked around but saw no one. The birds ceased their cries just long enough that she could hear voices descending down the rock face to her left into the fog. She peered down over the edge and saw three eggers with rabbits draped around their necks like fancy be-stoled ladies going to an opera.

"Hey there!" she yelled down. "Those rabbits belong to Richardson." The men paused their thievery briefly, but after seeing her size and distance began to laugh. One waved a dead rabbit over his head like a lasso.

"Come down and get them, then." They continued their deft descent.

Olive paused only briefly before making the way down herself. She had to grip the rocks with her fingers in an awkward, unsure way to find holds, imitating a crab with arms and legs akimbo. She slowly descended, the fog rolling in all around her and gulls hanging in the air nearby, pausing in curiosity to check her out before letting the wind roll them past like kites. Almost at the bottom near a miniscule sand beach, she became caught with one foot searching for purchase but could find no niche to settle her weight. She finally found a small lump on the cliff with her toe, but when she tried to stand on it, the rock crumbled and she tumbled backward and fell about five feet down, landing hard on her back in the sand. The contact with the earth flung her empty rabbit-collecting basket some feet away. She gasped for breath with a quiet opening and closing mouth like a fish on the deck of one of the Greek fishermen's boats that circled the islands, but no breath came in or out. She had knocked the air completely out of her lungs. As her lungs refused to fill, she closed her eyes and waited for whatever was next.

When she opened her eyes again, there were three bearded men standing over her, laughing.

"Looks like we caught ourselves a grouper." One gave her a kick in the side. "Good eating, I hear."

"A little small," another chuckled. "Mostly bones."

A hand reached down and pulled her up. She finally gasped and could get a trickle of oxygen into her lungs.

"Now why don't you go back up that cliff now, boy," the tallest one said, stroking the rabbits surrounding his neck like a king would his stole. "At the rate you were moving, by the time you get back up there those traps will be full again."

"Give me my rabbits," Olive squeaked, her voice cracking high from lack of breath.

"Look at the pluck on this one," the tall man said to his friends. "Sounds a little like a seal pup, doesn't he? Looks a little like a lady, if you ask me."

"He sure is pretty," said the shortest one, stroking Olive's hair.

"Prove to us you're not a pretty lady," said the quiet one, giving her trousers a yank. They had her surrounded and she had her back to the cliff wall with nowhere to run.

"Yeah. Just prove us wrong, boy." The tall one dragged his boot up the inseam of her trousers. The balanced rabbits shifted and one fell forward, its foot swinging out and catching her on the cheek. It was still warm.

"Leave me alone." She lowered her voice and put up her fists.

The men laughed at the thought of fighting the tiny creature but were cut off from their fun by a rifle shot in their direction, above their heads. A fourth man emerged from the fog and said, "Leave him be, boys." He was taller and wider than all the men, with an even wilder beard and black hair that reached his shoulders in dark curls. "Take those rabbits back to the tent and get them undressed for dinner. No need to undress the new lighthouse assistant before you go." He gave Olive a little wink and gestured the barrel of the gun back toward the eggers' meager tent camp. "Back you go, now. Go."

The men looked hard at Olive before retreating and making their way back up over some rocks and back to the next beach down.

The man towered over Olive and looked her up and down, unsmiling.

"Oliver, is it?" he asked. "Richardson's new assistant."

"Yes, sir."

"Well, you'd be wise to steer clear of those three from now on. There's a reason some men became egg men, and it's not because their mothers taught them proper etiquette."

"What's your name?" she asked, hoping to catch a moment more with this man before making her way back up the cliff.

"Warren. Charles Warren."

She laughed. A loud laugh from deep in her diaphragm. A full, deep breath of air finally entered her lungs and felt delicious as she exhaled in a chuckle. It was the first time she'd heard her own laugh since her mother passed.

"And what's so amusing about my name?"

"You sure found the right island to call home with all these rabbits running everywhere."

He laughed and slung his rifle back onto his shoulder.

"Ah! A clever one. Indeed. Give my regards to Richardson." He took five eggs out of a pouch in his vest and handed them to Olive. "Put these in your basket with some weeds as padding and take this trail up here." He pointed to a clear switchback on the far end of the little beach behind them that wound its way back up to the ridge. "Tell him if he wants some more eggs as payment for those rabbits to come see me and not go taking them directly like last time. He'll know exactly what I mean." With that he stepped away and was enveloped by the thick fog.

The trail switchbacked up the rock and met up with the footpath that led back to the lighthouse. The men were right—by the time she made it back up the hill, there was already another rabbit in the trap. But there was something different about this rabbit. Its fur glowed a beautiful silvery blue in the late-afternoon light. She unclamped the trap and put the animal in the basket at her hip. There was no blood on the fur, but the rabbit lay limp in her hands. She wished for a moment that she had the power to reanimate the creature, to see it jump off into the distance unscathed. She put its body into the wicker basket, briefly laying her hand on its silky back before securing the clasp.

Back at the lighthouse camp, Richardson was seated at the table trying to write a letter, rubbing his eyes in the dim light. Light poured in behind Olive after she opened the heavy door and stood there, unclasping the rabbit basket from her hip. Her illuminated outline lent her the kind of beautiful halo that halts a man. It was the kind of diffuse light on a womanly form that tears a man's heart asunder and wrests him from the mundanity of living. He looked at her with his hands paused mid-rub of the eye as though caught by a strange notion.

"I swear there must be some impurity of blood I'm experiencing, for my eyes are playing tricks on me."

"What kind of tricks?" Olive said, setting the blue rabbit on the kitchen block.

"Oh, never mind, boy," Richardson said with impatience, as though Olive had imposed on a conversation with himself. "What's this? A Russian blue? I thought they'd all been trapped out. Nice work, boy. They are the most delicious of all the island rabbits. They're a vestige of the Russians who trapped all the fur seals out of existence back in the early eighteen hundreds."

"There were more, but some eggers took a few right before I got there." Olive took out the speckled murre eggs and laid them on the counter next to the rabbit. "Warren sent these to make amends for his men. Said if you wanted more to come talk to him."

"*His* men, you said?" Richardson laughed. "They are no more *his* men than these eggs belong to any human. He's just one of the boys, no more than nineteen years of age. But he does seem to strike fear in the hearts of meeker men than he, does he not?"

"I just assumed he was in charge."

"He's a good man, that Warren. I figure if anyone can keep peace between the eggers and us lighthouse folks, he's our best bet."

"What is the source of the conflict?" Olive asked, pushing the rabbit to the edge of the cutting block to make room for potatoes.

"Well, there used to be a lot more open fighting before the Egg Company took exclusive rights to collection on the island. Now the trouble's just gone underground. A'brewin'."

"How so?" Olive asked.

"They complained to the inspector that we lighthouse men were collecting and selling eggs against the law, and other falsehoods against my character. But I wrote to the inspector myself recently and I showed up those egg men in their true light."

"I see."

"But now the rugged Egg Company fools think they own the island with the divine right of kings. There's a war developing between the lighthouse keepers and those dastardly egg men. Did I tell you what happened to my last assistant?"

"No, you didn't," Olive said.

"He fell and broke both his legs after being cornered by some rough eggers. He was out collecting abalone near the cave on the west end and they cornered him and tried to take the shells. Shots were fired. He got away, but fell and broke both legs."

"So that's why we stick to rabbit stew, then," Olive said, gingerly peeling the skin from a potato.

"We haven't retreated in fear, Oliver, and I'm remiss to hear you say that." Richardson sat up straight in his chair. "Those men thought they could frighten me into subjection. But I'm not that man."

"I only jest," Olive said, returning her eyes to the task at hand, noting how her vocabulary had taken on the Richardson hue.

"In fact, I'll prove it by going to gather abalone tomorrow after we've attended to the lens, if you'd like to join me. We can visit seal rock while we are at it."

"That sounds nice," Olive said, setting to free the potatoes from their little green-sprouted eyes. She heard a rushing noise loud as a tsunami wave crashing over the island. She leaned over the sink to look out the window to see what kind of monstrosity might conjure such a sound. Just then, the blue rabbit twitched and sat up, as though it had only been sleeping the whole time.

"My god, boy. It's not dead." Richardson pointed at the rabbit, who looked Olive in the eye only briefly before jumping off the counter and under the table.

"Get it!" Richardson shouted.

"I'm trying!" Olive scrambled after the rabbit. On the floor, both on their hands and knees, they met eyes one more time before the blue rabbit jumped toward the crack in the door, pausing in the dark entry before bounding into the wild night. Olive ran after and followed it outside. She saw the rabbit bounding smooth and cool under the moonlight, then paused by the pathway back to the traps.

"Don't go that way," she yelled. "That's where the traps are."

But the rabbit just jumped around in a circle and finally came back to where Olive stood as though waiting for a treat. She leaned down and picked the rabbit up and held it in her arms.

"You're more of a bunny than dinner," she said, glancing back at the house to make sure Richardson wasn't watching from the doorway. "Let's find you a safe place."

And with that, Olive had herself a pet. She found a little rock outcropping far behind the barracks and stacked some rocks around as a makeshift cage. She left the Russian blue there and petted its head, promising carrots and maybe some dried apple if she could swing it.

Once back inside the barracks kitchen, she threw her arms in the air and said, "I'm sorry, Richardson. He got away."

"Well, damn. Those rodents are fast. You know, Oliver. You have a knack for the kitchen life. Something tells me you can make a stew fine even without meat."

"Thank you," Olive said, returning to memories of her mother's warm kitchen, her soda bread and preserves. She could feel the tang of the baking soda on her tongue, in her chest.

That night, Olive snuck a carrot or two and some dried fruit out to the rabbit and watched him consume them with the brutal veracity of hunger. The carrots were gone in mere seconds. She secured some planks around him to keep him safe from predators—what exactly those would be on the island were beyond her ken. Back inside, she snuck a few of the dried and tanned rabbit hides into her room and covered her body under the blanket, pulling the thin wool over to keep them in place. Within minutes she was warmer than she had been since the day she arrived at the windy, foggy Farallones. The soft fur against her skin let her drift into a warm, gentle sleep.

At first the dream was idyllic. There were rabbits jumping everywhere, over one another and into holes and out. The field of green grass was full of them as far as the eye could see. She found an apple tree and picked an apple. In the dream, it was the most delicious fruit she had ever eaten. She threw the core for a rabbit to enjoy, but the scene turned dour. The first rabbit began to consume the apple ravenously until a second and a third tried to steal it away from the first. Then the rabbits started consuming one another with the same rabid ferocity with which the first had bitten into the core. A chain reaction started and the rabbits began eating each other in a huge cannibalistic mass of blood and skin and fur. Olive jolted awake and flung the blanket off in a sweat. She examined her arms for signs of the bloodbath she'd just experienced, but she was free from stains. She let the rabbit skins slide down to the floor and pulled the wool blanket back over herself, creaking as she changed position onto her side and closed her eyes, trying to think of anything else she could. She settled on Warren as she tried to reconstruct his swarthy features in her mind.

She put together the puzzle pieces of the tall, rugged egger and his gentle tones, the shotgun slung over his shoulder, as he called her clever. She could hear an echo of her own laugh and how for just a moment, the first since the passing of her mother, she had felt freedom from trouble. Lingering on his curly dark hair and beard, she wondered what it might feel like against her cheek, soft or raking, and speculated what he was doing at that very moment in time. She hoped she might catch a glimpse of him again the next day when Richardson took her to the abalone caves. She cringed at how the handsome egger must have thought her a silly little boy, guffawing with the clear pitch of a giggly girl at her own joke.

The next morning, Richardson and two other lighthouse assistants wrestled with one of the heavy iron attachments for the Fresnel lens— many giant, magnificently curved pieces of glass that fit together perfectly to project light unlike any other prism on man's green earth. Through the magnifying prism, the beam extended its long arm of warm light into the darkness of the ocean nights with the fearless might of an ancient god. After mending the attachment, they swore and sweat as they tried to return a slat of giant rounded glass back into a secure position. Richardson asked Olive to come take a side and she did, the weight of the thick glass seemingly impossible to uphold. She would almost have thought that the other men were not pulling their weight if she couldn't hear their grunts and smell their sweat as they struggled under the weight. But the heft of it felt good despite her screaming muscles. She could feel herself alive under the pressure not to let the magnificent glass tiers drop. Her blood pounded into her neck and she could feel her heartbeat in her ears as she strained to keep upright. They finally returned the lens to its position and let the glass down gently into the newly mended attachment. It stared back at her with its concentric circles like a crystalline cyclops. She wondered if men didn't fall under its spell out here, thrust into servitude to its spectrum. One of the other lighthouse men patted her hard on the back, breaking her free from the daydream.

"This work will grow some muscles on you, boy. How old are you? Thirteen?"

"He's a small fourteen," Richardson offered. "But more sturdy than he looks."

"Well, we'll see some hair on your chin soon, I suspect," the lighthouse man said in a less than convinced tone.

"I suppose so," Olive said, hoping dearly this would not be the case.

"And if not, he's a pretty great cook, so at least he'll still be useful in the kitchen." Richardson winked at Olive in a way that made her fear he might be beginning to suspect her deception. She glanced back at the lens and its opened glass eye, silently asking for some help in upholding her thin ruse.

Wild Ginger

Burning Woods, Oregon, 1977

THE BABY GROWING INSIDE her reminded Alice of a parasite. It sapped her of energy and kept her hungry, but the nausea made eating anything except toast or pretzels unbearable. She continued to be enervated day by day, slipping into a dull and thickening fog and resenting the "thing" as it drained her of her life force. It wasn't until she made a discovery in the patch of earth on the far hill behind the filbert orchards that things started to improve. Wandering out where the coyotes were rumored to den and the barn cats dared not go, back on the steep slope of sedge and alder giving way to Douglas firs and even a few small hemlock, she found a patch of dense earth that held some potent magic.

Confronted by Alice's sallow face every time they opened her bedroom door, her parents decided to ease up on their forced confinement and allowed her daily strolls—*for the baby*. Alice suspected this had been her father's idea when he winked at her one morning and said, "Enjoy your stroll, hon," in his quiet timbre. On one such morning walk, as she tried to keep one step ahead of the nausea to give the slip to brain fog, she found wild ginger growing around the base of a Doug fir. The flower was different from the run-of-the-mill wildflowers that grew in the area—the asters and the blue dwarf lupine, the Douglas's catchfly and Indian paintbrush. The deep blood-purple petals tapered into long fine points that curled up and out. She pulled her finger along the exotic edges of the curled petals. She dug out the leaves a little to see the half-hidden flower better, noted its hirsute petals and white interior, and just by chance, put one of her dirt-covered fingers in her mouth. It was the best thing she'd tasted since the morning sickness had hit. The fecund flavor of the black earth was at once bitter and sweet. She dipped her finger back into the roots and tasted the earth again. The flavor was delicious and somehow smacking of the forbidden. *Good girls don't eat dirt*, her mother's voice hissed in her head.

But eat dirt she did, fingerful after fingerful, until she became full in a new way. Full of earth like a freshly potted houseplant. Full like the swelling of the earth toward the moon. The flavors in the dirt changed with her imagination. She held the idea of a cherry in her mind, and up little flavor seedlings pushed through her taste buds. She thought of chocolate, lemon, and heartache. She thought of loneliness and there it was on the tongue—reminiscent of almond or marrow. And so it was that Alice found her energy and solace in a spoonful of dirt. She upped her trips to twice a day and snuck an antique silver jam spoon from her great-grandmother's silver set into her pocket and into the hills to taste away her worries. She ritualized the trips, looking forward to them for hours before she allowed herself to go. And after a few weeks, the little tiny seedling baby inside her stopped making her as sick, apparently also pleased by the strange nutrients and minerals. The color returned to Alice's cheeks and the fog parted just enough for her to feel that she might survive the most bizarre turn of events in her young life.

She tried dirt from different aspects of the hills on her parents' property, from the shade of the canopy to direct sunlight, from mossy to dusty, but her favorite dirt by far was that which clung to the roots of the only wild ginger bloom on the property. She scraped the spoon along the white fragile root system, careful not to completely uproot the flower, and delivered the spoon to her mouth slowly, her taste buds stinging in anticipation. The first bite was always the best. The spice of the dirt and root residue felt like miniature lightning finding its way along her tongue. After four spoonfuls of dirt, she kneeled on all fours and stretched like a cat curling her back toward the sky and then the earth. She was free and wild. And then she heard her mother's voice calling her in to eat dinner from across the field like an arrow finding its way to her side. She sat back up as though hit, but obediently went back to the house to eat. The nausea was starting to subside and she was hungrier than she'd ever been in her life.

"You're three and half months along now," her mother said, gesturing with a stiff hand for her to sit down at the kitchen table. "And your father and I think it's time you told us the truth about how this happened."

"I did already," Alice said, slumping in her chair. "Donnie. The comedian who left for Vegas. I honestly don't remember his last name."

"Well, dear," her father tapped the back of her chair with his cane to indicate she should sit upright. "We just don't buy what you're selling." He looked at his wife as though for approval.

"I don't know what to tell you." Alice interlaced her fingers in her lap. "I'm not trying to sell anything."

"And not to change the subject, but what are you always doing in the backwoods there?" Her mother put a steak down hard in front of her with a pat of butter and boiled potatoes on the side. "Eat," she said forcefully. Alice was suddenly less hungry.

"I don't know. I just like it back there."

"Well, your father and I think we need to raze a few trees to make room for a burn patch back there."

"A burn patch? Why does it have to be there?" Alice was horrified.

"Why *not* is a better question," said her mother. "Tell us what's so important to you back there and we might reconsider the location."

"If you tell us the whole truth—everything—maybe we can think of putting the burn patch somewhere else." Her father looked at her with wide, soft eyes. Her mother sat herself down the chair opposite Alice and stared her down with dark eyes.

"I already told you." Alice looked at her plate and tried to pull the tears back into her sockets.

"Tears are a sign of weakness," her mother said.

"The truth will set you free," her father added. "To quote our Lord and Savior. Now we bow our heads and pray."

Alice sat in silence the rest of dinner, feeling as though she might just be able to get away with avoiding the subject and that everyone might forget about the whole thing. She went to bed and prayed to God that He might spare her sanctuary and her beloved flower, its filaments providing her the only lifeline she had left. But the next morning she woke to the sound of faraway chainsaws and shouts of the arborists' coordination. "Headache!" she heard just as she went to the window, pulled back the curtain, and saw the top of the first Douglas fir from the far back lot fall, the impact bouncing and uprooting all the nearby plants. Her wild ginger was surely torn up and crushed by the behemoth's weight. The whole area would soon be destroyed. Heat rose in her neck. She would never tell her parents the truth, she decided. And she would no longer bend to their rules.

That afternoon, she went to inspect the damage in the back lot, the ground littered with wood chips, completely torn up. The entire lower half of the hillside was stripped bare, the smell of fresh sap and pine needles hanging in the air. She searched around on the ground among the chipped wood, but there was no sign of her wild ginger. She had just given up hope of finding anything when she heard her mother calling her name. Her eyes darted toward the house, then up the hill into the canopy of the alders and Douglas firs. She ducked behind a downed log and looked back one more time to make sure no one could see her before scrambling up over the tree corpse and up the hill away from the house, the orchard, her parents, and life as she knew it, deep into the trees. She put the spoon into the pocket of her thin fall jacket and headed west toward the point where her parents' property met state forestland, the tiny compass inside her flipping like a new salmon toward the sea. She would walk all the way to the ocean. And when she got there she would become a waitress, or maybe join a fishing fleet. She would be something new and never look back.

She didn't really start to get hungry until it got dark. But as her hunger grew, a summer night alone in the woods felt like a reckoning with God. With each crack of a branch, she dared Him to come get her. Curled up on a mossy place, she pulled the thin jacket around her, but was still cold, so she pulled some downed Doug fir branches into a pile and used them as a blanket. They worked surprisingly well and she curled up with her head on a pile of fern fronds and moss and waited for sleep to find her. Every noise made her tired body leap to attention, but when she finally fell asleep, she fell deep into an exhausted slumber and slept through till the morning. When she awoke in the predawn hour, the hunger that took over her body was unlike any she'd ever experienced. She thought with longing of the dinner she had picked at the night before—the warm steak and buttery potatoes—and her mouth filled with saliva at the mere idea. It felt like some animal inside her was tearing at her stomach. But there was something deeper to the hunger, like a presence behind her, a ghost, whispering that she must eat or die. And so she set out to find food.

Early summer foraging in the Pacific Northwest is not so bad. Bears do it. Birds do it, she told herself. *So can I.* She first came upon some huckleberry bushes with a few early ripened berries which filled the wrinkled cup of one hand and went down her throat in a flash. She then found some scant thimbleberries that tasted like the most amazing rose candies, melting sweet on her tongue. She found a few salmonberries, their unique tang lingering on the palate. But the very thought of salmon made her salivate. She would have to find some protein, and quickly. She sat on the banks of the Siuslaw River for a little while listening to it talk and briefly wondered whose land she was on. The land didn't announce its owner like the little patchwork green-and-white squares did on a map. To the animals, each hillside belonged only to itself. She listened as the stream spoke of things she did not know and never would. She fell under the spell of its rhythm and nodded her head in time. The watery sermon was more interesting to her than anything she'd ever heard in church, but with some of the same gravitas. It was Sunday and everyone she knew would be at church. They would be whispering about the wayward runaway girl and those in the know would be *tsk*ing and clucking about her poor, bastard unborn child.

She pushed their judgment and ignorance from her mind and tried to listen only to the stream, to let it pour over her thoughts and cleanse them. Down below, she watched an eddy and imagined what delicious fish flashed in and out of the shadows, playing hide-and-seek with the sun. In the middle of the stream, she saw a group of fish swimming over one another to try to avoid some sort of blockage in the middle of the stream. Flashing finned backs jumped over one another around the blockade, their bright silver scales catching in the sun. There must have been at least six fish, and from their large size she guessed that they were the first returning Chinook salmon of the season.

She moved down the rocks toward the river's edge and as she approached she noticed what the blockage was—a perfectly camouflaged net made of sticks, held out from a much longer stick on shore. The fish tried to avoid the triangular basket made out of twigs woven together by flopping in and out, but someone had made a rudimentary weir—a triangle of river rocks that siphoned them back into the net once they'd escaped. The fish moved their bodies over one another in such a sensual way that Alice almost felt as though she were intruding. She leaned farther out over the river, but there was no way she could reach the net without venturing in. She would have to walk into the swift water, so she took off her pants and waded into the stream, her toes gripping the slick rocks. She clung to a thin, bending branch of a willow as a lifeline as she waded in. The water rose up her calves as she reached the middle of the stream, then finally rose up over her knees, at which point she felt like she was more in than out of the water. *Note to self—the river takes over control when it covers your knees.* She closed in on the basket net slowly, trying to keep her shadow from falling over the fish. Their large bodies rolled up and over one another in a pile, in and out of the basket. Set on the long pole smack dab in the middle of the main rapid with the rough weir on either side, the fish would have to go either up or down to avoid the pit. The fish flopped against one another as though possessed. She let her feet find purchase slowly on the smooth stones and told herself that steady was just a state of mind. The water was almost at her thighs. There was a small waterfall and rapid just downstream in the swiftly moving current, and she knew if she were to let go or slip, that could be the end to her baby and more than likely to her as well.

But she was mesmerized by the fish and their flashes of silver and green. They almost seemed to be teasing her with the temptation of pink flashing flesh just below the surface. The predator rose strong in her throat and brain. She was no longer thinking in words and phrases, acting only on instinct—triggers and sparks of color and longing. She eased her feet down onto a rock above the fish and finally let go of the branch she'd been clinging to for support. It rebounded hard and a flurry of green leaves rained down. She bobbled, then steadied herself and waited for just the right moment before lunging her hands down into the water and net. The fish separated and bounced, finding their way out of the basket and into the weir's shadows with lightning precision. All but one smaller fish bounced out of the net, the small fish flopping once or twice against the woven sides before Alice got her hands firmly around the head and fins. Before it could bounce back into the water, she slowly retraced her steps through the water back to shore holding the flopping fish around the gills with one hand, steadying herself like a tightrope walker with the other outstretched arm. Once on shore, she pinned the fish's tail against a rock with her fist. She brought her hand down hard on what should have been its head, but the fish flexed up and the side of her fist hit only rock. A throbbing rose in her rattled hand bones. She wrapped her fist with her scarf using her mouth, keeping the struggling fish pinned to the shore by its tail with the other hand.

She had the animal firmly trapped. It writhed and raked at capture and she couldn't help thinking of the small, blond man in the moccasins, how he'd kept her pinned among the coats. The fish's mouth opened and closed, so much oxygen available but none filtering in through its gills. Its body struggled to gain breath—suffocation amongst bounty. She looked into its desperate fish eye and recognized the shock, felt it in her past. *Is this what they call compassion?* The moment of communion was taken over by a predator fist as she paused above the now tired, slowed fish, bringing her scarf-wrapped hand down in a hammer motion on its head. Fresh red blood trickled from the gills and stained the scarf, blooming in the wet fabric like a wild poppy.

The spirit drained from the fish and she fumbled for her hunting knife in her pocket. As the slick entrails slid out from the salmon, she decided that it was her life, and she would live it how she wanted. She was the fish and she was the man in the moccasins and she was wrested from the false promise that life would be simple if she just believed in some martyred ghost. It was all just a story. And she knew that stories change each time you tell them. After gutting the fish, she scaled the skin with her knife and let her mouth sample the raw pink flesh underneath. It tasted as delicious as anything she had ever eaten. She plunged her mouth in for more, feeling no remorse. She was blooming and she was free. As the fish filled her belly and evaporated the pains of hunger, she made a decision—she wouldn't let anyone else tell her story for her. She would be her own captain.

On the way back up the banks, heading to her fir-needle bed, Alice spoke her first words out loud to the baby. Her belly was full of salmon, gurgling and galloping through the nourishment, and the baby, maybe the size of a small avocado, made its first puttering motion from side to side in her belly. The shock of the sensation caused her to stop. She put her hands on her belly and said, *Thing. You are a lucky little thing. You weren't even an idea and then you were. Some babies are a series of hemming and hawing before they are made. They are a series of: Are we ready? Should we wait a year? You? You simply jumped the line and came from the strangest of all cannons into my womb. And me? I've just now decided that I love you. I know that your being here is not your fault and I promise I will never make you feel that it is. You are a lucky little thing, aren't you?*

Moments after Alice spoke the words out loud, she looked up and there was a young man, maybe in his mid-twenties, with a long black ponytail and a baseball cap with "Toledo Boomers" crouching on a boulder above, watching her. He looked like he was probably from the nearby confederated Siletz tribe. It occurred to her that she very well might be on tribal land.

"Hello," he said. "Did you enjoy that salmon you just stole from me?"

"I'm sorry." Alice looked around to see if there were more people, as if she were suddenly surrounded. "I didn't know it was yours."

"I'm just teasing you," he said, jumping down off the rock. "Looks like you needed it more than even the bears, the way you ripped into that fish."

The reality that she had been unknowingly watched during her most primal, private of moments made Alice's heart race. She wiped her mouth with a delicate motion as if to hide evidence of the carnage with her sleeve.

"Come and I'll show you the best salmonberry patch nearby. Name's Alex, but people call me Boomer." He pointed to the embroidered beaver-like creature on his hat and held out his hand.

"Thank you, but I think I should be on my way." The whole strange-man-offering-fruit thing was all too familiar and made Alice extremely uncomfortable. "Do you know which way the ocean is from here?"

"It's that way," he pointed up beyond a ridge to the west. "But you're a good thirty-plus miles from the ocean, here."

"Damn," Alice said. "Thought I'd walked halfway there already."

"Looks like you found an old road, so good on ya. Did you know this was once a highway out to the coast? Around the time of the model T's. Ran right between the rez land," he waved with his left hand, "and state forest," he motioned to the other side of the trail with his right hand. "But now all that's left is a half-collapsed covered bridge and this little trail here through the old growth."

The way Boomer looked up and regarded the trees with awe as he said this, the way his face was open to what he saw up there, made Alice feel like maybe she could trust him enough to guide her to some berries. But she decided to keep the thought to herself and busied herself looking at the ground instead. She dragged a foot over soft soil and through a patch of false Solomon's seal, revealing a black millipede with yellow spots along the edge of its body.

"Hard to imagine a car ever driving through here," she said, finally letting her neck crane back and letting her eyes follow Boomer's gaze up a hundred-year-old Sitka's peeling bark to the sky. As they watched, a small fat-bodied bird came careening out of the sky from the west and landed without an ounce of grace into the tree canopy. It settled onto a mossy branch out of sight.

"Ah!" Boomer pointed. "A marbled murrelet. They come all the way in from the ocean to nest in these old trees. That's a good omen for you and your baby. Very good spirit to have around." He smiled up at the sky but didn't look at her as he said this.

How did he know she was pregnant? She squatted and inspected a drooping pink wildflower next to her, a bleeding heart, and weighed her options. *She had no idea where she was and this man could help her find food. He knew about the baby. Had he heard her talking to it? Should she trust him? Or should she just walk away and hope she could find her way to the coast where she would do what? Find some sort of job and never go back to her parents? Run away and become a waitress or work at the mill?* Boomer interrupted her thoughts.

"You know, my grandmother was a very wise woman and well respected in the tribe. She used to tell me that even when life gives you shit, you can use it for fuel."

Alice looked up at him, her expression a mixture of amusement and confusion.

"I'm paraphrasing of course." He smiled a wide and self-satisfied smile. "So, do you think you'd like some berries and then maybe we can talk about when you'd like to get back to your parents?" Boomer stood up and extended a hand down to her. "I think that's probably wiser than running away to become, what? A seal in the ocean? Was that your plan?"

Alice stood up and dusted off her jeans and thin jacket. She heard another bird come flailing into the canopy and wondered where they had been all night and why they would come home so early in the morning. What were those little beasts up to flying over the ocean, under the stars? She was suddenly flooded by images of her parents praying together for her return, pacing the neat rows and rows of the orchard looking for some clue as to where she had disappeared to, hoping she wasn't dead. They would have the entire congregation looking for her, while surely planning how to kill her when she did return.

"Okay," she finally said. "Let's take a look at those salmonberries then we'll talk parents or seals."

"Sounds like a worthy discussion," Boomer said, handing her a half-eaten granola bar from his pocket, which she shoved into her mouth whole.

"Fanks," she said, chewing, as they walked single file along the overgrown road.

"Don't mention it."

"Just curious. Why do they call you Boomer? You hardly make a sound as far as I can tell."

"Yep. Stealthy and silent. You know what a boomer is?"

"Not exactly. No."

"It's a mountain beaver, a species found in the northwest. My parents said I always wanted to be down by the river or sitting among the ferns as a kid, so they started calling me Boomer."

"Ah. Things haven't changed then, have they?" Alice said, looking at the fern-covered hillside and nodding back at the river quietly shushing its retreat in the background.

"I guess not." Boomer put his hands on his small potbelly. "I wasn't exactly a skinny kid, either."

"I bet you were adorable," Alice said, her guard falling hard to the forest floor. "A little chunky Boomer."

"Not a whole lot changes, I suppose, when it comes right down to it." He led the way up a hill, the two moving together naturally through the underbrush, Alice using the same footsteps as her guide. "There are some parts of ourselves formed early in our lives that we just can't shake. Like, what did you love most when you were a little kid?"

"Hmm." Alice paused. "I think I've always loved birds. They can go wherever they like. On a whim they can fly to another state, or hell, another country. Total freedom."

"Then I'll call you little bird," he said. "And you," he paused to point and speak directly to her belly, "are the littlest bird of all."

They walked in silence for a while before coming to an area with the densest salmonberry bushes Alice had ever seen, almost as though someone had cultivated them. The plump orange-pink berries hung as heavy and thick as raspberries and the two ate quietly, side by side, until they could eat no more. When they were done, Alice followed Boomer out of the forest and to his truck without discussion. As she watched the green blur by along the highway, she knew that when Boomer took her straight back to her parents, her mother would probably grab her arm, pull her in, and yell at him to get off their property. She might call him a pedophile or a dirty Indian. Her father would stand by and say nothing. They would lock her away again in her room and she would let the bloom and beautiful chaos she felt newly opened in her chest slowly fade until she was an old bouquet, desiccated and dried like her mother's awful dusty cornflower decorations nailed to the wall. She had always disliked those displays—the crucified cornflowers gathering layers of dust like little flower corpses. The green blurred more and more as she blinked back the tears brimming in her eyes. She put her sleeve up to her eyes to catch the tears and cracked the window to let the air dry away the pink.

"You okay, little bird?" Boomer asked as they bore left off the highway onto the gravel of her parents' driveway.

"I will be, thanks," she said, unconvinced by her own words.

And so, as she had predicted, upon return to the orchard and her parents' doorstep, her mother did grab her away from Boomer with her vicelike hands, powerful from years of trimming trees and harvesting. She then asked who the dirty Indian was. Boomer backed away from the front porch with a closed, inscrutable face. Her mother slammed the door and threatened to bind her with the belts again, but seeing as she wasn't resisting, and at the quiet request of her father that she take pity, at the last minute she decided that a deadbolt on the outside of her door would suffice. She shamed her daughter for leaving and shamed her for returning. In a way, the predictability of her mother's response felt like a security blanket. Alice would have been thrown off if her parents had behaved in any way other than their strict, bigoted manner. The silence of her father in such matters often confused Alice. If he didn't feel the same as her mother, then why didn't he speak up? Why didn't he put his foot down when her mother went too far? Instead, he just retreated into the shadows like a troubled narrator in a stage play, as if to say, *But this is not my story to tell.* He would retreat into the orchard to trim and measure and try to make sense of things alone. Meanwhile the door to her room shut behind Alice and was locked, her mother's footsteps resounding hard as they retreated down the hallway. As Alice lay back on her bed, the little baby flipped around like the salmon she'd killed.

A package had come for Alice while she was away in the forest, "flaunting her heathen ways before God and nature," as her mother had said. After her mother had already gone to bed, Alice heard the bolt slowly unlatch from the outside, and her father slipped in with the package tucked under one arm. He handed it to her in the cover of dark and whispered, "From your friend Sal. I saved it from the incinerator. Don't tell your mother and keep it hidden under your bed."

"But why does a present from my best friend have to be secret, Dad?" Alice whispered, made bold by the dim light, as she glanced at the return address.

"I'm not sure, hon. You know how she is. Best not to poke the beast."

He slipped out and latched the door gently from the outside. Alice sat up, turned on a desk lamp, and examined the package. It had been half-opened, presumably to make sure it wasn't drugs, pornography, or worse. The postmark read Needles, Arizona. She finished unwrapping the brown paper and unpacked the box stuffed and well padded by little Styrofoam peanuts and wadded-up newspaper. She tore the wrapping the rest of the way to reveal a little antique beveled collection box with velvet lining and little wooden dividers separating bird eggs into their own sections. Some were big and speckled, others small, smooth or taupe. One egg was no larger than a curled-up potato bug. The great variety of sizes, colors, and shapes brought a smile to Alice's face. A little card inside read simply:

Thinking of you.

Love,

Sal

The baby fluttered excitedly in her belly as she laid her finger on the smooth surface of the largest egg. Alice placed the collection on the shelf and looked out her bedroom window over the green belt in the direction of the ocean, remembering what it was like to be out there in the wild, to be in bloom. Regret flowed through her. She should have at least made it to the ocean before she came back to her prison cell. Her parents had never taken her to the beach and she had always wondered what kind of salty magic might be held in the place where such vast, watery mystery met the shore. *Why had she not asked Boomer to take her there before returning to the orchard?* She put her hand on her belly and promised the littlest of birds, her very own, that she would help it find patches of salmonberry and seek that thing in life that would make it feel alive, always. She would help it fledge and learn to fly, even if someday that meant it would fly away from her.

Waking

ALICE'S PARENTS DIED ONE after the other, their exits from the earth like one tree falling in the forest and knocking the other flat to the ground in its wake. First it was her father who died of a heart attack while working the rows, and then her mother one week later of an unknown ailment resembling—the romantics postulated—heartbreak. Others blamed her mother's passing on shock. Alice secretly wondered if her mother hadn't given up the ghost on purpose, as she had found an almost empty, small bottle of arsenic inexplicably mingling among the cordials and sweet wines in the cabinet after their passing. To compound the mystery, her mother had drunk more raspberry wine in the week after her husband's passing than in the rest of her life combined. Inebriated one night, she grabbed Alice by the arm and almost told Alice she loved her. Instead, she looked into her face and asked very seriously if Alice planned to do all her chores for the week or just laze about like a damn cat all day. Holding the little bottle in her hands, Alice remembered the mad gleam in her mother's eyes as she asked this inane question, then Alice threw the poison bottle in the trash and put the idea out of her head. There were plans to be made, boxes to be filled, and funerals to plan.

Before their deaths, Alice's parents had taken on a significant role in raising her young daughter. But an infantilized Alice had always struggled with their dominion over Lily. They told Lily that God's wrath was full of fury. Alice would whisper to her before bed that God was a jokester, for how else could one explain things like giraffes, four-leaf clovers, or love? Her parents told Lily she had to eat her liver even though it made her gag. Alice passed her a small ziplock bag under the table and, before they got up, tucked all the chewed up liver pieces away in her cardigan pocket to dispose of later. She was more like a big sister to Lily than a mother. So when they died, Alice spent a lot of mornings looking into the mirror and telling herself she was going to be fine, that it was time for her to become a woman, to become a mother. On the outside she was ready to take on the role, but a kernel of doubt stayed planted deep within.

She projected a confident, womanly countenance to the nosy, overly dramatic people of Burning Woods. She let them know that she was in control by the way she steeled her face when they rolled out their condolences, and with them an array of their own anxieties. It seemed to Alice that each person projected their own sense of mortality and experience on her parents as they whispered the story over and over in grocery lines or after church. It became a sort of absurd game of telephone as the tale stretched and evolved and moved from ear to ear. Alice kept her face stoic, steady. She stopped going to church and whisked her way through the store like she was on a mission.

People who hardly knew the family speculated on every minor detail of their passing. It is in this perverse way that the newly dead spin into fame. But in a world of mill accidents, logging mishaps, farming imbroglios, and assorted other hardscrabble exits from the earthly plane, the passing of two young grandparents in succession ultimately was not completely out of the ordinary. They were just two more grandparents led back to the earth—or, in the parlance of their church, to their maker. In death, theirs was a dramatic fifteen minutes of fame.

As the story was told and retold, the deceased farming couple became symbolic of God's wrath and righteousness. They had been either called to a higher purpose or brought down by vice, depending on who was spinning the yarn. There was a lesson to be learned, though no one could quite pinpoint it precisely. Their church hosted an elaborate double funeral at which the weeping and wailing was appropriately dramatic. Somber hymnals were sung and traditional black worn. Alice sat in a sort of shock in the front of the church, flat-back perfect posture on the hard pew as her parents had taught her, but never once shed a tear. She straightened tighter as she felt a ghost tap of her father's cane on the pew. Five-year-old Lily sat next to her and cried in what Alice suspected to be fear at seeing her grandparents made up with layers of thick makeup, chemicals filling their veins, lying still as the day in their satin-lined boxes. As a large housefly landed on her mother's nose, then buzzed and flew over and landed on her father's forehead, Alice held Lily's hand and told her it would be okay. She held her breath, trying to create tears. But no matter how hard she tried, she could not shake a single tear from her dry eyes, even as she met the suspicious, turgid gazes from the congregation.

That evening at the funeral reception, held at the orchard farmhouse, it became a sort of unspoken bet among the guests to see who would be the first to get the young, tragic daughter to crack.

"Your parents' dedication to St. Timothy's was so admirable," an ample, purple-haired woman said before piling stuffed mushrooms into her mouth. She swallowed and shook her head. "Absolute pillars of society. You must just be so *sad*, honey. It's okay to let it out, you know."

"I know," Alice said cautiously, secretly trying to tie a knot with the string of a celery in her mouth.

"You really shouldn't keep it all inside," another taller woman with significant chin hair chimed in. "T'isn't healthy."

"Yup," Alice said, glancing outside at the rain streaming down the windows in rivulets. *Was that the kind of waterworks they wanted from her?*

"What on earth will you do with this whole orchard all by yourself?" A man joined the circle. Perhaps a scare tactic might work. Alice stood, slowly blinking.

"Excuse me," she said, pushing her way to the kitchen. *Why were people such sadness succubae when it came to mourning? It's like they were trying to get off on her pain and wouldn't be satisfied till she'd filled their cups with her salted tears.* In the kitchen, she dodged a couple more attempts to convince her into emoting and rooted around in the drawer until she found, way in the back, the little jam spoon she'd used to taste the roots of the wild ginger. With the spoon in her pocket and a copy of Italo Calvino's *Cosmicomics,* she slipped out the back door and into the rainy pasture. She had picked up the book at the local thrift store, God's Closet, a place that mysteriously provided her with interesting reading from time to time. She often wondered what local Burning Woods citizen shared her passion for fringe literature. They certainly weren't any of these folks gathered inside her parents' house. She glanced back at the farmhouse and paused briefly to wonder about her daughter and her whereabouts but kept going, because Lily was surrounded by people. She would be just fine.

At the back of the orchard, where the burn pile had supplanted the Doug firs and alders, the once-haven for wildflowers, she took out the spoon and found a nice scorched patch. The earth was full with moisture and carbon. She scraped the spoon along the black dirt and lifted it to her mouth, something she hadn't done in a long time. She closed her eyes and smiled as the blackness spread over her tongue, because this, this dead, absent flavor, matched exactly the feeling she had inside. She put the spoon back in her pocket, sat down under the umbrella of an evergreen, and cracked her book. It was marked on a passage about falling into the void. *Perfect,* she thought. *Let us fall and keep falling.*

Back at the house, young Lily wandered all over the floors looking for her mother. She wondered if this wasn't what death meant—people just wandered off somewhere and were never heard from again. Perhaps her grandparents were now off wandering in the hills toward the ocean. It was how her father had gone out of her mom's life, just wandered off on a barren Nevada highway, so maybe he was "dead" too. She went upstairs and then down into the basement, where she played quietly with a croquet set, setting the balls to *click* against one another, then back again, before noticing a small, half-covered secret little cupboard in the wall. She moved the boxes from in front of it and turned the small brass finding on the closure. It opened a minute door that led to a lightless room under the back porch. The opening was just big enough for her to get her body through. Certainly no adult could follow her. She climbed inside and closed the door behind her. Through small slits in the wooden slats, she could see full-grown legs milling about outside beyond the porch, smoking cigarettes and talking in quiet tones as they sipped chablis. She looked at the shape of each pair of legs but didn't recognize any of them as her mother's extra-long, muscular limbs. She decided she would stay there until she saw her mom, watching the stems of strangers wander in and out of view.

The search party for Lily didn't begin until Alice had returned from her reading break in the woods. Everyone had just assumed they were off somewhere together. When she came back, she started asking around about Lily, who had seen her or talked to her, was she playing with older kids or younger. The snowball of paranoia developed quickly as people heard the little girl was missing. People experiencing grief are primed to let in whatever wild horse of emotion comes to the gates, whether it be fear, lust, or the histrionics of blame. The members of the reception checked everywhere in a manic state, even the basement, but the secret little cupboard door was shut tight to the room under the porch. The local police were summoned. Lily might have heard the search party calling her name both inside the farmhouse and out if she had not fallen asleep under the porch a good hour and a half before and slumbered the sleep of the dead. So to speak.

When Lily woke up, she felt a sharp pain on her chest just in front of her armpit. There was a little bit of swollen flesh throbbing and she felt sweaty after a swampy slumber. Her curly fine white hair was matted in little curls to her head. It was the small, painful flesh bite that prompted her to find her way out of the dark room and back upstairs. The first person she met at the top of the creaky stairs was a tall uniformed policeman sitting in the kitchen writing in a notepad. When he looked up and saw her telltale shock of curly, rumpled hair, he looked, appropriately, as though he'd seen a ghost.

"Mister," Lily said, padding her way over to his lap and putting her hot hands on his leg. "My armpit hurts."

There were wild rumors in the town that next week about Alice and Lily. The spider in the basement that had bitten Lily was speculated to be a brown recluse. She had been bitten on her chest just in front of her armpit and the area swelled up and out in a bull's-eye pattern of red rings that later turned dark in little parts, concentric circles of deep irritation extending out over her heart. It was the talk of the town. She might die, they said. The venom had weakened her heart, they said. Some clucked that Alice was unfit to be a mother. Some said that she abandoned her young daughter at the reception to run off and have relations with one of the harvesters in the shed. Others still said that Lily had been possessed by the spirit of mourning and had been trying to find her way underground to be with her grandparents, as they had been the only upstanding citizens in her family. What was common among the stories was the disdain for Alice and her methods of child-rearing. *Heathen*, they murmured in line at the market. *Elvira. Spiderwoman.*

For Alice, the next few weeks were spent packing things up in boxes and rearranging the house, trying to ignore the unfortunate events after the funeral. She ignored the judgment in the faces at the bank, the post office, the grocery store. "Nice to see you, too!" she would say, contorting her beautiful, wide mouth into a grimaced smile. "Lily's just fine! Healed like a champ!" she would say. "Did you know we don't actually have brown recluses in this part of the country?" she asked total strangers in an attempt to stem the flow from the rumor mill.

Lily asked her mother one morning, mouth full of cereal:

"Why'd you leave me, Mama?"

"When, honey? I never left you."

"Yes, you did. After Grandma and Grandpa wandered off. You left me alone with the strangers and then the spider bit me."

Alice had no response to her young daughter's accusation. She had, in fact, left her daughter behind in order to quell her own selfish rage. She had left her, and Lily had lodged herself in a small dark place like an unweaned animal. She poured her daughter some more cereal and kissed her on top of the head.

"I'm sorry, honey."

At the bank she took out a little extra to buy Lily a new toy. She had been asking for a Lite-Brite for longer than Alice could remember. The guilt had weighed on Alice for days as Lily recuperated at home. Lily had started to grow tired of her old toys and asked her mom to give them away with the many other items piled in boxes. Something in her was changed by the incident. She sighed and gave away her blankie, her favorite stuffed bear, and all her plastic horses. Often she sat at the window watching the rain come down. It didn't even occur to Alice that her daughter could actually be mourning the loss of her grandparents. Alice figured she could fix things by giving her something new. With the Lite-Brite she would give Lily the power to rearrange the stars in the night sky. A little astral meddling seemed like just the doctor's orders.

Alice was grateful that her parents had at least waited to exit the stage until after harvest was complete. They had left her enough in the coffers to figure out what to do by the time next spring rolled around, when she would need to start the process of trimming and spraying the trees on her own. Lily asked her mother one day whether Grandma and Grandpa would be coming back, or if they had wandered too far. Alice looked puzzled, then stared her plain in the face and said, "I sure hope not." Lily didn't ask any more questions about that and instead asked if she could have their old bedroom, to which Alice said, "Of course," and leaned down to kiss her on her pouf of white waves. "You couldn't pay me to sleep in there."

A letter came in the mail about three weeks after the funeral addressed to Alice with a postmark from Green Valley, Arizona, and a hand-drawn golden eagle soaring over a canyon on the back seal.

March 12, 1983

Dear Alice,

> *Greetings from the Sonoran Desert spring! The desert is sleeping down here, which is one of the quietest and most incredible things. I wish more than anything I could transport*

*you down here to see it. I heard about the passing of your
parents and it's long overdue that I send you a letter. My
deepest condolences, dear friend. I know you didn't always
get along, and that their passing brings complicated emotions
for you. If only I could be there to hug you right now, to just
help you in any way I could. We could perform a spiral dance
on the commune, drink red wine, and make fun of Kenneth's
newest driftwood sculpture. We could climb a hill until it was
hard to breathe, or just lie back and listen to the pond frogs.
Unfortunately, I am broke as a joke, so I am unable to come
home. Just know I am there with you in spirit.*

*Arizona is mixed—amazing land, but often intolerant and
difficult people. I'm still out traversing the wild places like some
furless wild dog looking for meaning. I've lived so many places
over the last five years since I left Burning Woods, and each place
holds its own magic. But in that half a decade I've never really
belonged to a place, nor the place to me. My college semesters
were short and brutish, bookended by time interning for
conservation groups as a field tech. The footprint of my tent is
always temporary. I think of you walking among your hazelnut
groves that were your father's and your father's father's. I think
of you sleeping for twenty-two years in that same old leaning
farmhouse. It's a romantic feeling for me, to imagine those kinds
of deep roots as I walk along yet another new arroyo or come
up over another aspect of a mountainside. When my feet are
throbbing with blisters and I still have four miles to walk over
uneven ground before I even get to my old truck parked by the
side of the highway, I think of you sleeping gently in your bed, the
curtains rustling in the morning breeze. It is a beautiful, cool,
calm dream. I do miss you, and Oregon, and all that that means.*

*When I have a long way yet to walk I also sometimes
talk to the trees. Any kind of tree—a mesquite, aspen, or
ironwood. Chilopsis is a favorite conversation partner because
if you're lucky it will make a little hiss back. Do you ever talk*

to the trees? I'm kind of forgetting what normal people do and don't do. I find when the wind is very low, just whispering, then stopping, is a good time to attempt a discussion. Sometimes you can just perceive an answer in the stillness. And then the wind rises again and takes that moment with it, on into the future and is gone. Say hello to the evergreens from me, and give one a squeeze when no one is looking. Although, really, who's left there to shame you for tree-hugging now? Hug away, and with abandon. It's your land now.

My deepest regards to you and to that teeny little beauty, Lily. I wish I were there with you. Thank you so much for the drawing of her. She's getting so big! I keep it with me always.

Love,

Sal

Lily was back at kindergarten and Alice found herself alone for the first time since her parents' passing in the truly empty farmhouse. Alice let her eyes linger on the word *love*, then folded the letter and put it back into its envelope, smoothing the seal with her fingers. Every time she received one of Sal's letters she felt a mix of resentment washed over by an upwelling of affection. It was the tapping of a long buried stream that rolled within. Over the last couple weeks, the food train of helpful (read: nosy and judgmental) neighbors and church friends had slowed to a stop, and she shed her black mourning clothes for her much preferred jeans and T-shirt and started packing up things she no longer wished to have around in order to donate them to charity. Sitting there with a giant cardboard box filled with crucifixes at her feet, the stillness felt like the eye of the storm. In the calm, she waited for someone to tell her what she was doing wrong, or what she should do next. She tucked the letter from Sal into a tin box she kept behind a row of never-read encyclopedias way up on the highest shelf in her father's drawing room.

She surveyed the room and decided it would no longer be called a drawing room—too stuffy. From then on it would be called the library, a more egalitarian word for the space. She glanced back up at the tin on the shelf. Only she knew the tin was up there, and by far the tallest of everyone in her family, only she could reach up there without a stool. She realized as she stretched up on tiptoes that she no longer had to hide herself away in tiny boxes stuffed into dusty corners of the house. Carefully she brought the tin back down and left it open on the coffee table, the contents of her secret self unhinged and open for anyone to see. Inside sat a few letters from Sal, some cigarettes, an expired condom, a couple ancient joints, a collection of Gustav Klimt postcards with thin naked women in broken doll poses, and a miniature copy of the Anaïs Nin erotic book *Little Birds*. The clothbound book's paper was thin as tissue paper and utterly rippable.

Alice started a small fire in the fireplace and put Clifford Brown on the record player, sorting through the records and starting a pile for church music (headed to the donation box) and a pile for jazz (keep). Brown's trumpet filled the room and Alice paused to consider how even when his music seemed happy and upbeat, there was an underpinning sadness to the chords and progressions that she appreciated. It was almost like a secret melody hidden underneath the blanket of sound. The music felt tended, tacked down by melancholy, as though it might float away into the ether if left to its own devices. After lighting the fire, she sat down in what had always been her dad's chair and lit one of the joints, her legs splayed out in a most unladylike way. She waited for someone to yell at her from the kitchen, or rap her on the leg with their cane, indicating she should get up out of their chair. But she was alone and it felt good. Due to an inefficient flue, the smoke from the fire filtered into the room a bit, mingling with the smoke from her joint. She took off her bra, threw it on the floor, and cracked the miniature copy of *Little Birds*. As the haze of her new life filled the room, she was transported to France in the thirties and New Orleans in the forties, where the brassy women in the book did all the things they were told not to and enjoyed every moment of it.

She was far away; her hand slid down the front of her pants playing with what God had given her, the weed spinning patterns in her brain, when a loud knock on the front door brought her back to Burning Woods, away from the wild sexual abandon of a painter's studio in Paris. She pulled her shirt down and got up to see who dared interrupt. There on the front porch stood a church friend of her parents', Char, with a casserole dish and huge smile pasted on her face.

"Hello there, honey!" Char bubbled, her smile tightening a bit as she noted Alice's undone top button of her jeans and erect, braless nipples under her thin, rumpled T-shirt. "I thought you shouldn't be alone on an overcast day like today."

Char pushed her way in past Alice, slipping easily under her long arm into the foyer. She headed straight for the kitchen but stopped and peered into the hazy, warm library with its box of crucifixes glinting and reflecting in the firelight as though itself lit.

"You really ought to fix that flue, honey." Char's smile shrank as she waved away a thin plume of wandering smoke. She changed course and entered the library and put down the casserole on the coffee table, sniffed the air, and wrinkled her nose. "Redecorating?"

"Um. Sort of," Alice said, nudging the box of crucifixes with her foot as if to hide them behind the couch and quickly closing the tin of sin on the coffee table.

"Well, maybe we can redistribute these to the people of *our* church who would love to have them." She emphasized the *our*, lingering, with her lips pouting for a moment. "How 'bout I take them to the church thrift shop?" She picked up the box and cradled it like an abused baby. "Unless, of course, you want to keep them."

Alice crossed her arms and said, "Thanks for the casserole, then."

"Hey," Char's voice softened. "Why don't you keep just one of these." She handed an all-wood, crudely carved crucifix to Alice. "To keep you rooted."

"Thanks," Alice said, taking the crucifix and stuffing it in the back pocket of her jeans. "You know, I just remembered I have some chores to do before I pick Lily up from school." She cocked her head and opened her arm toward the front door.

"Of course, dear. See you soon. God bless."

Alice closed the door behind Char and watched her retreat toward her car through the front door's wavy turn-of-the-century glass, original to the house. Through the filter of weed smoke, Alice saw Char bounce to the beat of Clifford Brown's trumpet and through the waves of glass do a little cha-cha with her wide hips before she slipped into her station wagon and rolled up the dusty road. Alice sighed and slunk back into the library, lifted the tin-foiled edge from the casserole, and dipped a finger in. It was delicious. She got a fork from the kitchen and came back into the library, eating almost half of it in one sitting, sans plate. She examined the crucifix with one hand and shoveled chicken and noodles drenched in homemade gravy into her mouth with the other. *Why was it so good?* she wondered. *What kind of culinary witchcraft?*

Her eyes rested on the fire and the crucifix grew warm in her hand. She sat back in her dad's chair and twirled the little Christ figure around and around between her fingers like a ballerina in a music box, the flames flickering behind it. He danced and danced in the flames. She looked at the walls and couldn't think of a single place in the house to put the crucifix that felt right. And so, finally, she laid the crucifix in the only place she knew would send her old life into the past forever. *Why did everyone romanticize her rootedness?* All she wanted to do was rip up everything she'd ever known from the ground and burn it down. As she watched the fire grow, she was a wildfire, germinating seeds as it tore through the pines. She was a maelstrom of possibility. She watched the wood turn black, the smoke of what had once been herself rising up and out into the cool air. She decided then and there not to live in a manner that made her feel dead. She went over to the shelf and replaced an icon of Mary on the mantle with the egg collection Sal had given her when she was pregnant with Lily. And then she lit the rest of the joint and listened to the rain start to click on the stones and trees outside, a staccato plucking of the strings that made everything new again.

All About Taking

UNDERNEATH THE DARK OUTLINE of scattered redwoods, a nighthawk sailed through the beam of a loud, buzzing streetlight outside the town hall, making a loud, sharp "peent" call followed by a low boom. The lower, rasping sound brought to mind a miniature dragon bent on destruction. The bird flew in and out of the light on pointed brown wings with white illuminated stripes, its silhouetted image flashing on and off in the moonless night like a strobe as it dove in and out of the beam of light. The bird swooped and caught insects in its mouth, engaged in the arduous task of providing a meal large enough for both itself and its new offspring. A second nighthawk sat atop a fence post outside the front doors to the hall, blinking its inky, black eye in the darkness, resting, waiting its turn to swim upstream on the river of survivalhood.

Inside the small hall, the summer heat hung in the air. An impassioned speaker, one Mr. Randolph Collier, pounded the podium as he said the words he wanted to accentuate. Gold. *Thunk.* Copper. *Thunk.* Ours. *Thunk.* Action. *Thunk.*

"These hills are filled with ore. We have to get roads built to access the deposits or we're going to have wasted our whole lives as fool paupers sitting atop a *gold mine.*" He slammed both fists to accentuate. "It's time we started talking again about statehood. I'm talking about the new State of Jefferson, folks. It's time to secede from the big government city-folk states to the north and south."

The audience erupted into skeptical murmurs and shouts of agreement as he drew his speech to a close. The air in the room had become stagnant and hot over the last hour of the community meeting and the crowd of mostly men fanned themselves with their pamphlets like señoritas watching flamenco. In the back, an old man named Warren and his wife, Olive, both in their seventies, sat in the last row of chairs listening to the meeting take place. Olive was the only woman in attendance but dressed like everyone else: jeans, wool shirt, and warm cap for the ride home through the cool night. The couple had said nothing to anyone, but kept their hot, calloused working hands clutched in one another's the entire hour.

"These secessionists seem to take in more air than the average man," Olive whispered to her husband as the men filed up the aisle and out into the night. "Makes you understand why they call them 'windbags.'"

"They'd take the oxygen out of our very lungs if it would fetch the right price," he said to her, patting her hand before they slowly rose up out of their chairs.

"Greed for greed's sake, my love." She took his arm as she straightened up.

The couple were strong and lean, dressed in matching, sensible work shirts, though he stood a good head and a half taller than her and then half again as wide. He helped her escape the tight row of uncomfortable chairs and held her arm as they filed out, the very last two bodies to leave the room.

Outside the hall, the men were riled up, talking about the idea of seceding to form a new state. Not everyone was in agreement, but the men talking the loudest were by and large defending the idea. The couple moved through the crowd and most men moved out of their way, except one. A plump, blue-eyed farm boy turned around on his heel and looked right at the old woman.

"I'm not sure where you think you are, ma'am. But this here was a men's meetin'. Bake sale's next week."

"Excuse me, young man," Olive said. "But you are an ass. Now let us through."

The young man scoffed but stepped just far enough aside to make room. He made sure to let his shoulder find hers hard as she passed by. She winced as a pain ripped through her middle, a string of lightning bouncing through her organs and up her spine, but did not want to give the whippersnapper the satisfaction of seeing her in pain, of seeing her weakness. She gritted her teeth and let the pain from her old injury subside as she walked over the fence and rested with both hands on the post. Looking up at the nighthawks swooping in and out of the light, she felt a deep affection for their perseverance and grace. It was hard not to admire the way they went about their business. *Boom.* Warren watched her, admiring her upturned face holding the light. She looked like a painting when she watched the birds.

A shot rang out above her head. The nighthawk fell from the air mid-swoop as the man who had checked her shoulder lowered his rifle slowly. The second bird on the post scattered into the protective blanket of night.

"Damn bull bat," the man said, "Couldn't get a word in edgewise." He swung his rifle back onto his shoulder and took a swig off his flask. "Just like my wife."

He was looking right at Olive as he said this. Message sent. His friends laughed and patted him on the back like he'd just slain an attacking bear. One of them hopped the fence to retrieve the trophy from the ground. The group of secessionists ambled off down the road toward the bar to finish the night in similar fashion to how they started it. The dead bird flopped off the shoulder of the man who'd shot it, a small trail of blood dripping a dotted line in the dusty road.

"He should be arrested for that," she said to the rapidly dispersing crowd of onlookers. "So says the Migratory Bird Act of 1918."

"I'd like to see them try," a man said. "There'd be more than that one shot fired around here if they took a man into custody for killing a bird, I'll tell you."

"Boys will be boys," said another. "Let it go."

Warren and Olive walked silently a ways in the other direction toward their horses. It was time to get back to their farm, to their llamas, goats, and sheep. They rode the three miles home in silence under the stars. As they slipped down the road, she looked out over the trees and into the unknown. The trees made a dark line like a seismograph against the skyline, wildly oscillating jagged edges registering unknown shifts. As she traveled along slowly, moving with the lope of the animal underneath her, she thought of an article she'd read in one of her periodicals on the increasing use of coal since the turn of the century. Consumption showed no sign of stopping. She wondered as they turned up the gravel road to their house if maybe it wasn't all about degrees of taking. Humans just kept taking resources but never considered the outcome. *All these goods we take from the land,* she thought, *they have to grow, settle, and age. The rate of taking exceeds that of growth, which just can't go on forever.* The couple arrived at their sanctuary and stabled the horses. When the husband saw his wife's dark, furrowed brow, he told her he would check in on the animals. "There you go thinking too hard again," he said. "You go fall into bed." He kissed her on the top of her head.

The next morning, the sun came up with the intensity of a desert heat as the couple went about tending to their farm chores. Warren mowed the expansive lawn around the garden with a push lawnmower, moving the blades through the grass with the strength of his core body. It was getting more difficult with each passing year. He had paused to wipe the dripping sweat off his neck when he noticed not far in front of him a ground nest with small green-and-brown speckled eggs. He took out a string from his pocket and marked the area with a little stick planted in the ground, so he would remember not to mow over the area in the future. Making a wide semicircle around the nest, enough to give it a nice buffer, he continued cutting the grass.

Back at the house, he found his wife in the kitchen, embraced her with an extremely sweaty hug, and said, "How ya like me now?"

"You brute," she said and snapped him with a wet dishrag on the behind.

"Ow," he said, crumpling his face up. "That smarts."

"I fed all our ungrateful bovids," she said. "But I think you should take a look at Shorty. He's been pretty lethargic lately. Hardly touched the fresh hay."

"I'll look in on him in a few," he said, unclasping a bottle of beer from the cold box. "Seeing as you are our resident bird expert, ma'am, what do you reckon nests on the ground in the tall grass and has little green-blue eggs with brown speckles on them? I found a nest and mowed around it out in the back by the garden where the sagebrush starts up."

"Hmm," she said. "I suppose it could be a few different species. You didn't see a bird hanging around or making noise while you were peeking in on the nest?"

"Coulda been," he shrugged. "There was one of those funny green birds with the red spot on the head skulking around in the sagebrush at the edge of the yard."

"Green-tailed towhee, maybe," she said. "Beautiful bird."

"Whatever you say, love." He picked her up gently and twirled her in a circle. "But you're the only beautiful bird I know." The lightning lit up in her middle again as he swung her in a circle, but she said nothing. She gripped onto the counter with white knuckles and let the pain dissipate, then moved out of the kitchen and slowly down the steps out across the grass toward the nest, her curiosity piqued.

The couple had chosen to buy this land because it marked the place where biomes met, the line between forest and desert scrub. She loved that she could look in one direction from their yard and see small tanbark oak in the foothills blending up into the redwoods, Sitka and hemlock. If she looked the other direction, she saw the great expanse of sagebrush wandering out into the great basin. A creature with a wandering spirit, she had always loved these liminal places. When they arrived in these parts well before the turn of the century, there was nothing but trees and desert for miles in either direction. She had immediately fallen in love.

She bent down to look in the nest and saw that one of the eggs had a small puncture in it. She picked up the green speckled thing, just bigger than a dime, and examined the smooth sides and painterly decoration. It always amazed her that this was the way birds came into the world, from painted packages as fine as any marble sculpture. She examined the small hole in the shell, probably made by another bird. A wren, perhaps. She put the egg into her pocket and breathed in the strong, brisk sagebrush air.

Back at the house, she drained the unviable egg by puncturing the other end and blowing out the yolk. This one particular possibility of life was, like all her own eggs knocking around inside her, never meant to develop into young. Long ago, her monthly had abruptly stopped due to complications from an injury. In replacement of her role as mother, she found herself taking care of wounded wildlife in a special shed next to the other farm animals. Inside the shed was a rotating cast of songbirds, hawk, deer, rabbits, and, one time, a baby raccoon. People from all over the area would deliver half-gone wildlife to their steps and the duo would do what they could for them. Survival rates were low, but the release of a rehabilitated creature gave her more joy than she could express in words. It was a sight to see: a posse of rehabilitated animals following her around from place to place on the farm as she went about her business.

She clucked at a robber jay hopping on the back porch railing and said, "You can't come inside, now. Remember what happened last time?" The sky-gray jay hopped up onto the top of the screen before scolding her once and flying off to harass a bluish-grey rabbit hopping around near the shed. She came inside and handled the egg carefully over the kitchen sink basin, turning it back and forth in the light. She blew out the last of the yolk and carefully left the empty husk to dry on the sill above the kitchen sink. As the speck of clear white and deep orange yolk swirled and found its way down the drain, she marveled at the scientific tricks required to transform such simple ingredients into life. She went into the living room and examined her old silver egg collection sitting on the bookshelf next to her field guides. There was more than enough room for a new member in the assembly, and the little towhee token would look nice in there. She picked up the most recent copy of *Nature Magazine* and sifted through the articles, stopping on one called "Helping Birds to Migrate." She made it halfway through before the day took its toll on her and she fell asleep in the chair with the magazine laid open on her chest, her brown hair streaked with lines of grey flowing loose over her men's shirt. The magazine, a picture of white parrots on the front, rose and fell on her chest gently as a boat on the calm ocean.

The People Collector

T O ALICE IT FELT like standing before a blank canvas, paintbrush poised to fill in the space with invention. For years Lily had been begging her mother to tell her a little about her father, and one evening after a long day driving the husker in circles to collect the hazelnuts for harvest, Alice, dizzy with fatigue and three glasses of cheap bordeaux, finally caved to Lily's request for the story of Original Donnie. She paused and stared into the fire in the library, sipping deep from a tall glass of red, and composed the lie. She could make him a centaur, or a Pegasus with a typewriter for a head. Who was left to refute such a truth? In the story Alice finally decided on, she embellished with just enough details to make it plausible, adding that in the strong tradition of wild and rebellious Christian daughters, at fifteen, the same exact age as Lily was, she pointed out with a note of warning and a wag of the finger, she had left the farm with an older aspiring comedian named Donnie to go make her fortune in Las Vegas.

As she sketched in the details, Alice felt swept up as an actress might be on the first night on stage of a big production, her heart beating faster and her voice growing dramatic in the telling. Alice claimed Donnie told her she had "showgirl legs," drawing her fingers up her indeed lovely legs, and shrugged her shoulders and said that that was enough for her. She lingered on the invented minutiae. She had packed up her small houndstooth carpetbag and crept from the creaky house so early in the morning that the birds hadn't even begun to sing yet. The way Alice told it, she and Donnie only made it as far as northern Nevada before she threw up her breakfast and realized she was pregnant. When she shared the news with him, he said, "I'm not headed to Vegas to be that kind of daddy," and put her on a bus back home to Oregon. Alice claimed she never even knew his last name (a morsel of truth) and told her daughter that their sorrowful parting in front of a diner was the last time she ever heard from him. Alice finished her glass of wine in one final, dramatic gulp, feeling a sense of pride in the storytelling. It seemed like an airtight story to Alice—a man on the run and a woman scorned make a tearful final break somewhere on the loneliest highway and part ways forever. The story was not a new one, as far as stories go.

Alice had looked deep into Lily's eyes as the fire licked gently in the glassy reflection of her pupils and emphasized that Lily looked exactly like her and nothing like him. But that evening after hearing the story, looking at herself in the mirror upstairs in her room, Lily felt there was clearly something else in there, like two dark half moons under her eyes waiting to rise above the surface and tell a bad joke, or start a fight. Compounding this distrust of her own genetics, Lily lingered on the elements of the story she'd heard Alice telling Darla about her attempted in-utero assassination of her daughter. As the evidence mounted, there was something even more sinister yet undiscovered about the foreign features staring back at her. She played with the fleshy knob at the end of her upturned nose and pulled out her ears to inspect the shape of the lines, as though there were some map hidden within her singular topography. Her mother was simply not telling her the whole truth, and a familiar hot anger welled up in her face, making her skin hot to the touch. She sighed and put her forehead against the mirror to feel the coolness. Her third eye, her mom would call it. She closed her eyes and tried to disappear into the mirror, to let the cool reflection give way like a diver into moonlit waters. She wanted to disappear. Her mother's half-truths weighed her down like a suit of lead. All the information and misinformation was not helping Lily mend the kind of self-loathing that can walk girls hand in hand into adulthood like a shadow friend.

The next morning, Lily squinted into the sun and put on her sunglasses as her mom drove her to school. From behind her glasses, she glanced sidelong resentment at her mother in the driver's seat. Her mother's stories just didn't add up. It felt like a growing chasm of lies between them eating up the days with silence. They passed the grocery and the bait and tackle and, of course, Dickerson's Feed and Seed, with its slick, expensive signage and line of glossy tractors in primary colors for sale in the yard. *Grass may be gold in Burning Woods, but well, then, chemicals are diamonds.* She had heard her generally quiet grandfather say this one evening after a hard day of spraying the orchard, his fingers stained blue from the fungicide. The Dickersons, of Dickerson Feed, Grain, and Fertilizer, were by far the wealthiest family in all of Benton County. They drove a fleet of Dodge dually pickups, and when they would stop at the only stoplight in downtown, they'd rev up all six cylinders under the hood to let everyone know they were there, the engine growling like it might devour whoever dared cross its path.

Every morning in front of school, Dempsey and Todd Dickerson poured out the back door of the extended cab, all arms and legs swinging like two baboons, carrying their takeout breakfasts in paper bags. Their older brother, Slay—no one knew his real name—gunned the gas and took off like he was late for an important business meeting.

As Lily and Alice drove up to the curb, Lily tried to adjust her sunglasses as if she could hide her identity from the boys sitting up high on a cement wall, swinging their legs, punching each other, and laughing. As she passed the boys on her way into school, she half expected feces to be flung.

"Hey, your mom was in the other day buyin' pesticides. I thought hippie freaks didn't use that stuff."

Lily raised her sunglasses on top of her head and looked back at her mom idling in her diminutive aqua truck, clearly straining out the window to hear the exchange but pretending to check out something on the side mirror. Her hair was pulled back tight in two braids, but the blonde fringe around her face surfed the wind coming in the window like it was trolling for trouble. Lily glanced back and could swear Alice was flexing her biceps.

"Boys," she paused. "It's way too early to talk shop."

Both Dempsey and Todd held sixty-ounce sodas and looked like they were on meth, they were so jacked up on caffeine, despite it being only 7:43 a.m.

"Well, tell your mom she can come by any time and I'll give her a personal tour of the feed barn," Dempsey, a fifth-year senior, said, nudging his younger brother.

"I'll be sure *not* to do that," Lily said, lamenting the weak comeback.

"Not!" the boys pounced on her weakness. "I thought you were like a brain or something. Where's that brain now?"

The boys took synchronized pulls off their sodas and filled their cheeks to capacity without swallowing. Lily felt justifiably worried they might spray down upon her a fine mist of whatever disgusting drink they held in their cheeks when Max came out of the front doors. He was wearing dark jeans and a tight, black vintage shirt printed with a bouquet of wildflowers underscored by the word Montana in pink. He squinted his eyes at all three of them, assessing the situation. Lily's chest tightened at the mere sight of him.

"Dickerson central out here," he said. "Tell me, guys, is it true that 'erson' means limp? Or is my Old English slightly off?"

The second bell rang and the hall monitor waved everyone inside, the Dickerson boys swallowing the warm liquid they'd been saving in their cheeks and mumbling something inaudible in baboon speak before jumping off the wall, throwing their emptied cups into the trash with two close-range cheater jump shots before walking inside.

"Thanks, flower," Lily said. Max smiled. "All of nerd-kind is reaping the rewards of your rain dance. Those dopes are totally afraid of you."

"Don't mention it," he said, putting his hand over his chest and bowing dramatically. Lily glanced back at the street and saw her mom still sitting in her truck watching them with a dark face as they walked inside the school doors.

∾

WHEN MAX DROVE LILY home that afternoon, it was unseasonably warm and muggy. Birds sang in the trees with a manic intensity, like they had missed the memo that it was spring and were trying to catch up by performing double time. Lily smiled as they eased up her long gravel driveway, content with their emerging ritual rides home, but when they pulled up next to her mom's parked truck, she noticed someone had crossed off the word "bicycle" on the bumper sticker and written in a childish font "blow job." The message seemed little changed, as she imagined fish had little need for those either.

She could just make out her mother spraying fungicide in the far orchard, dressed in head-to-toe protective gear, full blue suit and bonnet, face mask and booties. She waved them inside and came down off her ladder and across the orchard. Despite the voluminous blue suit, the urgency in her brisk movements was apparent.

Once on the stoop, she was flushed and sweaty as she stripped off the suit and left it outside in a quarantined bin. She wore tiny jean shorts and a tank top with no bra that left little to the imagination. Lily was just relieved she was not entirely naked under the suit.

"Hi, there. I'm Lily's mom, but you can call me Alice," she said, taking off her gloves one by one like an inspector.

"I'm Max. Nice to meet you." He stuck out his hand but she waved him off.

"Poison fingers, sorry." Alice waggled her fingers and went over to the sink to continue the conversation, yelling over the sound of the water as she washed her hands with goo from an orange container for what seemed like a very long time.

"You spraying for bugs, then?" Max sort of yelled.

"Not bugs that are the problem right now. Fungus. There's a blight that has all the filbert growers up in a tizzy. We lost almost half our crop last year."

"Wow. Lame," Max yelled, the word "lame" booming in the silence as Alice turned off the faucet.

"Totally," Alice said, smiling and leaning back against the sink. "My grandparents didn't exactly choose the best land for growing filberts up here in the mountain foothills, but I suppose they didn't really know any better back then."

"So the biome is better down in the oak savannah, then?" Max asked, almost in challenge.

"I suppose the valley floor supports a stronger growing environment, yes." Alice cocked her head to one side.

The two locked eyes for what seemed like way, way too long to Lily. The two were in a sort of bio-speak battle. She glanced back and forth between the two of them, quietly mesmerized by her two closest people finally meeting. There was probably something she could say to break the silence, but she feared another "you bet your quarks, buddy" moment and chose silence instead, settling her feet on the carved lion paw feet under the table. It was her mom who finally wrested herself from the gaze of Max and went to open the fridge.

"Juice, anyone?" She didn't wait for a response and got three small handled mason jars down from the shelf. "I hate to use so many chemicals but it's use them or lose them these days," she said. "The world of filbert farming is just not what it used to be."

"I suppose that could be said of a lot of things," Max said, sitting down at the table and crossing his hands in his lap demurely. "The unnecessary occupation of foreign countries, the recent Rwandan massacre, the greenhouse effect, what have you. It's a messed-up world in general."

"I suppose it is now," Alice said, looking pleased. "Would you like to stay for dinner, Max?" she asked in a hopeful, childlike way. Lily would bet money there was no hot meal planned to back up that offer. "Stay a while." Alice waved in encouragement, having conceded the battle.

"Thanks, but I have to be going. I have a date with my uncle to dehydrate an unfortunate elk. I'll take a rain check, though." He flashed them both his widest smile.

"Yes, do," Alice said, and as the screen door closed behind him. "Don't breathe too deep on your way out to your truck, dear," she added.

"See ya," Lily said with raised, perturbed eyebrows long after he'd gone, digging a bobby pin into a preexisting rut in the wooden kitchen table.

"Lily, don't," Alice said, swatting at her daughter's hand.

"No. YOU don't," Lily responded under her breath as her mom got the newspaper from the front porch, letting it fall on the table with a thud on her return.

"Excuse me? Please, speak up."

"Mmm." Lily put the bobby pin down but pressed the flesh of her thumb into the widening divot on the table. The table was so scratched and worn it must be have been hundred years old, she figured. When Lily was a kid, she used to hide under it when her grandmother and mom were fighting about boys, God, the righteous path, or whatever else they found to fight about, and she would play with the carved wooden lion paws, stroking them fondly. She would pretend that the table could come alive and carry her off into the forest where they would hunt rabbits together and the lion would raise her like its own cub. She concentrated and waited for the wood to turn to soft fur under her fingers. Then she would be free.

"Wow. Freaking hot suit." Alice interrupted Lily's thoughts and fanned herself with the paper, inspecting the face of her sullen daughter but deciding to sidestep an argument. She chugged her juice before going to the fridge and refilling her glass with wine. "Seems like a nice boy, that Max."

"Yeah, I guess." Lily pretended to read the comics page.

"Interesting and smart."

"Yeah, I guess."

"Handsome. With a bit of *drama* to him."

"Mmm. Hadn't noticed his *drama*," Lily said. "Whatever that means."

"Yeah right you hadn't noticed." Alice rolled up the rest of the newspaper and slapped her gently on the arm before heading to shower off the day, refilling her wine glass on the way. In the stairwell, she paused and leaned against the doorway, pushing her chest out like someone in a dirty movie.

"Just be careful with that boy, Lily. Don't do anything I would do."

"Mom. Gross."

"I just don't want you making the same mistake I did." She shook the rolled up newspaper like a long, pointing finger at her daughter.

Lily raised her head slowly from her pretend fascination with the comics.

"And I suppose I'm the mistake to which you refer?" She raised her nose and used their mutual mock professor voice with a combative question mark at the end.

"You know what I mean. Don't be smart."

"Can't help it." Lily returned her eyes to the paper. "I must have gotten it from Original Donnie."

Original Donnie was a useful moniker in distinguishing Lily's biological father from Donnie Jr., her pet duck. Donnie Jr. had been a present from a traveling worker with stringy sun-bleached hair, named Lobo, who sold drums out of his VW Vanagon and had an unshakable scent of old curry. After working side by side in the orchard during one fall harvest, Lobo had it pretty bad for Alice. Lily had just turned seven, and at the end of harvest when the job was over and it was time to go, Lobo lingered a week or two, unpaid, half-assedly fixing things around the farm.

One day, Lobo presented Alice with a duckling in a little ribbon-wrapped basket, a faint glimmer of hope in his watery blue eyes. But Alice could hardly stand to look at Lobo, as he reminded her of the long-gone but never forgotten weed-and-speed dealer who had assaulted her among the wraps and coats on the commune so long ago. She refused to eat strawberries, spurned any and all beers, and was certainly not about to date a doppelgänger to her rapist. She turned around and immediately regifted the duck to Lily, who squealed with joy. Then Alice told Lobo with certainty that it was time for him to hit the road.

All Lily had been told at that point about her father was a name—Donnie—so she named the girl duck after her long-absent dad. Her mother remained tight-lipped and veiled about any other pertinent facts. As far as she was concerned, sitting in the long grass playing with her new downy duck, seven-year-old Lily felt a duck was as valid a replacement for her father as any creature on the planet. Donnie the duck would have to do.

~

THAT NIGHT IN HER bed, thinking about Alice and Max's eye lock, Lily felt troubled. What she had overheard her mother saying to Darla started to settle into her brain for the first time: she was an unwanted child. Heavy thoughts settled under her thin lids. The moon was almost full and had the intensity of a searchlight, frozen and bright on her bed. Lily regarded her two partners in insomnia—a poster of a glowing zombie, almost animated in the moonlight, and a coyote on the far hill just beyond the orchard's border winding his long song up toward the light in the sky. She thought about what should happen next in her life, and after rejecting a couple pretty good career options (fortune-teller, tattooed lady), she finally decided that she should probably continue on with her earlier plan to get Max drunk and make out with him. In the middle of the night with the cold moonlight on her face, it just seemed like the right thing to do. She had never been kissed, but she could imagine the lapping and swirling as clear as a Siuslaw River eddy.

Making a plan helped to ease the burden. The blueprints for an evening of drinking and kissing developed quickly as she worked out the important elements on paper. She decided the liquor should be drunk out of teacups, that it would have to take place during the upcoming lunar eclipse to maximize romance, and that her outfit should not be too complicated to get into, but not too easy to get off, either. She drew diagrams and made lists. Undoubtedly, her classmates did not have such planning and foresight with their own first engagements with drinking and fucking. She had heard stories in the hallways at school of kids drinking electric-blue Boone's Farms and doing donuts in their four-bys, then having sex in the back of oversized cabs or throwing up on each other, or sometimes, on off days, both.

Naked Antiques

Deep in the Mojave Desert, 1978

Dear Alice,

How have you been, my dear? How's that little bean growing inside you? I'm down in western Arizona right now working for the USGS doing bird surveys. It's hard work and a real strain on the body, which is starting to make me feel old way beyond my years. My bones ache. But still, I love my life, as it is the one I chose.

Have you ever heard of the sacred datura? It is a plant that grows here in the Mojave Desert and is a powerful hallucinogen. Well, it's too strong for most people to take it straight (remember how loopy I get off two pulls on a joint!), but another field tech told me about using the petals steeped in water to help with sore muscles, and so I decided to steep a bath tonight at the field house to ease my aching legs and back. Even though I'm not, I feel like I'm too old for this all-day off-trail trekking shit, I tell you. Post holing through the desert sand really puts strain on the ankles. Ha! I sound like such a Golden Girl. But which one? I'd like to think I'm Rose, but I'm probably Dorothy, right? Obviously, you are Blanche, you sexy lady, you.

I digress! Back to the bath. I put the flowers and steeped them in the hot water before lowering my aching body into the tiny, cramped field house tub. What happened next was something that is hard for me to describe. I never quite had the way with words that you do, but I'll try. The only way I can explain what happened is that I became a butterfly. As my muscles relaxed I suddenly felt as though I had these wings attached to my back. I knew that they had always been there, but I had just never noticed. When I got out of the bath, I let my wings flutter and dry and then I put my clothes back on and went out for a walk just before sunset. My skin sang in the warm winds and my wings bounced as I stepped over the uneven mesa. I walked along and let the strong oily scent of the creosote expanse fill my senses. I inhaled deeply and dragged my fingers through the little tough bunches of leaves and stood in the warm breeze, feeling the relief of the sun dropping below the horizon. I stood there alone and content just listening to the desert breathing. And then suddenly, without warning, I felt this great emptiness within myself revealed. After that, as though it were the most natural thing in the world, I could feel you standing there with me. I thought to myself—I wish more than anything I could hold Alice in my arms right now. I wanted to wrap my new wings around us and cocoon us into the darkness. I wanted to fly away with you forever. Just then a sidewinder struck up its mechanical rattle nearby and brought me back into myself. The snake passed in front of me with its strange sideways slither and carried on into the darkness undisturbed. And just like that, my wings were gone.

So here I sit in front of this piece of paper, writing this strange tale to my oldest and dearest friend. I'm not sure if it sounds crazy because spending so many hours alone in wild places has sort of dampened my ability to judge such things as what's "appropriate" or "sane." But I know that you will accept my tale and not ridicule me for it. You are the most accepting person I know and I miss you terribly and feel as though there is purpose in the different turns our lives have taken. I would love to see you again soon. Maybe after breeding season is over? I miss you something fierce.

Thank you for being a friend,

Sal

Sal paused before the only mailbox in the town of Needles, Arizona, with the letter half in the slot, the sealed and signed message to Alice growing warm between her thumb and forefinger. She pulled it back suddenly from the darkness, the foreverness of the mailbox belly. Perhaps her judgment wasn't sound. Perhaps the datura hadn't worn off yet. This admission of her long-held affection for Alice felt too bold, too hotheaded. She was a scientist and needed to think like one. How might pregnant Alice respond? The outcome felt unclear. Risky. She would collect more data and process her thoughts. Perhaps it was wise to hold onto the letter another week, and maybe next time they rolled through town, she would have the courage and confidence to send it. Then again, maybe not.

Whenever she and her field partner Ed came into town, they split up to "get shit done" as Ed would say in his crooked-toothed smile. Ed had been a stock car racer, a bartender, and a lobster fisherman before he started as a biological field tech, and he wore his different life paths as topography on his leathery, wrinkled face. What he did during his days off, Sal didn't need to know. Women, booze, or gambling—she didn't judge. She stuck to her own path, and she preferred others to stick to their own, too.

Sal shopped at the only grocery store for food staples she would need out in the desert wilderness the next week—tortillas, cheese, eggs, peanut butter, carrots, celery, oranges, gorp, five gallons of water, Tang, ice, and a couple six-packs of beer. These two full bags of groceries and water would keep her alive another week, she supposed, as she threw the ice into the cooler and the canvas bags into the back of the huge silver work truck before stepping up into the cab. She glanced at the letter again and threw it onto the dash. She felt her thinking clearing up, as if there had been an impetuous fog hanging in her brain. Alice would surely think she'd lost her mind if she mailed such a manifesto of love. The letter landed neatly under a growing collection of items she and Ed contributed after each day in the field, a shrine to their own scientific gods that included some dried wildflowers, a small rodent skull, some Long-billed Curlew feathers, and a perfect quartz heart. She stared out the front window of the truck before turning the key, but just before starting up the rumbling engine, she paused, something across the street catching her eye. Scrambling back down from the seat, she made sure the cooler was shut and secure, so the desert heat wouldn't spoil her groceries, and walked across the street. No need to look twice for traffic in this small town.

NAKED ANTIQUES read the worn wooden sign. Sal opened the door and was hit by a cool, musty blast of air. She looked around the small shop at the old saddles, photos, tin cups, Navajo weavings, and a glass showcase with medals, coins, and old jewelry. She was admiring an old Victorian hair brooch when she heard rustling behind the counter. A small, old man with bright blue eyes looked back at her, with tanned brown sagging skin and not a stitch of clothing on except a tiny sack on his junk held up by a string that went around his waist. Around his neck he wore a pair of reading glasses and a collection of necklaces with various animal teeth and shell fragments hanging from them.

"Welcome to Naked Antiques," he said, smiling as though nothing were out of the ordinary.

"Well, sir," Sal smiled and looked him in the eye. "You've already answered my first question."

The old man laughed. "Glad to hear it. Let me know if I can be of any other assistance to you, dear." He put on the reading glasses and started sorting and pricing some old postcards. The combination of his nudity and reading glasses on a silver chain started to give Sal the giggles so she had to find something on the other side of the store to occupy her attention. She looked the shelves over one by one until something on a high shelf caught her attention and she reached up onto her toes to get it down. It was a beautiful antique silver collecting box with beveled glass and reddish velvet lining. There were five different windows cut in the side that allowed an admirer to look in as though through a portal. Inside sat a three-quarters-full collection of bird eggs, all perfectly drained and nestled into the soft velvet bed, separated by thin wooden dividers. It had a tag hanging off it clearly marked NOT FOR SALE. She brought it back over to the old man who had since opened a can of beer and slipped it into a bright blue koozie sleeve reading: *Why Limit Happy to an Hour?*

"This is a fascinating object," she said. "Does it have a story?"

"Uh-oh," he said, peering over the tops of his glasses at her. "You have great taste."

"This has to be some sort of hummingbird egg," she started out by pointing at the littlest one. "And this bluish, speckled one with the pointed end looks like a seabird. Maybe a murre or a guillemot. This one looks like a green-tailed towhee, if I'm not mistaken? But it could be an eastern towhee." She looked up at the man whose twinkling eyes showed approval. "Not a bird from around here."

"You are not mistaken. Hummingbird, murre, and green towhee. And this one here I'm told is a hermit warbler." He pointed to a speckled brown-and-white overgrown jellybean of an egg. "My favorite. Hermit warbler that I am."

"We're birds of a feather," Sal said.

"So how does it come to be that a young woman such as yourself knows so much about bird eggs?"

"Bird gun for hire." Sal smiled, tipping her dirty, sweat-stained USGS baseball cap. "I'm out here studying birds for the government." She waited patiently for the laugh, or snide reaction she usually received when people in the area discovered that their tax dollars were going toward this girl cataloguing the desert avian populations.

"Finally. Some action by the powers that be that I can get behind." He smiled.

"Thank you for saying that."

"You know, I can't sell you this collection, unfortunately."

"Oh, I know." Sal smiled, sliding the collection back his way. "I was just so interested if you knew anything about its origins. I love a good story. Especially one that involves birds."

"Well, I can tell you there's a great story associated with this collection. All you might want in an epic tale—death, love, a war over eggs, pirates, daring escapes, and more death."

"That sounds like quite a tale. But I would imagine that death and more death might apply to any number of items in this store," she said.

"And you would be absolutely correct." The naked man looked hard at Sal before walking into the back room. She heard a rooster cry from the back room as he puttered around with boxes back there, and the naked man gently clucked back at the rooster. He brought back with him a box and set it on the counter. He offered no explanation for the rooster pecking around his stockroom. "Like I said. I can't sell you this collection because it is not the kind of thing that should be bought or sold."

As he said this, an enormous truck rumbled past outside the shop, cutting him off. He looked stunned for a moment as if lost in memory or remembering something important. After the rumble died down, he came back to reality and looked back at Sal who seemed utterly unfazed by the sound, almost as though she hadn't heard it at all.

"But I do believe this collection belongs with you. If you'd like to buy something else in the store," he put his hand on a forty-dollar saddle hanging on the wall, "then this will be yours to take with you free of charge."

"Deal," Sal said, resting her fingers gently on the counter.

The old man put his hand on the collection and sighed. "I knew someday I'd have to give her up. But parting is such sweet sorrow." He packed the box up inside another box, padding the space between with balled-up newspaper. Sal saw a flash of a picture of some judges and the headline, "Supreme Court Grants Women Freedom of Choice" just before the naked antiques seller crumpled up the paper and carefully tucked it into the side next to the collection. She instantly thought of Alice. The rooster crowed again from the darkness.

"I've always liked the company of roosters," he said with a sly smile. "Good friends, no judgment." His seemingly permanent smile was suddenly gone as he looked very seriously at Sal. "Take good care of this artifact. And I hope you can add to the collection. There is still some room in there for another leg or two of the story."

Sal nodded as though she were being knighted, or sentenced.

Ed waited for her back at the truck and laughed huge belly laughs when he saw diminutive Sal cross the street with a saddle under her arm and a box wrapped in string held firmly in her other hand. She threw the saddle in the back of the truck and set the wrapped and twined box in her lap.

"All right, cowgirl. Where's your horse?" Ed asked, as they started up the truck and rumbled out of town into the pastel pink, blue, and orange sky of a cloudless Mojave night.

"None of your biz, man. Let's blow this pop stand," Sal said, popping in a cassette of Black Flag and turning it up.

That night, after Sal had dropped Ed off at his starting location a few miles away where he would be surveying the next day, and as she unrolled her thin sleeping pad and lay it out under the stars in the desert wash she would call home for the night, she decided not to send the letter to Alice after all. Instead, she would send her the egg collection, and the gift would have to speak for itself. But first she would have to add to the collection, and she knew just the egg to add.

A cactus wren nest she had been monitoring had been depredated just two days before. The nest was settled deep into a jumping cholla in what seemed like an impenetrable fortress of spines but had still been torn apart by some larger bird, most of the eggs cracked, whitewash sprayed over the wreckage, and minute droplets of blood cast as though some final act of birdy Santería over the whole thing. Previously, the nest had been incredible—lined with downy feathers, soft green arrowweed leaves, and grasses, with a leaf hanging, inexplicably, by a spider web at the entrance in what seemed like an unusually welcoming way. Bird #36 had a flair for interior decorating, it seemed. Sal didn't usually get torn up about things like nest depredation, as it was part of the reality of being a bird and the biologists who love them, but this nest had been especially beautiful and she couldn't help feel a little wan as she marked down *depredated 4/20/78* on the nest card. Alone in the night, Sal lay down on her soft bed and let the sound of the elf owls courting nearby draw her into a quick and heavy sleep.

The next day, she woke a full hour before dawn in order to have a moment to sit with a cup of sock coffee before walking to her first point. She boiled the water on her camp stove, squatting in the wash, and poured the water through the coffee sock, the smell of the hot black liquid filling her nose. She popped a couple aspirin to ease the stubborn pain in her ankles and hips and pulled on her gators over her boots and field pants for added protection from the desert's dangers. The little bit of extra clothing was worth sweating it out under the hot afternoon sun. Surely, there was nothing worse than a stray jumping cholla ball sticking into your ankles. And it sure did seem to jump sometimes, from the ground and into the shins, wounding the flesh with its ungodly barbed thorns.

She gathered up her map, compass, first aid kit, her pens tied to flagging, binoculars, range finder, thermometer, nest cards, data sheets, clipboard, camera, sunglasses, hat, snacks, and extra water bottles. She double-checked everything, reviewed the exact latitude/longitude coordinates, checked the township and range lines, and marked the location for the truck before leaving the campsite and heading out toward her first point. As she loped uphill in the sand, the dawn chorus erupted into a manic cacophony of birdsong. A slender pink line appeared on the horizon as she scaled a small cliff out of the wash, walked through some joshua trees, cholla, and into a creosote patch. Soon the hot sun would surface and she would have to shed her warm layers, so she enjoyed the coziness of the desert cold and tried to keep it close, as though she could store it up for later. Her boot slipped through the sandy ground up to her ankle where a ground squirrel had dug a tunnel long ago, but she picked it up, shook it off, and kept going. She was a woman on a mission.

By the time Sal arrived at the depredated nest of Bird #36, the sun had only been up a couple hours but was hot enough that she had already sweat completely through her bra and peeled off all but the protective layer of a thin, long-sleeve shirt. She set her backpack on the ground and surveyed the nest hidden among the folding, labyrinthine, thorny branches of the cholla cactus. It took a trained eye to notice what had been the entrance to the nest, a small, grass-lined round opening just big enough for a small mirror to go into. She took a stance in a deep squat and pulled out her mirror pole—a compact mirror glued onto the end of a telescoping car radio antennae. Still squatting, she slowly allowed the mirror into what once had been such an inviting entryway but was now relegated to a mess of grass and feathers. Sure enough, she could just see in the mirror that one sage-green-and-brown speckled egg still remained. She leaned forward carefully and slipped her hand into the hole to grab the egg. And just as she did, she lost her footing and fell forward just a few inches. She yelped as pain seared through her chest. She pulled the egg out and dropped it into her pocket. A round cholla ball had found purchase, its barbs sinking unforgivingly into her chest right between her armpit and her heart. She yowled, screamed obscenities, and bounced on one foot in a demented dance of pain. She used one of her layers to pull the largest part of the spiky cholla ball off her chest and flicked it away using a pen. A dozen or so spines still remained staunchly rooted in her flesh, sticking out like acupuncture needles. She got out her tweezers from the first aid kit and painstakingly removed the needles one by one, pulling unnaturally hard to get the spikes out. Little droplets of blood rose to fill the void as she pulled the hooked barbs through her skin. When she had removed the last one, she looked down, amazed at the pattern on her chest. If one were to connect the dots, the little red droplets of blood formed a perfect spiral inward. As if some kind of hypnotists had lured her into this mess.

"I'll be damned," Sal said, taking a picture with her camera before wiping off the blood. Some twenty meters away, she heard a cactus wren begin its harsh rising song. *It must be #36*, she thought. *And I thought she had sung her last song.* The sound reminded her of a scolding from the beyond—the winding, cranking pitch upping intensity and culminating in a final *chaaa* before pausing just long enough to let the listener think about what they'd done. Sal thought that perhaps she was being punished for the sin of love. Or perhaps the bird was scolding Sal for doubting her resilience. Sal tried not to apply human emotions to the subjects of her transects, but the fact that #36 was alive and well brought tears to her eyes, just to the point of warping her vision. She wiped the tears away and inspected the egg in her pocket, finding it unscathed. Wrapping it carefully in a handkerchief, she stowed it away in a safe pocket of her backpack for later. She would add it to the collection, a subtle token of her longing for Alice. Then, as Sal moved through the desert with the solitary lope of a coyote, the cactus wren wound up its scolding song all over again. The sound wandered upward and dissipated into the waves of heat, the crashing of wavelengths, the melding of modes. The song left her and found its place up in the blue.

Blood Moon

Among the Siuslaw's Sitka, Oregon, 1994

THE MORE OF AN effort Alice made to assuage her daughter's resentment by cleaning, cooking, or offering to play games, the colder Lily grew. Lily's unshakable feeling that she had been betrayed deepened with each clear attempt at bribery. Alice spent money she didn't really have to buy Lily presents: a new PJ Harvey CD, a subscription to *National Geographic*, some new jeans she had been talking about for over a year. Lily neatly stacked all the presents in the library and put a note on them that simply stated, "Not interested." She wanted answers from her mother—the truth, not trinkets.

Lily was on her own path. She would seduce Max in her own way, with no help from her lying mother. So she went shopping in Toledo at the only nearby thrift store, aptly named "God's Closet," looking for an appropriate outfit in which to lose her virginity. A huge mural on the parking lot outside the thrift store depicted a preacher floating on a hill, the valley below filled with followers who all appeared to be in nightgowns. The anatomical dimensions on the followers were a bit off, making them resemble pinheads.

Inside God's Closet, Char, dear Char with the dyed-red perm and ceramic nails painted with American's flags or cats depending on the season, puttered around pricing items. She greeted Lily as she entered the store and perused the racks. Lily held up a pair of vintage ruffled underwear that went all the way down to her knees and said, "Char, I think it's just perfect that in God's Closet I can find ruffled women's underwear."

"Honey," Char smiled, "God's got even more goodies in his closet than we can ever imagine."

"Too true." Lily held up a suit jacket and tie.

Lily and Char were never *exactly* on the same page, but somehow they always found an easy way of chatting.

"What are you lookin' for today, Miss Lil?" she asked.

"Well, something with a little style. Maybe even some sex appeal," Lily said, feigning embarrassment and raising her eyebrow a little.

"Ahh. It truly is spring, isn't it, lamb? Here, try this. I actually thought of you when it came in." She pulled out from behind the counter an old plaid housedress from the fifties with a little belt and buttons up the front. Lily held it against herself and admired herself in the full-length mirror. She never ever wore dresses.

"Look at that," Char said. "It's just your size."

Lily remembered the last line on the outline for losing her virginity she had drawn up a few nights prior:

Be something NEW

"How about three dollars," Lily offered.

"Done," said Char, ever the dealmaker.

Char and Lily found themselves yet again approaching from two very different roads, but meeting at a comfortable junction. To Lily the dress was an ironic, iconic statement. To Char, she had finally gotten the local tomboy with the black nails and lips tucked into a dress.

"Take anything in that box, hon. It's all donated stuff I can't sell in here, but maybe you or *your mom* would want some of it." Her tone lingered and dipped deep into the well of judgment on the words *your mom*. "I know how you two love the kitschy stuff." She pronounced "kitsch" more like "quiche."

Inside the box were a couple of bodice-ripper romance novels, a Rastafarian figurine smoking a rolled "cigarette," a brass ashtray with a naked lady perched on the lip, and a poorly printed pamphlet called *Animism: a guide to breath, blood, and life.*

"Wow, Char. Can I take the whole box?" Lily asked.

"'Course, love. Get it out of here. Most of our customers don't have room for that kind of stuff, now, do they." This was phrased like, but was not, a question. Lily rolled the dress up and tucked it among her newfound treasures.

∼

THE NEXT DAY, MAX brought to school the two-pronged velvet antlers from the poached and butchered elk that had bumped in the back of his truck and laid them on the counter next to Lily during science club.

"For you, my queen."

Lily stroked the soft, brown slopes and considered the gift to be a very good sign. In their developing friendship, Max had pegged Lily as mildly obsessed with death, which, as she pointed out, wasn't exactly new as far as obsessions were concerned.

"Now you can think of me and think of death." He grinned a terrifying smile like that of a skull.

"Aw shucks," Lily said, punching him on the shoulder gently.

Their science teacher, Mr. Janowicz, approached and touched the antler gingerly.

"Amazing specimen, Max. Did you kill it yourself?"

"Nah," Max said, "someone poached it on Rez land. My uncle chased 'em off and I helped him process it."

"Ahh." Mr. Janowicz looked relieved. "Did you know that velvet antlers grow up to an inch a day? Isn't that incredible? At the cellular level it's the fastest reproducing bone cell in existence."

The teacher and his two students all stood with a hand on the antler to ponder its miraculous growth, abruptly halted. Lily thought for a moment she could feel the soft antlers shiver and move like a Ouija under their fingers. She thought about something she'd read in the animist pamphlet that said it was a misconception that only humans housed souls, that animals and objects housed spirits in equal ways. She wondered what kind of messages the antler was trying to spell out, what kind of tender plea.

~

WHEN MAX DROPPED LILY off after school, she tucked the antlers under her arm and nonchalantly leaned up on the truck. On the drive home, Max had stripped down to his Garbage Pail Kids T-shirt with Roy Bot on it, the little cabbage patch robot shooting flames out of his hands. The way it clung to his strong form made Lily shudder a little as she asked him if he wanted to come by her house on Saturday to watch the lunar eclipse. She had to clench her jaw to disguise her involuntary clattering of teeth. The result might very well be perceived as contrariness.

"It's late, like eleven p.m.," she told him. "But if you come earlier we can drink some whiskey up on the hill, maybe have a picnic or something."

"Where'd you get the whiskey?" he asked her.

"Don't worry your pretty little head about it," Lily said.

"Aw. You think I'm pretty," he said, shimmying his shoulders a little, bringing Roy Bot to life.

"You in?"

"Sure. What should I bring?" he asked.

"Just your fine self," she said. She could see a slight flush on his neck under his golden brown skin. She felt momentarily jealous that his pigmentation acted so successfully as camouflage. If they were ducks flying along together, she imagined, she would be the first glowing white orb shot out of the sky.

On Saturday morning, Lily went around the house collecting materials she'd need for the evening's festivities. But when she got to the liquor cabinet, really just an old paint-peeled cupboard under the stairs, the half a bottle of whiskey she'd seen there two days before was conspicuously missing. All that was left was a bottle of cooking sherry and a tiny amount of ouzo knocking around in the back. She popped the cork out of the sherry with some difficulty. It smelled terrible, but it would have to do. She put it in a wicker basket along with mismatched teacups, some cloth napkins, pickled vegetables, salami, some crackers, and cheese.

Lily originally bought the basket as a birthday present for Alice's thirtieth birthday. At the time, Char gave her a toothy smile with little dots of lipstick on her teeth and said, "What an *interesting* woman that Alice is. A little collector of all of God's people."

"People collector. That's a good one, Char. I'll have to use that," Lily said. On the way home from God's Closet that day, Lily swung the empty basket and thought of all the people her mother had collected over the years, from Original Donnie, Randy, and Lobo to Sal and herself. There were many whose names she never even knew. She pictured her mother tossing folks in like berries one by one into the basket, letting them bump around and mush together. She saw all those people, the good and the bad, just rolling around having a collected people party, drinking collected people cocktails, having collected people fights. She also realized that day, that *her* basket was empty. It made her feel like an egg, an inkling, a mere suggestion of the woman she would someday be. It made her want to start collecting, stat.

She packed up all the materials needed—binoculars, blanket, sherry, teacups, picnic foods, animist pamphlet—and the full wicker basket creaked in time with her anticipation at an evening of teenage deviance. Though she had told Max to drive in the back way and to meet her up on the back hill, she still had to avoid her mother's inevitable line of questioning.

"I'll be out on the far hill," she told Alice in her cramped and messy office. Alice was filling in little squares on a black bound ledger book, nervously pulling a piece of her long hair, winding it around her finger. Her brow was knit tight.

"I'm going to go watch the eclipse on the far hill. Sarah is joining me," she lied. "Don't wait up for me."

"Oh, I almost forgot. The eclipse." She looked up, distracted. "Tell you what, I'll come join you when I finish my books tonight."

"I kind of wanted some alone time with Sarah. She said things are bad at home again," Lily lied again.

"Oh." Alice sat up straight in her chair as if taking notice of her daughter for the first time since she entered the room. "Nice dress. Is it new?"

"Yeah. Another Char special," Lily said.

"I haven't seen you in a dress since you were a little kid." Alice narrowed her eyes a bit and cocked her head to the side.

"Well, change does us good, right?"

"I suppose so," Alice said, not entirely convinced by this line of reasoning.

In the harsh light of the office desk lamp, Lily saw the fine wrinkles around her mother's eyes and mouth clearly. Her skin had begun to sag under her chin and she looked tired. There was a whiff of loneliness in the room. That, and whiskey. It occurred to Lily that these might be one and the same—that her untouchably beautiful mother, the flawed and brazen people collector, might actually be growing old alone.

Lily laid out the blanket in the twilight out on the hill and practiced sitting in the womanliest way she knew how. But no matter what she did, the dress lay flat on her front like a little boy's school uniform. She lay back on the blanket and gazed up at her favorite Douglas fir, known affectionately as Dougie. She read from the animist pamphlet as the sun sat just above the horizon.

> The root of the word Animism comes from the Latin word anima, meaning breath and soul. Animism may be one of man's oldest beliefs, with its origins thought to date back to sometime around the Paleolithic age. From its earliest manifestations, animists held the belief that a soul or spirit existed in every object, even if it was inanimate. Trees, rocks, or clouds could all harbor a soul the same way people or animals could.

She looked up at Dougie and the other nearby trees—a few ash, a big-leaf maple, and the shrubby bitter cherry. They all shimmied their leaves in a rising breeze and Lily could immediately identify their personalities. The maple was a showgirl, fluttering leaves like sequins in the low light. The bitter cherries were, well, bitter, not quite bush and not quite tree. Then there was Dougie. She felt he had a real humility to him. He didn't ask much except to dance a little in the wind from time to time and sway like the tallest kid on the dance floor. She turned her head and thought of the orchard trees down below all lined up in tidy rows. They were the golden retrievers of trees—compliant, loyal, but prone to illness and genetically flawed by inbreeding. She continued reading.

> *Then, after leaving an object or being, this soul or spirit would exist in a future state as part of an immaterial soul. In effect, the spirit was thought to be universal. No one being or creature held spiritual dominion over another, as it was known that this spirit would be transferred at death.*

The sun went down behind Dougie as she leafed through the rest of the pamphlet, taking note of an animist breathing technique for "sharing breath" with a partner that looked a hell of a lot like making out. She looked up as points of light caught in Dougie's needles like cartoon stars. She pulled on her hooded sweatshirt against the spring's sudden turn from warm afternoon to evening chill and closed her eyes for a minute, breathing in the resin-scented air. Before long, she fell asleep.

In her dream, Dougie bent down and pulled her up into his branches. He tickled her feet with his soft green needles. She laughed, then slipped into a panicked gasping as she couldn't breathe. She told him to stop, that she's a fainter, that he'd be sorry when she fell from his branches and died, but Dougie told her not to worry in this huge, booming tree voice. She patted his trunk and felt very, very small. He lifted her, then set her down on a sturdy branch and slowly slipped a small branch up the hem of her dress. The bark felt rough on her thighs as he moved his way up her legs. All her sense of dimensions seemed off, like her hands and feet were huge and then suddenly very tiny. Her whole being was in flux. Her body folded in on itself like origami and she resisted the flushed feeling that flowed into her like golden beams. There was an image of Roy Bot the Garbage Pail Kid shooting fire through her body and she felt her body break apart into a thousand confetti pieces of light and bones, scattering into the strong winds. She was flying.

Just then, she was awakened by a howling and shaking in a nearby bitter cherry. It was completely dark and she flailed around on the blanket confused by the awkward reality of night. She tried to extract herself from the blanket but couldn't. A high-powered beam of light moved across the blanket and landed on her face. She recoiled like a prisoner under interrogation.

"Halt, little lady. What are you doing there?" a deep voice asked from behind the light.

She tried to untangle herself and muttered, "I think I just had a sex dream, or something. About a tree." She instantly regretted the statement.

Max howled again, this time with laughter.

"Oh, you are a precious, precious thing, Lil. Only you would jack off to a tree, my friend."

He sat down next to Lily and patted the blanket smooth, tacking the corners straight.

"I didn't say I jack..." she broke off. This was not an auspicious beginning to their evening of romance. "It was just a dream," she said softly.

"There's an old myth my grandma used to tell me about a woman who fell in love with a cedar tree," he paused. "But I can't totally remember what happened in the end. I think she either became a bird or drowned." The cadence of his voice was so sweet it could drown a person.

"Thanks for the reassurance."

"What you got in your basket, little blue riding hood?" he settled into a spot on the blanket and patted Lily on the point of her hood. He was also in a hooded sweatshirt, but his read Minor Threat across the chest.

"Well." Lily took out the teacups and sherry ceremonially. "This was all I could scavenge."

"Sherry? Like for cooking? Oh, that is classy, sis." He pulled the cork and made a painful face. "Smells like a couch that's been left out in the rain and peed on by bears."

The moon had just risen above the horizon when they poured out the pinkish liquid into the cups and took their first sips. There was a slight sweetness to it, but it punched at the taste buds like Whack-a-Moles. The heat forged a hot trail down Lily's throat and by the second cup she felt warmed enough to throw back her head and pronounce, "Max. I'm officially ready."

"For what, officially?"

"To try the animist breathing technique."

"Say what?"

"There's a diagram in here." She pulled out the pamphlet and turned to the back where the recommended activity for "experiencing another's breath" showed line drawings of a man and woman acting out the technique. She took his flashlight and shone it on the drawings.

"Hmmm," he studied them for a long time without looking up. "Looks weird."

"I thought you were the lord of the weird."

"True," he paused. "What the hell. Let's try it."

They opened their mouths in the oval shape as per the directions and slowly leaned in toward one another. Lily could smell his breath when they get close, the odor of something like onion, or even earthier, mixed with sherry. When their lips touched, they waited there a moment, neither one breathing at all. Lily tried to tell him to breathe in, but the words were garbled without the use of her lips. He pulled back.

"What?"

"You breathe in first," she said, "then I will."

"Oh."

They placed their lips back together and they were both dry, kind of sticking to one another in patches. As he tried to breathe in, Lily could feel the suction and pull of his inhalation at the back of her throat. Her body didn't want to cooperate and for a moment they were stuck in a breath stalemate. Then, her nose opened and she felt the rush of resined night air rush into her nose, down into her mouth and out into Max's mouth and body. He breathed out and the air reversed, back into her own mouth, almost making her choke. Before Lily knew what she was doing she pushed her tongue forward like a shot into his mouth and moved it around awkwardly, unsure what exactly she was looking for in there. She slammed her hands down into his lap in a clumsy hammer motion and searched blindly for something, anything. He grabbed her shoulders hard as he pulled away from her.

"What the hell are you doing?"

"What? I don't know. Just."

He was still holding her shoulders hard, keeping her at arm's length.

"Are you trying to make out with me?"

"Yeah. Sort of. Maybe."

"Did you honestly not realize that I'm gay, Lil?"

"Shut up. You are not."

"It's pretty obvious. I am *so* gay."

"No. You're not. Stop messing with me. You can't be." She shook her head in denial, but it occurred to her that, of course, he was, in fact, gay.

He laughed. "I can be and I am. It's not like I advertise it at school or anything. I mean, would you if you were full gay, half-Native from a disappearing tribe? Think about all the possibilities for awkward social speed bumps, there." He looked at Lily hard, eyebrows up. He seemed all of a sudden to be made of stone, the perfect sharp angles of his face glinting in the moonlight. "But I very much am," he softened a little. "I guess I just thought you knew because, well, because you seem to know me better than anyone else around here. Remember when you called me flower?"

"You were wearing a damn T-shirt with damn flowers on it," Lily grumbled.

"I thought it meant you knew."

"I was just making fun of you. Because I liked you."

Lily sat there quiet for a minute and looked up at the sky. A crescent of orangey red had just barely pulled itself over the corner of the moon like a blanket slipping off the edge of a round silver bed. She took a deep breath and closed her eyes as the blood rose in her neck, focusing on not fainting, on breathing deep. But instead of fainting, she let out a deep and resounding howl, a "nooooooooo," her voice pulling loud out of her body like a long chain up into the sky. She pulled and pulled until the knot around her heart gave way. Max joined in with her, then some coyotes on a far hill. When they finished, they collapsed onto their backs and looked up at the disappearing moon.

"Sometimes I just see what I want to see, I guess," she told him.

"I love you, Lil." He pulled her close and wrapped his arms around her back, nestling her head into his neck with a warm hand. "Just not like that." This position was far more intimate than any diagram, or anything she'd ever known with any man, for that matter. They lay down and held each other for a while, and as they lay there entangled, a crashing made its way up the grassy hill.

"Stop! Don't do it! Stop it right now."

Alice came lumbering through the sedge to their left, wagging her long hands in the air before her.

"I'm not too late, am I?" she fell down onto her knees before them looking serious. "It's not worth it, you guys. It's just not."

"Hi, Alice." Max sat up and looked amused.

"What's so funny? I heard screaming. Or yowling, to be more exact." Her breath smelled strongly of whiskey.

"Oh, nothing. I was just telling Lily how gay I am." He rubbed Lily's back in a slow circle, saying this in a way that made Lily want to implode with embarrassment.

Alice sat there on her knees, eyes locked once again in a stare with Max, sussing him out. She let out a deep whiskeyed sigh and placed her hands on both of theirs. She was out of breath but still managed a look of calm.

"I could have told you that, honey. But it doesn't mean you wouldn't try it out one time with a girl, just to make sure. It doesn't mean you wouldn't knock my daughter up."

"Not to worry," he said. "Our girl's chastity is intact."

Max started humming Madonna's "Like a Virgin" like a slow and baleful dirge, and Alice threw her head back and laughed in a loud, uninhibited way Lily hadn't heard from her in weeks, maybe months. It occurred to Lily that Alice might be way drunker than they were. Her embarrassment softened to pity. Her mother—the withholding, secretive woman she loved, but whom she was learning to resent— was revealing herself to be a hot mess.

"Hey. Look up, you guys," Lily said.

She wanted everything to stop. She wanted them to stop talking and she wanted to shrink away into the dark of the woods, to denature and unfurl and disappear. She felt herself recoiling from her affections for both Max and her mother. They both sat there, oblivious to how much they hurt her. Her mother in particular seemed oblivious to the daily pain and suffering she dragged her daughter through. A deep rage settled heavy in Lily's middle as she thought about her mother's withholding of the truth about her father. They sat there, all three of them in a circle, looking up at the moon with necks craned and prone. The globe Lily thought she knew appeared to be dying in the sky. The color bled a slow orange pool through the facade and it looked like the man in the moon was changing into a costume, perhaps to play a role as a blood orange in some overacted space drama about fruit murder. Then she thought that maybe their dear moon just needed a change, to feel like someone else for one night. She smoothed out her dress over knobby knees, reached into the basket for the binoculars, and took a closer look. Through the glasses, all the craters on the surface looked deeper and darker in the changed light of the earth's shadow. He was so beautiful she longed to pluck him from the sky and put him in her basket. Feeling decidedly unwanted by the two humans lying next to her, Lily decided someday, if all else failed, she would marry the moon.

Siren Song

A FTER A MONTH AT the job, Olive found herself relegated to the kitchen in the lighthouse keeper's shared quarters more often than she felt comfortable with. In addition to her confinement to the kitchen, there was the disturbing fact that Richardson began using terms like "tender" and "intuitive" to describe her cooking, which led her to believe that she was in grave danger of being found out, or perhaps already had been. "You have an uncanny, intuitive way around a stew," he would say. Or, "These blackened rabbit haunches are simply the most tender I've ever tasted." Despite the fact that it meant she was perhaps revealed, she took some pride in the compliments, as her culinary skills were part of the small, intangible parcel she had left of her mother.

She began plotting her escape plan, should she be officially discovered. And whenever a whiff of fairer-sexed terminology made its way off Richardson's tongue, she quickly changed the subject.

"A fine sort of cook you are, dear boy," he began, "I've said it before and I'll say it again."

"Richardson," she diverted. "You mentioned you might show me to the abalone caves soon."

"I did indeed and I have not kept my word. I do apologize, but I've been kept busy with those rapscallion eggers trying to work out some sort of deal so they don't make me 'pay' for eggs that are my god-given right to collect." Every time Richardson began to talk about the Pacific Egg Company men, he grew red in the face and poured himself whiskey. "Liars and thieves, the lot of them. They have tried every means in their power to effect my removal. But I've started my own plea with the inspector, did I mention?" He poured another two fingers of brown liquid, "And have made headway by sending documentation of their untoward activities on this island to Washington. I expect these men will soon know who, in fact, is the true keeper of the Farallone Light."

Olive let Richardson snort and harrumph his way through the end of his tall pour of whiskey without interrupting, satisfied that at least he was off the subject of her fine and tender anything. He rubbed his eyes and ranted, shifting in his chair or laying a hand flat on the table when he wanted to punctuate. As she scrubbed the dishes clean, she tried again.

"Perhaps, Richardson, you might just oblige me with directions to the abalone cave so that I may visit it on my own tomorrow. I do believe it's my afternoon off."

"Of course, boy. I'll draw you a map and leave it on the table tomorrow morn. And if you wouldn't mind bringing some abalone home tomorrow, I know you can manage some delicious and tempting cioppino for tomorrow's dinner. That's Italian for seafood stew, if you don't know. My grandmother was Italian."

Olive craned her head back a little to release the little cricks in her neck as she finished up the dishes.

"Of course, Richardson. Despite my mother being Irish, I know it well. She was a fine cook and not choosy over the origin of a good recipe. I'll come up with something." Talking about her mom made Olive feel that she was close at hand, in one form or another.

The next morning the map was there, as promised, drawn in the crude hand of what appeared to be a seven-year-old. There was a dotted line indicating the trail that traveled past the eggers' camp and past a little shed she knew was called the egg house by the eggers. After that, the line curved around seal rock and up and over a steep series of pinnacles with steep inclines, and finally all the way on the far side of the island an X marked, "Jewel Cave."

The air felt particularly cold and close that morning, like it was trying to spirit its way up her sleeves and into her bones as she started out on the trail with her collecting basket and knife, her warm pocketed sweater on with a small leather pouch of salt and a small silver spoon she had kept from her mother's silver set. It was the only relic of the set still in her possession. She decided to bring her blue rabbit with her and extracted him from the secret makeshift cage she'd constructed for him behind the barracks. He moved around in the basket, jostling and startling, poking his eyes up above the edge of the basket in the inch allowance if she lost her footing or jumped from rock to rock.

"I'll have to figure out a name for you," she whispered to him as they neared the bend where the trail passed above the eggers' camp. "You deserve a name after that stunt you pulled the other day."

She was tumbling monikers over like a stone in the water—Velvet, Salt, Skipper, Blueberry—trying each one out loud when a booming voice startled her.

"Hey, you! Lighthouse boy."

She turned on her heel to find Warren, the tall egger who had shot the gun into the air to stop the others from their inquiry into her pants last time they met. His canvas vest was full to bulging with speckled murre eggs. The effect on his gruff countenance was more than a little ridiculous.

"Yes?"

"Heading somewhere in particular?"

"And what business is it of yours, yolk beard?"

"Yolk beard? That's a first," he laughed. "I just wouldn't want a repeat of the other day."

"I should thank you for that, I suppose," she said.

"I suppose you should, but there's no need. That's just what good men do for each other, right?" He was still smirking a little from the yolk beard comment and patted her hard on the back.

"Well. I was headed over to the abalone cave Richardson is always on about." She took the map tentatively from her pocket.

Warren leaned in and looked at the childish scrawls, his smirk widening into a full-blown laugh.

"That Richardson is a card." He shook his thick black curls in the breeze and looked up into the salty sky as if looking for what to say next. "I'll take you there. This map will leave you stranded on the edge of a cliff like those seal pups that climbed up and got stuck last year. They died there, poor souls, yelping for days for their moms to get them down."

"Sounds like a tall tale, or a fable, if I've ever heard one," Olive said, folding the map back up and into her pocket.

"But it's all true." Warren gingerly removed his egg vest and stashed it in a divot in the rocks, covering the openings with a cloth from his back pocket so no gulls would recognize the contents and seize the opportunity to plunder. "You mentioned fables. A fan of literature, are you?" Warren asked as they started down the trail together.

"In so much as I enjoy a good tale as much as the next...kiiiid." She said the word "kid" carefully and slowly, as her mind had almost not sent the message to her mouth and she had been very close to saying "girl."

"Well, I'm a great appreciator of Greek mythology myself. Spent some time on a Greek fishing boat," he adjusted his Greek fishermen's cap in punctuation, "and those men could sure spin a yarn, I tell you. On the boat's where I first heard of sirens. You familiar with their story?"

"Afraid not," she said.

"Well, the sirens are beautiful creatures that were thought to be the daughters of the river god Achelous, who the Greeks say was the son of Gaia and Oceanus, but that's a whole other story for another time."

"So they were beautiful women," Olive prodded him back onto the story of the sirens, glancing in her peripheral vision at this strange man, sizing up his hulking presence. *Nineteen years old, Richardson had said. Hard to believe.* No one had told her a good story since her mother had died and she was like a parched and eager wanderer at a well. "Then what?"

"So the sirens were the most lovely of all women." He made the sign of an hourglass with his hands. "There were two or three, and their names were very hard to pronounce, so you'll have to forgive me, but these beautiful creatures had something of the sinister in them."

"Go on." Olive's mouth was getting dry with anticipation.

"They sang a mellifluous song, always at midday, when the winds would calm. Their long flowing hair glided on the wind, turning circles in the air as if to compel the sailors toward the rocky shores like hypnotists. The song was sad and seductive and called the men closer, even when their sailor sense heralded them to steer clear of the rocks. The siren song would possess the men so completely they couldn't help but dash their boats to splinters on the sharp cliffs, their bodies littered at the feet of the lovely, serene, yet evil, ladies." He drew his hands in the air like a magician and made the sign of crashing boats on the rocks.

"Oh. I love it," Olive said, lost in the world of the story.

"Well, as a young man you are supposed to heed the warning, not revel in the carnage of tempting women, or something like that. But maybe I'm telling the story wrong."

"No, I think you told it just right." Olive smiled to herself.

"The oldest fisherman on my ship, Alexio, always told the story with a horrifying ending where the sirens devoured the flesh of the sailors and their earthly blood spilled down their beautiful bodies as they sang and ate, sang and ate to the bodies of the foolish men." He shook his head in memory. "The way Alexio spun it, this final scene could go on for a long time. Made me wonder about that man's head a bit."

"The storyteller lingers where they choose to dwell, right?"

"I suppose you're right." He snuck a glance at Olive, admiring her fine neck and chin. "Well, I think we're almost at Jewel Cave."

Olive had been so caught up in the story she'd forgotten to look out for the landmarks. They had passed the egg house completely unbeknownst to her. The blue rabbit rearranged himself in the basket. Warren had not yet seemed to notice the third member of their party.

"Over there." Warren pointed to a narrowing in the trail that disappeared over a ledge. "We're in luck that the tide is negative today."

As the pair approached the edge of the island, the water roared and raked against the rocks. A line of enormous elephant seals with their broad faces and long flubbery noses heaved great bodies into the water with what looked like enormous effort. Once in the ocean, however, they sailed out of view as if on wings. There was a sense, to Olive, that on this edge, the continual pounding of the rock by the surf served the purpose of informing humans that this was a place of great change, the liminal space between land and sea. It was a site where the burden of flesh translated into flight.

Warren descended first down the rock face and after finding footing reached up to help Olive down to his level. He held her hand and she saw his eyes linger on her long, thin fingers and small wrist. Their shape betrayed her secret. He looked back up at her with a sort of detective's eye and held her gaze for a long second. A panic struck her. Perhaps the day had finally come where she would be revealed, as she could not hide the delicate, womanly bones of her hands. She felt in that moment, with the sound of the surf filling her ears, her biology exposed. The thought of it made sweat break out on her tightly bound breast. She wondered if she were to heave herself into the sea like a seal, might she transform and escape the danger of the situation. Her mother had often told her of selkies, the women who turned into seals and escaped the world of men by flying into the unknown salted sea.

Olive took a few deep breaths and scrambled the rest of the way down. At the bottom of the climb, there was an entrance to a cave that must have been completely hidden under the surface of the water during high tide. She pulled the sleeves of her sweater down over her thin wrists and buried her hands in her pockets to try to conceal her dainty hands. Luckily, Warren seemed less concerned about her feminine hands and more concerned with the task at hand of entering the cave. He inspected the opening and looked out to sea with a faraway look. Olive secured her precious blue rabbit in his wicker cage into a divot in the rock by the entrance to the sea cave.

The tide pools brimmed with anemones in all the colors of the rainbow—from large green tentacled things, to smaller orange ones, to teeny glowing red ones that looked like delicious wild berries. There were layers of pink and iridescent seaweed waving in the water as sea stars, chitins, and urchins mingled as though at a costume party. Bright yellow sea slugs dotted the rocks and made their glacial, merry way over to the dance floor. Olive was caught in her own reverie, swatting at the kelp flies as she combed the rocks, crouching and peering into each pool and imagining the party taking place. Suddenly Warren's great paw lifted her by her collar and brought her away from the edge of the island just as a wave crashed up and over the rock she'd been squatting on.

"Never turn your back to the sea," he scolded. "Unless you wish to become part of it forever."

"Thank you," she said, acutely aware that this was the second time he'd kept her from harm in as many weeks.

"Let's enter the cave on the left side. Always keep your eyes open and aware. I wouldn't want you washed out to sea like a piece of flotsam."

The entrance was small enough only one person could fit through at a time, but once inside, the hollow rock opened up like a great hall. It took some time for their eyes to adjust to the dark once they'd passed the threshold. The air was instantly cooler by degrees and Olive was glad she had worn her wool sweater. The scent on the damp air was strong—fecund. They stood there for a moment before venturing farther and waited for their eyes to adjust to the darkness. On the ceiling of the cave, there was a small hole in the rock that let in just enough light for shapes to take form, the water reflecting back little stars of light catching on the wind rippling over the pool. As their eyes attuned to the dark, forms began to appear beneath the surface of the water. The delicate oblong curve of thousands of abalone shells began to appear. Each shell had a rippled pattern emanating from the apex and a line of small, evenly spaced holes along the outside near the opening.

"You see that line of holes on the abalone?" Warren asked.

"Yes."

"The fishermen once told me these sort of snails do everything through there. They breathe, excrete, and reproduce all through those tiny windows to the outside world. What a strange existence."

"Ensconced and protected from the world," Olive said, reaching her finger into the water to trace the outline of one. She felt a kinship with the snail, veiled and protected by her secret.

Warren peered down at her with a look of scrutiny as she traced a finger gently over an abalone that made her wriggle in her own scratchy wool shell as she stood back up. She felt suddenly exposed, and the idea of hiding like an abalone appealed more and more. Warren broke his gaze to pick up an empty shell and show her the dancing lines of pearlescent pink, white, and blue—colorful even in the low light of the cave. He found a small chink of light and held the shell up to it, letting the colors move and change with the deftness of a hypnotist's wand.

"Not a bad place to spend your days." His eyes smiled as he watched the iridescent movement in the shell. "Dancing in the glittering ballroom of the self."

They watched the colors change in the shell and Olive felt the movement reflected in her own chest, the rise and fall of colors folding in on themselves. She could hear Warren's breath next to her and she found it harder and harder to control her own. The anxiety over being discovered softened as the colors danced before her. She wondered, eyes fixed on the shell, if this were perhaps a cave-borne illness taking over her body. She might drop dead at any moment from asphyxiation. Or hypnotism. She wondered, then, as she gathered her breaths one by one enough to calm her heart, if perhaps she were simply falling for this gentle, observant man.

"They call it a sea ear," Warren said. "Should we listen?" He placed the shell over Olive's ear and she heard the distillation of the sea bend its way into her head. The sound was calm and sure and led straight ahead. She found it within herself to raise her eyes and look into Warren's. What she found there were his thick-fringed brown eyes telling her she was not alone in her feelings. Her costume felt suddenly absurd and unnecessary.

"You know," she started, then stuttered. "You know, I'm not…"

"I don't care what you are not," Warren said. "Because I know what you *are*." He put his hand on his heart.

As if afraid of her response, Warren sidled away toward the edge of the pool and set to cutting an abalone away from the wall. He brought it over and sliced the shell open, revealing a very slimy blob. He cut away at one side.

"This here is the guts. Best to remove it before eating."

"Hmm." Olive was not sure her stomach was settled enough to eat this creature. Was it still alive? She was not sure. Warren pulled a lemon out of his pocket and sliced it in half, squeezing the juice onto the now gutless abalone. Olive had never met someone who kept lemons in their pocket. In fact, she had never tasted a lemon at all. The first one she had laid eyes on was at the market in San Francisco a month ago with Hazel by her side. Who she had been then, and who she had become, seemed a lifetime apart in their realities. Warren made crosshatch cuts in the flesh with his knife as Olive watched him. She let herself consider what might happen were she to reveal herself. The idea felt suddenly magnetic, enticing.

"The tang of the lemon helps bring out the flavor." He pulled the floppety white flesh from the shell and held it quaking near Olive's mouth. "Quick now. Down the hatch."

Olive paused only briefly before catching it in her mouth like a seal. She chewed and the flavor was salty and tangy, maybe even a little like butter. The flavor was so fresh and smooth she closed her eyes to better allow her taste buds to experience the ribbons of changing flavor on her tongue. There, on her tongue, she felt the moment approaching when she might safely reveal herself. When she'd swallowed the abalone, she opened her eyes and looked into Warren's expectant eyes for just a moment before he leaned in and kissed her on the mouth.

His unruly beard and mustache poked into her soft cheeks and upper lip, but the softness of his lips landed perfectly on hers. She finally knew what the beard felt like on her skin, and it was softer than she'd imagined. The salty flavor from the mollusk lingered between them as they kissed. She felt his arms fold around her and she let his warmth wrap her in iridescence. He held her for a long time and finally whispered:

"Is your name truly Olive, then?"

"Yes, Olive," she said softly.

"Well, Olive. Will you run away with me?"

She paused and said more loudly, "We won't get too far on this island."

Her head rested on his chest, and the sound of his laugh as it traveled through his bones and blood, past muscle and skin, finally into her ear, filled her with a sense of satisfaction. Enclosed in the cave together, like a single creature in its shell, she felt that the tides could come and go through their little portal holes, but she was content to simply sway in this glittering ballroom as long as the fates allowed. There was relief in the telling of the truth.

"I have a plan," he said, leaning back and holding her at arm's length to look at her face again, smiling like a little kid. "Are you ready to be a pirate?"

"Aye aye, matey," she said. She would have been the peg leg, parrot, or the very ship, if he had only asked her. "Let us plunder and pillage the sea."

He took out of his sack a beautiful bottle with light amber liquid inside. It had the name *Coors* printed into the glass on the outside.

"Beer. Have you ever tasted it?"

"No."

"This company just started bottling a year ago. Just hit the San Francisco markets. I bought a case back on my last trip in the city. Go ahead and try," Warren said, offering her the bottle.

The delicious bitter taste of the bubbles on her tongue washed down the lingering salty flavors of the abalone. Her mind hummed with the sound of her own heartbeat and the sly possibilities love

whispers to the newly bewitched. The two sat on a rock outside the
entrance to the cave and silently watched the clouds move across the
horizon. They traded pulls off the bottle and Warren took her hand in
his. After a while he revealed the details of his plan to steal a shipload
of eggs from the Egg Company. He figured if they got away with it,
there would be enough money to buy some land up north, maybe
start a little farm in Northern California near the Oregon border.
Olive considered the plan as the sun slunk weary below the horizon.
They paused their strategizing as an enormous being, a blue whale,
surfaced its silver-spotted back into the air and took an audible breath,
the power of it pushing spray high into the air loud as a steam engine.
She looked up again at Warren and examined the way his wild beard
grew and coiled in every direction possible. The whale, she thought,
lived under the ransom of their world. It had to come to the surface or
die. And love, it seemed, perpetuated similar acts in those compelled
by its force. She breathed deep like the blue whale. She would steal
and cheat, plunder or murder, in order to keep this thin grasp she
had on beauty. Raising her face upward, she let herself bask in the
unknowing blue, the sky and ocean reflecting the absence of answers
back and forth on one another.

Season's Quake

Yreka, California, 1941

THE WEATHER FELT UNSEASONABLY warm for November on Highway 99 heading north toward the Oregon and California border. Men with rifles blocked all lanes on the north-south route of the two-lane highway and a long line of cars at least a half mile deep waited to be let through the barricade. Each driver was handed a pamphlet reading:

Proclamation of Independence

You are now entering Jefferson, the 49th State of the Union. Jefferson is now in patriotic rebellion against the States of California and Oregon. This State has seceded from California and Oregon this Thursday, November 27, 1941.

Patriotic Jeffersonians intend to secede each Thursday until further notice.

For the next hundred miles as you drive along Highway 99, you are travelling parallel to the greatest copper belt in the far West, seventy-five miles west of here.

The United States government needs this vital mineral. But gross neglect by California and Oregon deprives us of necessary roads to bring out the copper ore. If you don't believe this, drive down the Klamath River highway and see for yourself. Take your chains, shovel, and dynamite.

Until California and Oregon build a road into the copper country, Jefferson, as a defense-minded state, will be forced to

rebel each Thursday and act as a separate State. (Please carry
this proclamation with you and pass them out on your way.)
    State of Jefferson Citizens Committee Temporary State
Capitol, Yreka

The late fall sun baked down on the crowds. Eyebrows were lifted.
Leather seats stuck to the skin. People started getting out of their cars
and wandering up and down the grass shoulder, pacing confusedly
with the pamphlets just handed to them by the state of Jefferson
secessionists crumpled in their hands. Insults flew through the air
between stuck motorists and the Jeffersonians blockading traffic.

Some two acres away from the stopped traffic across a fallow
field, an old man sat on his front porch smoking a tobacco pipe and
reading the newspaper. "Damn secessionists," he muttered to himself.
"It's just greed for greed's sake." The acreage between the man and the
now crowded highway included a field with two old horses and a young
border collie trying to get the horses to let him chase them around, the
horses blatantly ignoring his pleas to play. All three animals seemed
particularly excitable, pawing the ground and shimmying their manes.
The man looked up and listened to the string of muffled car horns across
the field and stroked his clavicle-length white beard with only a thin
streak left of the dark black it once had been. He sorted his mustache
hairs evenly on either side of his nose before sighing, then rising from
his chair. Struggling up the front porch steps, he went inside to repack
his tobacco laid conveniently on the mantle above the fireplace.

Next to the tobacco pouch sat a Victorian egg collection. The
man wiped the five beveled sides with care every time he laid eyes
on it. His wife Olive used to call the oval windows "portals to the
unknown." He peered in one of the windows and saw the blue-green
speckled murre egg and sighed. The collection was the last earthly
vessel that embodied any concrete representation of her, the singular
being he'd loved most in the world. A small lock of her hair tied with
a ribbon sat at the front of the egg collection, mingling its fine protein
forms among the cotton and silk of the smooth pink velvet.

A worm of darkness rimmed in light ripped through his mind and the man tried to remember why he had come into the living room in the first place. *Where was Olive? Was she tending to the hens?* He couldn't remember. He looked down at the collection and slowly recalled as he wiped away the nonexistent dust, pausing to think about his wife's hair. The brown lock was hers. *Was it true that she wasn't outside in the yard brushing the horses? Was she not about to come up the front steps in her clodhoppers to fix dinner?* It seemed hardly possible that she was gone. Another worm of light traced its way through his brain, and he remembered that reality was cruel and it was up to him alone to feed the dog. He ran his finger along the brown lock of hair, as it held within its chemical makeup traces of meals and drinks they'd eaten together, laughing and toasting, long after they'd retired from raising bovids on their small farm. They had never had children, but had instead collected a group of animals on their farm that would make Noah green with envy. They had everything from llamas to emus, rabbits to rehabilitated wrens.

He stroked the hair with his forefinger. Perhaps what he was feeling was the residue of the pasta primavera he'd prepared for her the Valentine's Day before she died. They'd spent a romantic evening delivering a pair of baby goats together in the bitter cold. They named them Valentin and Valentina and collapsed exhausted and full of life into their two chairs before the fireplace, devouring the simple pasta and opening a well-deserved bottle of Sauterne, clinking glasses to a day well spent. He missed the way she laughed before she'd fully produced a punch line, always "ruining the joke" as she liked to say. He remembered it clear as a bell, and then, as if in imitation of one, the memory faded like sound waves into air.

As he looked at the collection and lost himself in half memory, a collection of shooting stars ripped through his mind and the entire house began to shake. The glass rattled in its silver frame, the eggs inside bouncing on the velvet. The vines on the filigree legs of the collection were alive as the earth moved below. The house swayed a bit—the dance every object unable to move of its own accord waits in silence for. The trees outside shed clouds of golden and brown leaves into the air. He thought he could hear faint cries and gasps from the crowds down on the highway as their cars must have bumped and jumped out of their neat rows. And then, as abruptly as the quaking had started, it was quiet again.

On the mantle, the silver filigree box settled out of its wild dance. The largest of the eggs, the common murre's masterpiece sixty-some years old, revealed a crack the size of a thumbnail splitting the past from the present. The man stared at the egg in a sort of disbelief before going outside to check on the horses, an animal that never seemed to do well in an earthquake. *That was an earthquake, right?* He couldn't trust himself anymore to know what was happening at any given point in time, and it made him angry with himself. The horses trotted a circle around the field and neighed in mild discomfort but otherwise seemed unfazed. The border collie was nowhere to be seen. *Was there really a dog to feed or was that a lifetime ago, too?* The man stroked the neck of the mare and whispered calming nothings to her when he noticed a figure with a very large knapsack on his shoulders walking up the drive.

As the figure approached, the old man noticed how young he was. Could hardly call him a man, really. He couldn't be more than seventeen. He had the air of a wanderer, with stains on either legs of his jeans and greasy hair tamped down under a Greek fisherman's cap and tucked behind his ears. The sight of the cap made him smile with memories of days spent with actual Greek fishermen. He remembered a story of sirens told by an old Greek, the way they had devoured men after dashing them on the rocks, blood from the sad, simple men roaring down their lovely necks. As the boy approached, he shook his head to unearth the memory and try and settle the lightning worms in his brain. *Behave,* he hissed at the half thoughts inside his head. The boy looked tired but approached him with a friendly smile, dark wavy hair, and earnest clear blue eyes, a color that had been burned brighter yet by long exposure to sun. The old man swore he smelled salt on the air for a moment as the boy approached. *What a strange thing*, the man thought, *to smell a memory like that.*

"Hello, sir," the wanderer said, putting his hand out for a shake.

"Well that's a fine start, son, but you can drop the 'sir.'" The old man returned the handshake. "What brings you up my drive? You're not a secessionist, are ya? Because if you, are you can just turn around right now and march back out."

"No, sir." The boy shook his head. "Unless you count seceding from my old life and hitting the road, then, yes. I am."

The old man laughed, and the surprise of the sound inside his ribcage rattled him. He hadn't laughed out loud in months. At least, if he had, he couldn't remember doing so.

"I'm glad you think that's funny," the boy's blue eyes crinkled at the edges, lines baked into his skin beyond his years by the unkind sun. "Coulda gone either way."

"Name's Warren," the old man said. "Why don't you come take a load off and have some water. Sorry I don't have anything else to offer you."

"Thank you kindly," the boy said, avoiding speaking his own name, as the sound of it had come to make him uncomfortable. The two lumbered up the steps with matching creaky joints and tired movements.

The old man walked carefully through the front door and went inside for water. The boy set his heavy pack down on the porch and sat down in an actual chair for the first time in days. In the kitchen, the old man turned on the faucet and immediately a flash in his brain erased all memory of the boy. He opened himself a can of beer and stood staring out the kitchen window into the backyard where someone's dog, a border collie, was running wildly around in a circle. *Who did that damn dog belong to again? Probably a secessionist.* On the front porch, the boy put his feet up on a footrest and waited for his water, his mouth parched and dry. He wasn't sure how long it had been, but he closed his eyes and listened to the rustle of leaves overhead. Before he got any water, with the car horns blaring down on the highway and the sun beginning to set, he fell fast asleep.

An hour later, Warren came outside to get the newspaper and was surprised to find the boy sitting on the porch, a flash of recognition reminding him of the situation. He went back in to get a glass of water, muttering admonishment to himself, and let the old screen door slam into its frame. When he returned with water, the boy was sitting upright, his arms stretched upward, yawning.

"Must have dozed off," he said. "Mr. Warren, can I ask you..."

"Just Warren," the old man interrupted.

"Warren. Can I ask you a favor? Please feel free to say no."

"Doesn't hurt to ask."

"Can I stay the night on your front porch? I haven't had a good night's sleep in quite some time, and it's fixing to rain tonight." The warm afternoon had led into an overcast and increasingly cold evening.

"How about I do you one better and you stay on the couch instead?"

"I won't argue with that."

"Do you know how to boil pasta?"

"I do indeed."

"Then we better get started on dinner."

Warren felt a sort of desperation to stay in the moment because as long as he was exchanging pleasantries with the kid, he felt he might be able to stay conscious of where, who, and what was going on around him. He wanted to tether time and keep it right there tied up on the porch like an obedient dog. *The dog! He hasn't eaten!* he thought, quite pleased for the moment with the idea that the dog was his. He knew just what to feed him and where it was kept, but when he went to the cupboard to find the food, all he found was an empty bag with big shredded holes at the base and rodent signs littering the cupboard floor. The sight of the torn-up bag empty as the day made him want to cry, but he gathered himself up and looked in the fridge. He found an old bone with some chicken still on it and some old hard rice, which he put in a bowl with a little milk to soften it, and asked the kid to take it out to the backyard. From the kitchen window, he watched the boy enter the yard and the dog bark in tight circles as he approached, until it realized he was bringing him dinner, at which point the dog reversed the direction of his circles and licked and licked his hands and ankles as though he were the best friend he'd ever had.

Warren took out a pen and paper and began a letter, putting it in an envelope with all the money he owned. The bank would be coming to take his house soon, he figured, as he hadn't paid a dime on it in almost a year. So those bills in the envelope, they were the rest of what he knew as wealth on this earth. Better pass them along before the bank came to claim them for their own.

Over pasta with butter and pepper, ancient Parmesan from the back of the fridge grated over the top, the men split the last two beers in the house. The wanderer tried to mind his manners, but the taste of a warm meal urged him to gulp and slurp beyond the reign of his control. After subsisting on rationed beef jerky and cold cans of soup, the simple flavor of pepper and cheese on warm pasta made his head spin.

"So, where are you headed?" Warren asked.

"Not sure. East toward the desert seems wise for the winter. The wetness of these western forests is getting to me."

"Seems wise. I've never been to any desert besides the Great Basin." Warren pointed out the window to the desert side of the house and paused to wiped his mouth on his sleeve. "I hear there are lots of snakes."

"I would imagine so," the wanderer said, wiping the grease from his mouth onto his sleeve in imitation, something he'd had drilled out of him by at an early age by his well-to-do parents. He adjusted the napkin in his lap nervously. "But there are snakes wherever you go."

"I s'pose so."

The two ate in silence for a few, the clinking of forks on china a sort of conversation in itself.

"Did you feel that earthquake earlier today?" Warren asked. "Just before you arrived, if I remember correctly."

"Strange." He wiped the last traces of delicious peppered oil from his plate with an old, hard crust of bread. "I can't say that I did."

"Well," Warren sighed. "Don't always trust the sensations of an old man. Might have been my stomach growling for all I know."

"No earthquake, no. But those secessionists were sure causing a ruckus out there on the highway. What can you tell me about them?"

"Don't get me started," Warren said, getting up and opening the fridge for a beer, forgetting that the last two had already been consumed. "Thieves, the lot of them."

"What's your experience with the movement?" asked the kid.

"Well, we're in the heart of the matter, right here." Warren said. "All's these men want is to get at the copper in the hills. It's not about anything but yet another gold rush by selfish men."

"Have you seen the Charlie Chaplin film *The Great Dictator*?" the wanderer asked.

"'Fraid not," Warren said, but he couldn't really be sure if he had or hadn't.

"Did you notice that the double cross symbol the Jeffersonians use is the same as the one the parodied Hitler, the leader of Tomania, used?" The boy's eyes sparkled as he theorized and conspired, waving the pamphlet he'd been given earlier. "What do you suppose that means?"

"I don't suppose I know," Warren said.

"Well, I don't think it very wise to align themselves with Adolf Hitler in any way. Even a parody. Not with what's brewing in the world and this country on the brink of war."

"Absolutely right you are," Warren sighed. He was suddenly feeling exhausted. "Boy. I'm too old to live through another war. I just don't think I can do it."

"There's a paragraph at the end of Chaplain's long monologue I've memorized," the wanderer said, ignoring the old man's flagging interest. "I think it has to do with what you were talking about earlier, about the greed of man. Would you like to hear it?"

"Sure," Warren said, easing himself back down into the chair with a sigh.

"'Dictators free themselves but they enslave the people!'" began the wanderer, sitting up straight in his chair and closing his eyes. "'Now let us fight to fulfill that promise! Let us fight to free the world—to do away with national barriers—to do away with greed, with hate and intolerance. Let us fight for a world of reason, a world where science and progress will lead to all men's happiness. Soldiers! In the name of democracy, let us all unite!'"

"Sounds like sense to me," Warren said.

"I think at the core of your argument, you feel the same way. As if the secessionists are just impeding the progress of man toward a more tolerant world and are simply concerned for their own pocketbooks' well-being. Theirs is a clear greed for goods in these parts. I can tell just from the conversations I've had hitching into the 'state of Jefferson.' They just want riches, not the betterment of mankind like they say they do. Isn't that what's ultimately wrong with our country? We propagate greed for greed's sake."

"I do believe you are the single most reasonable fellow I've spoken to in a long time. I admire your energy for the subject. And I hope you keep up the good fight."

Warren stood up with some difficulty and went into a room in the back of the old drafty house and returned with an envelope.

"Here's a little something for your travels." Warren paused. "Please don't open it until you are on the road. No need to thank me."

That night, as the young wanderer did the dishes, Warren played back the earthquake as best he could in his mind. It had rattled him, and he remembered the egg breaking. But when he went to fill his pipe with tobacco and peered into the portal of the collection, there sat the murre egg perfectly intact. *If I'm imagining earthquakes, this must be the end of it,* he thought to himself. *Surely I will be joining my Olive soon.* The very idea sent a shiver of anticipation through his whole body. He took the case down and opened it one last time, touching the lock of hair gently before closing the lid again. He withdrew the lock of hair and placed the strands on his tongue and moved it around, swallowing with difficulty the little gnarled nest of all that was left of the woman he loved. Perhaps he would be able to find her more easily in the great beyond if a part of her was inside him. He closed the lid and took the collection into the kitchen.

"I'd like you to hold onto this." He pushed the collection carefully across the kitchen counter toward the wanderer as he dried his hands on a towel.

"What is it?" he asked.

"It was my wife's. Her mother gave it to her. It's a very old collection of bird eggs."

"It's real nice," Victor said. "But I'm not the gentlest on items that get thrown into my rucksack. Isn't there maybe someone else who should have it?"

"I don't believe so. We never had any kids." Warren organized his beard nervously. "I'm nearing the end of my days and really this collection deserves to continue on until it's been completed."

"How will it be complete?" the wanderer asked, skeptical of the whole scenario.

"You'll know, I suppose," Warren said, sighing at the boy's lack of understanding. He grew impatient and stood up. "Just keep it safe. It's not to be bought or sold. When the right person comes to pass it along to, you'll know."

"What bird is this from?" The wanderer put his finger near a lightly speckled taupe egg.

"Ah. The hermit warbler," the old man sighed. "I collected that one just after my wife died, when I became a hermit myself."

"I see," the wanderer said. "I appreciate the symbol."

"Well, I hear the bed calling me."

The old man went up to bed, laboring with each step up the creaking stairs. The wanderer stood alone in the kitchen and opened the lid to the collection. One of the eggs rolled up and out of its divot and then settled back—the largest, a perfect blue-green brown-speckled egg with a sharp point on one end. He wrapped up the collection tight in an old T-shirt and placed it at the bottom of his rucksack, padded by his few, threadbare items of clothing. He moved the sealed envelope back and forth between his hands, holding it up to the light to try and see what was inside. He suddenly felt bad that he hadn't even told Warren his name—Victor. And here this man had been generous as a mother to an unnamed, dirty kid. He placed the letter back in the rucksack and forgot all about it as he lay down on the couch and slept the slumber of a stone.

The Followed Path

Spring in the Sonoran Desert, Arizona, 1983

ALL MORNING, SAL FELT pursued. By what, she was not sure. When she started her transect in the first dawn light, she stood before a steep wall of giant tawny boulders and took a deep breath to ready herself for the labyrinth ahead. Looking down at the dry, cracked ground, she saw cougar tracks, barely there, indications that a big cat had passed through recently. She started up through the spaces between the rocks, using blind handholds that quickened her heart rate, cutting a winding path among the boulders and scrub so disorienting she had to recalibrate her direction over and over with her compass to make sure she was on track to hit all her points.

Once she had navigated to the right spot for her first count, she stood and diligently listened and looked for all the birds in earshot, identifying each species and marking them down on her data sheet. Rock wrens perched high above her, black-throated sparrows chattered in the scrub, the acrobatic, inky-black phainopepla picked away at some mistletoe, and the colorful verdin delivered its short, straightforward song. With each turn of her body to hear a new bird, Sal felt a sense of danger lurking behind her. More than once she shivered and whipped around to see what might be creeping up. But she never encountered more than a horned lizard, keeping quiet and still so as not to be eaten by this strange, upright, and downright jumpy predator.

Sal, a scientist first and foremost, reminded herself that cougars preferred not to interact with humans. They were not hunting her because she was not their understood prey. And while she knew on an intellectual level that she was not being stalked by *a cat,* she just couldn't shake the feeling that she was being pursued. By *something.* When she was finished with the point count portion of her transect, she decided to take a seat on top of a flat boulder and eat some lunch before diving into nest-searching. The sandwich and hot sun made her sleepy, so she lay back for just a moment and closed her eyes. Her 4:30 a.m. wake time suddenly inhabited her body like a drug and she fell into a hard sleep.

In her dream, she found herself in a small boat on a rough, midnight-blue ocean sitting next to a pregnant Alice who had her hand up to her eyes looking into the distance. White caps licked at the sky as storm clouds brewed overhead. Very far away, a lightning bolt made its way into the water.

"Where does lightning go when it touches down on water, I wonder?" asked Alice.

"That's a good question," Sal said. "How are the fish safe?"

"Maybe all the electricity just bursts into a million pieces and all that's left is a tingle here, an inkling there."

"Like a memory of something fierce."

"Exactly," Alice said, smiling and folding her hands over her belly.

"I suppose it must dissipate over the surface until the charge is spent."

"Like all bright and dangerous things," Alice nodded, "it finds its way to calm."

The two women waited quietly together for the lightning storm to make its way toward them over the water.

When Sal woke, she was covered with sweat and felt a mild panic take over her body. She glanced at her watch. She had only been asleep about fifteen minutes, but she could hardly remember what day it was, or even for a split second *who* she was. The reality of herself in the desert came back to her quickly, like her essence had been dropped back into her body from a great height. She gathered up her things and scrambled down from a boulder and into the sandy wash to begin looking for nests.

It was only 11:00 a.m., but the sun was hot overhead and Sal's steps through the sand felt slow and plodding. She listened with one ear for birds' contact calling or acting erratic—two signs she might be near a nest—but she was still haunted by her dream and she couldn't shake the feeling of being pursued. She remembered a professor of ecology had once stressed that lightning, much like a stream, plant, or even an ice crystal, takes the path of least resistance. It seemed this idea could then be applied to any number of actions in the biological world. In general, energy winnows itself down smaller and smaller until it is dissipated. The plight of the earth's creatures, then, is to gather and use energy before it disappears into infinity. Every creature is subject to the first law of thermodynamics. Energy is always lost and so there can be no perpetual motion in any real sense. She sighed. It seemed that life and living, in this sense, were walled in by the natural course of things. Every living thing succumbs to an eternal and unending decay of energy, matter, and time. The path of least resistance is simply a gentle way of nodding toward death.

A nearby rattle juggled Sal's thoughts into dispersing seeds on the wind. A small western diamondback made its way along the sand, rattling at any nearby movement. Sal noticed that the snake's eyes were sheathed and cloudy, a sign that it was ready to shed its skin. She had read about this phenomenon but never seen it in the flesh. Having just woken from its long, winter slumber, the snake rattled along, jutting back and forth with poor eyesight, blindly announcing itself in the bright spring midday sun.

The snake's intense drive to survive snapped Sal out of her borderline-nihilistic scientific musing. She sat down on a soft bank and took out her notebook. Decay was inevitable, sure, but wasn't it beautiful, the infinite variety with which creatures raked and railed against it? As though she had hit the bottom of her own dark thought pool, she bounced back up toward the light. Every little live thing surrounding her suddenly shone and sang with the song of resistance. She plucked a bright orange wolfberry from a nearby plant and popped it in her mouth. The tang and sweetness echoed the sharpness of survival.

Across the narrow wash, a tiny yellow-headed verdin popped inside a sharp, barbed globe that hung from a low branch, revealing its nest location. Within the uniform ball of woven thorns held together by spider silk, the bird had made the tiny cup of its nest. The effect was that of a perfect fortress but for a small hole the bird popped in and out of. She knew that inside, where the eggs were nestled, it would be soft and cushioned by feathers, plant down, and soft leaves.

The idea of a home so safe gave Sal pause as she filled out her data card, marking the exact location of the verdin nest. Sal spent so many of her nights in a tent, picking up and moving from here to there. Maybe that was the source of this feeling of being pursued. She had moved around so much the last couple years her body and mind had finally been tricked into believing she was being followed. Why else would a person run so hard?

Sal couldn't conjure a place or person that made her feel as protected as those eggs, save Alice. She waited until the bird left the nest and poked her finger into the hole to count the eggs. She had to be extremely careful not to shake the globe or she might lose an egg out the entrance. One, two, three, four. Four perfect little eggs nestled in the fluff. What lucky birds to have such a secure spot to start out their lives.

The nest got her thinking. Sal had always told herself she was free, that she was the rolling stone that gathered no moss. But what if all her rambling had simply been an easy conceit to avoid any real commitment to one place, job, or, for that matter, person? Was she pursued, then, by her own lack of direction or dedication? The thought did not feel especially pleasant. She thought of Alice, back in the farmhouse with her parents, so rooted there now as a mother that she couldn't possibly find her way out to travel with Sal for a season, as Sal had often wished were possible.

Sal found a few more easy nests, the acrobatic phainopepla, some mourning doves, and a lesser goldfinch, before calling it a day. She walked back toward her truck and ran into her field partner, a baby-faced redhead named Eric with skin so pale he wore a sun hat with full neck and earflaps in combination with wraparound sunglasses and still managed to burn in the intense desert sun. She found him waiting for her curled up in the shade reading a fantasy novel about time travel and dragons. Sal often wondered if Eric would make it in the long term as a field biologist, so sensitive was his skin and, for that matter, his countenance. When she asked him questions he often shuddered before answering and avoided eye contact. But he liked the job, he told her, because he didn't have to interact with actual people most of the day.

The two were quietly riding the forty miles to their next transect site when Eric broke the silence.

"I forgot to mention, I picked up the mail from the PO Box in town yesterday. This came for you." He handed her a postcard with a watercolor of a little girl on the front that Sal instantly recognized as Lily. She was driving, so she put it on the dashboard to read later. As they drove along the highway, she noticed some virga clouds dotting the horizon, letting down moisture in a watercolor wash that never quite reached the ground. The effect was that of a motion interrupted. The feeling from her dream earlier in the day came back to her and she could see Alice's face lit by lightning. She still felt pursued, but traveling at sixty miles per hour on the highway helped put the day sufficiently behind her. Perhaps if she drove just a little faster she could outrun the darkening feeling. Eric braced himself on the dash like she was going to kill them both and Sal smiled a little as she pushed the little truck into the upper limits of its horsepower.

When she dropped Eric off at his tent site, he seemed especially relieved not only to be alive but that Sal would be moving on and leaving him alone once again. She laughed as she bumped up the dirt road away from him. What was it in her that enjoyed torturing the poor guy so? Maybe she was bored. But maybe it was biological dominance, pure and simple. She was older, stronger, more tanned and knowledgeable in the field. And she made sure they both knew it. She knew better how to survive in this place where survival was a desperate and difficult mission. Maybe it was important that someone else recognized this fact.

That night, after a lonely meal of dehydrated beans and rice, some carrots, and a single beer, Sal set up her tent to the side of a sandy wash near her next transect and settled in for the night. From a saguaro nearby, an elf owl hooted its high-pitched laugh of a mating call, but Sal couldn't hear a mate responding. She read the postcard from Alice again and again, wanting to understand exactly what to make of it. It read:

Dear Sal,

Both my parents have died. It's pretty inexplicable, or if there is an explanation I'm not sure I want to know it. Looks like I'm in charge now. Lily says hi, and that she found a new egg for the collection box. She doesn't know what bird it's from, so you'll have to let her know next time you are in town. We already had a service, so don't worry about trying to come back for it. Hope you are well.

Yours,

Alice

There was a crudely drawn picture of a little speckled egg next to the text, clearly added by five-year-old Lily. The emotionless tone of the postcard made Sal unsure what she should do next. There were mixed signals in the short phrases, a sort of *come, don't come* tone. But that was how Alice had been the whole time Sal had known her. Their relationship seemed to her an endless parade of green-and-red flags flashing, the moon hiding behind the clouds just at the moments she saw how beautiful and bright it shone.

Jump

L ILY PACED THE FLOOR of the kitchen practicing what she would say to her mother when she woke up. She could hear her snoring upstairs. Lily herself had hardly slept that night as she went over and over what she had overheard of her mother and Darla's conversation, her mother's drunken crashing of the eclipse rendezvous with Max the night before, and, finally, the questions that still remained to be answered. Her mother's behavior the night before had brought her to a boiling point. Why, when she looked in the mirror, did she want to start a fight with herself? Why did she faint? Lily needed answers about Original Donnie and she wasn't going to back down until she got them.

Alice came down in her gossamer nothing of a nightgown rubbing her eyes and sniffling like she was getting a cold or suffering allergies.

"Morning, pumpkin," she said, as though nothing had happened the night before. As though she hadn't just ruined her daughter's life.

"Mom. We need to talk," Lily said.

"Let me wake up first, please." Alice ran water into the teakettle and set it on to boil. "No shop talk before I've had my tea."

"We need to talk about Donnie. Now." Lily pulled the chair to the table, the little lions peering out from under the table in the dark as if watching from an arena cage before a gladiator fight.

"Honey. Let me wake up. I'm all cobwebs this morning." Alice stared blankly at the flame on the stove as though hypnotized.

"I would say you're more spider than cobwebs, Mom." Lily sat down at the table with her hands flat on the surface. "Black widow. Don't they eat their young or something?"

"What the hell are you talking about?" Alice said, pouring the water over her tea, a little splashing onto her thumb. "Fuck," she said, putting her burned finger under the faucet.

"Fifty cents," Lily said. "*Spiderwoman.*"

"Seriously," Alice yelled over the sound of the faucet. "You are acting insane. And it's the offspring who eat their mother in the species *stegodyphus lineatus*, not the other way around. Black widows eat their mates sometimes. Can't hardly blame them."

"I don't actually care how much you know about spider cannibalism," Lily said, unblinking. "Okay. So maybe I am insane." She tapped her fingers on the table as if to accentuate. "What I do want to know about is my father. Then maybe I'll know if I need to check myself into an asylum."

"What is this all about? Is this because Max is gay, honey? You can't take that personally, love. That's just who he is."

"It's not about Max. It's about *you.*" Lily slammed her hands on the table. "You trying to kill me in utero. You not telling me who my father is. You crashing your way into my personal life with your drunk-ass self every other day."

Alice made an exhalation like a leaky balloon.

"I need you to tell me about Original Donnie. Everything."

"There's really nothing to tell," Alice said. Her face looked deflated, her eyes clouded.

"I overheard you talking to Darla about how you tried to drink yourself to an abortion," Lily said.

"Honey," Alice said feebly, shaking her head. "I'm sorry you heard that."

"Is that why I faint all the time? Is that why I'm so small?"

"Honey. No."

"Who is Original Donnie?!" Lily screamed.

"There's nothing wrong with you," Alice whispered. "You're smart and perfect. Confirmed by everyone who's ever met you."

"Aagh! Stop lying to me. Who IS he?"

"I don't know," Alice said, looking down, away from her daughter's bright pink face and the scary blue veins sticking out of her neck. "I really don't even know."

"But you know more than you're telling me, obviously." Lily got up. "And if you won't tell me what I need to know, then I can't live here with you anymore."

"Wait, hon." Alice tried to move toward her daughter and grab her arm, but Lily slipped quickly past and grabbed a backpack all ready and propped outside the door on the deck.

"Come find me when you're ready to tell me everything," Lily said, pausing in the kitchen screen door. "I'll be with Sarah or something."

The screen door slammed its thick, mildewed wood frame with a thud as Alice watched Lily retreat across the orchard and toward the expansive back garden that once had been a burn patch, and before that, had been a sanctuary with a beautiful wild ginger growing among the trees. That acre was their own little experimental succession story. Alice felt encased by molasses as she watched Lily grow smaller and smaller in the distance. She was far too slow to chase after her. As Alice watched from the window, Lily disappeared into the same small greenbelt running toward the sea, up the hill and toward the low mountain foothills of the coast range. She walked right into the fold of dark evergreen and Alice could imagine her taking the same old overgrown road that she had when she was her age. From the look of her bulging backpack, though, her daughter was far more prepared for the journey than she had ever been. She sat at the table with her head in her hands for a long time, letting the gravity of what just happened sink in. She picked up the receiver from the yellow wall phone to make a call to the one person she knew could help. It rang for a long time before someone finally picked up.

"Hi, Boomer. It's Alice."

"Wow. It's been a loooong time, Alice."

"I know, friend. Mea culpa."

"What's going on?"

"Lily ran away."

"Like mother like daughter," Boomer said. "How do you suppose I can help?"

"Can you just make sure she's okay? Track her, maybe?" Alice sighed. "She's heading west. I can pay you somehow."

"No need, Alice. I'll check up on her. Where is she headed?"

"She's on the old road."

"Well, of course she is."

~

LILY WAS OUT OF breath by the time she reached the lagoon—a bend in the Siuslaw that held deep green, cool, rocky pools for swimming. It was always a good trek to get there from the highway, but the intrepid were rewarded by some of the best swimming holes in the area. The shortest way to get there was the half mile straight uphill from their orchard property, but it remained a closely guarded secret. The morning sun had broken through the fog and Lily was starting to peel off layers as she set her backpack on the small rocky beach. She was warm from the uphill hike, but when she stuck a toe in the water, it was cold as snowmelt. Going in would require a sort of madness, a need to wrest the self from one's own body for a moment. She was up for it.

Lily stripped down to nothing and scrambled up a ledge some ten feet above the water. She knew every inch of the pool from years of summer swimming and would aim for the deepest part. As a kid, she loved going in with swimming goggles on. There would be a brook trout or two cruising the bottom, and some crawdads and caddis flies trying to hide from the trout, which would inevitably find and eat them. There was a whole brutal hierarchy down there below the surface. Her mother told her there used to be salmon that would come up this far to spawn, but no more. Something had changed their course over the years and they no longer made it this far inland. She braced herself and gripped the rock ledge with her toes. Just as she was preparing to jump, her knees bent and Achilles sprung, one of the first butterflies of the season came and landed on her bare naked chest, right on the periphery of the scar left from the spider bite she'd gotten under the porch, just above her heart. She tried to stop, but the jump was already in motion, so she sprang up in the air, the butterfly clinging to her chest as she tried to wave it off wildly before they hit the water where its thin wings would be forever ruined. *Save yourself*, she thought. But the insect clung to her skin and refused to budge as she flailed her way down toward the water.

The shock of the icy water knocked her breath away as she plunged into the pool. She shot down into the cold and her toes just touched the pebbled bottom. She frog-kicked her way to the surface and hooted a few times in corporeal response to the cold. She briefly looked around for the butterfly but it was nowhere to be found, not on the surface of the water nor in the air. *Did I imagine it?* she wondered as she looked under the surface, then swam in brisk strokes toward shore. Back on land, she lay flat on the rocks to maximize sunshine-to-skin ratio. The spring sun felt warm, but not quite warm enough, as her thin skin goose-bumped all over. The scar on her chest, always more sensitive than the rest of her skin, throbbed with pain from the cold. She shimmied in the light and felt herself return to her body slowly, a falling leaf settling through the wind and finally landing on the water. The plunge had not succeeded; the darkness had not fully dislodged from her heart. She hoped her mother was suffering terribly with anxiety. She hoped Alice thought she was dead. She hoped Alice would learn her lesson this time.

Lily was almost dry as she put her clothes back on, but her underwear clung and rolled up as she tried to pull it up. She hopped on one leg and tried to unroll the now wet tangle to smooth it up over her backside. As she dressed, she suddenly felt as though she were being watched. The feeling was unshakable and she pulled on her shirt quickly without a bra, then her sweatshirt and jeans, in a matter of seconds. She looked around but saw no one. *Strange*, she thought. *I could have sworn there were eyes on me. I should get out of here in case Alice decides to show up.*

She made her way up the creek and onto a trail she had found once as a kid where she thought there might be some early wild fruit. She found a patch of thimbleberries, but they were all still green. There were salmonberries, huckleberries, and blackberries too, green, green, and green. If only she had timed running away to correct gathering season. But, alas, foresight and planning are not the fortes of most teenage runaways. In all the commotion at home, she had failed to eat any breakfast, so she sat on the trail and rifled through her backpack to find a snack. She gnawed on some beef jerky and threw a handful of trail mix in as she walked the trail farther than she had ever dared to go as a kid. She wondered how the trail had gotten there in the first place. It felt as though it must have once been a thoroughfare, like an old mine trail or logging road, long uninhabited and forgotten. The greenery was taller than she was and brushed her shoulders as she edged through the narrowing path. The vine maple grew more dense and arched over the trail, causing her to duck and weave as she stepped her way through. As she scrambled deeper into the dense understory, becoming more and more entangled with each step, she realized that she had no idea where she was headed, but also that she did not intend to go back. There was no map she knew of for this kind of journey, so she would have to draw in the wending lines and layers as she went along.

The trail continued to narrow until Lily lost a shoe, was grabbed by some vine maple, and tossed down under a dense patch of Oregon Grape. She groped around for her worn sneaker, the prickly leaves scratching at her skin, and found it. It was as she pulled her hand back and examined the thin scratch marks, some just barely filling in with small amounts of blood, that she realized that she would need to recalibrate her compass. The anger she had felt back at the orchard had evaporated off into the cool darkness of the forest understory. She sat down on a fern-lined log, pulled out her maps, and started to trace the river up from her house in order to figure out where she was. Wherever she was, she could feel the buffer of soft green between her anger and her future.

Within a mile or so margin of error, she made a circle on the map in pencil. There were two creeks and a ridge between them that wound its way fairly well west. She wondered why it was that she was inclined to move that direction, west, toward the ocean. *Go west, young woman.* Maybe it was because her mother had so often refused to take her to see it, as though there were something out there that haunted her. Lily would beg her mom to go to the beach and Alice always found an excuse or diversionary tactic. *Let's go to Chuck E. Cheese's instead,* her mom would say. *Or let's get some ice cream and watch a movie.* Lily's attraction to seeing the ocean felt suddenly inversely proportionate to her mother's aversion.

The map showed patchwork state forest and private land all the way to the Pacific. Something seemed to pull her toward the shoreline, as though that thin line drawn between the ocean and land might deliver the answers she was looking for. The internal compass of the downtrodden does seem to draw them toward water. She put her shoe back on, folded her map carefully, and pointed herself uphill so that she could find the ridge and follow it toward some sort of answer.

At the top of the ridge, Lily looked out over the slight valleys to either side and saw a small section of highway peeking through the layers of trees to the left. She squinted her eyes in uncertainty, but parked on the side of the road she could swear she saw Max's old red pickup with the rust stain on the door. She took out her binoculars and confirmed the truck's identity by the Dead Kennedys sticker on the bumper. *What on earth would he be doing parked down here halfway between his house and school? Maybe he was doing an extra-credit project on the microbial stream biome, or raptor migration, or something.* She scanned the small strip of road and the adjacent forest for signs of Max but saw nothing. She continued making her way up the ridge toward a spot that looked like it might be some sort of peak from which she could survey the surrounding land. Maybe she could even get a glimpse of the ocean from up there.

At the top of the ridge, the land flattened out and a trail appeared out of nowhere under her feet. It ran perfectly west and through the thinning trees on the balded crest of the ridge. One large fir had something large and squared off hidden in its branches. She approached the base of the tree to find a rope ladder hanging down.

"Hello?" she said, looking up the length of the ladder toward the darkness in the branches.

What appeared to be a platform of some kind lay flat among the branches some twenty feet up. A long black braid was the first thing to show itself, falling earthward through a hole in the board. Then a round face followed and a man with a familiar straight nose with an upside-down triangle on the end said, "Well hello there, Lily. So nice to finally make your acquaintance. Why don't you come on up? Or would you prefer that I came down?"

The man looked a lot like Max, she realized, but older.

"Um. Who are you?" Lily asked.

"You can call me Boomer. I'm your friend Max's uncle."

He shimmied down the rope and jumped the last couple feet into the dust and pine needles, wiping the dirt off his hands with loud claps.

"Hope I didn't scare you," he said.

"Likewise," said Lily.

"Not much scares me out here. Unless it's human, I'm pretty much okay with it."

"So you're the infamous Boomer," she said. "What's up there, anyway?"

"It's a sort of makeshift watchtower I built. Real clandestine."

"What are you watching out for?"

"You know. Fires, bears, birds, lost teenage girls."

"Ha," Lily said. "You find many of those?"

"You'd be surprised, my dear." His voice singsonged in the same beautiful cadence she always admired in Max. "You would be surprised."

Lily set her pack against the tree and climbed the ladder with some difficulty up to the platform, squeezing her body through the hole like a dog through a cat door. Up top, she stood up and could see 360 degrees. It was a clear day and only little puffs of cloud floated in the blue. On all sides, the swaths of evergreens leaned up on one another like a patchwork quilt of green and brown over a sleeping giant. In the far distance, she could just see the ocean glittering.

Boomer had followed up behind her and examined the way she lost herself westward, her spirit straining outward for something like a satellite unearthing a coded message from a distant star.

"You want to talk about it?" he asked.

"Not really." Lily snapped herself back inside. "What I'd really like to do is see the ocean. Maybe it's too much to ask, but would you want to drive me that way?"

"Not too much to ask at all." Boomer looked satisfied, like some sort of spiritual bounty hunter with his trophy in hand. He always regretted that all those years ago he hadn't delivered the peace of an afternoon at the ocean before he'd taken Alice back to her parents' vicelike ownership. Now he had his chance to make things right.

The two scrambled back down the ridge using a trail that Lily wished she had known about on the way up. They made it down to the truck in twenty-five minutes flat, whereas it had taken her an hour and a half to climb up through the underbrush. She sat in the familiar passenger's seat of the truck and tried not to ask about Max. They rode west on the highway and she suddenly felt as though she'd given up on some sort of goal she had never actually defined in the first place. A sense of sadness and self-doubt returned. She wished she had some sort of internal compass that could guide her onto the right path. Instead she was allowing herself to be washed back down the mountain into the flood of humanity.

They passed by a newly logged patch next to the highway. Boomer glanced at her dark gaze.

"Salvage, they called it," he broke the silence. "But that hardly seems the right word for it."

"It's just like a graveyard now," Lily said. "Each stump is like a little tombstone sticking up." She suddenly felt naked and wished she had her black lipstick to apply. She combed her fingers over her bare, dry, cracking lips.

"Max told me you had the poet in you." Boomer put his foot down on the accelerator to pass a Vanagon with surfboards on top. "And he wasn't lying."

"Thanks," Lily said, reapplying her imaginary black balm. "Cursed by metaphor, I guess. That's my lot." She closed her eyes and tried to rid her mind of the vision of Max among a graveyard of trees, as though she could séance the Sitka, smudge the serviceberry, or cleanse the ash. The embarrassment of the night of the blood moon rose high in her chest once again.

Once they reached the beach, they pulled into an almost full parking lot, including a long, antennaed news van. Lily had never seen so many cars gathered at once at the shore. They got out and joined a crowd walking toward a group gathered around something down by the water. They found a place on the side of the circle and gazed at a motionless, fat, black sea mammal maybe twenty feet in length. It raised its head an inch, then let it rest back on the sand. It was clearly very near death.

"What is it?" Lily whispered.

"Pilot whale," the woman next to her in a bright blue windbreaker with NOAA printed on the breast said, without taking her eyes from the gruesome scene.

"I wouldn't want it to pilot me anywhere," a man next to the lady said. She looked toward Lily and rolled her eyes.

"He has a point," Lily shrugged. "What is being done about it? Can they put it back in the water?"

"It'll just keep stranding itself," the woman said. "Something's thrown its internal navigation way off. They strand themselves in the hundreds elsewhere, but it's extremely rare to see, much less find one on shore, here in Oregon."

The whale had a little fat rounded forehead like a toddler and a mouth line seemingly stuck in a coy little upturned smile.

"At least he died happy," Lily said, turning to Boomer.

"It's like we're all awkwardly trying to have a conversation at a funeral," he leaned down and whispered. She felt simultaneously listened to and chastised for cracking jokes at a wake.

"I remember one thing from my grandparents' funeral," she said as her hand automatically rose to the scar on her chest. "I remember watching everyone's legs from under the porch and seeing how no one seemed comfortable in their own bodies. They just kept changing and shifting, crossing and uncrossing in order to try and find a position that felt okay."

"I think that's what a lot of people do their whole life," Boomer whispered. "Shifting, afraid to face reality." He turned to look at her. "Running away from their problems."

"Hmph."

"We'll all end up stranded on a beach taking our last breaths if we're not careful."

The two wandered away from the spectacle and back toward the truck. They got in and Lily sucked on a salty piece of hair in contemplation. She squinted out toward the huge expanse of gray-blue water looking for answers.

"Maybe I could just stay with you and Max for a couple days?" she asked. "Until I figure some stuff out?"

They sat quietly staring out to sea until Boomer started the truck up, the familiar rumble making Lily feel a little better.

"I don't see why not," Boomer said cautiously, rounding the corner out of the parking lot and getting back on the highway. "But you should call your mom and let her know you're okay."

"That wouldn't be completely true," Lily said. "Can you just call her for me? I need some more time before I talk to her."

"I guess that will do," Boomer said, switching on the radio. Merle Haggard sang a song about an "only rebel child" where "mama tried to raise me better" and "mama tried, mama tried, mama tried." The two looked at each other with wide eyes before bursting out in laughter. Boomer rolled the window all the way down to let the cooling evening air rush in and lift their hair from opposite ends of the chiaroscuro up off their heads like they'd seen a ghost. Lily threw her head back and sang along, yowling a little like a lost coyote.

Breeding Season

A TUFTED PUFFIN FLEW in a perfect straight line overhead, its long yellow ear tassels tucked flat against its head with the movement of its body through the air. Its mouth was full of silver sardines that bulged from either side of its bright orange beak and reflected the bright sun in glints, food destined for the hungry, gaping mouths of its young tucked deep inside the burrow nest. Olive regarded the bird with a sense of awe. The birds of the island had such a sense of purpose, especially so, it would seem, in breeding season. They appeared to know just exactly what they needed to do and never second-guessed their instincts. Olive felt the opposite in her gurgling, deep distrust of her own actions, as she paced behind the barracks with the Russian Blue tucked neatly on her hip in its basket. It was the day for which she and Warren had been preparing for weeks, but how could she know if their plan would put them on the right path? It could easily backfire if any single element of the strategy didn't go exactly as they intended. They could verily lose their lives by the end of the day.

The plan was that Warren would scope out the eggers during mealtime and make sure no one was near the brimming egg house, while Olive would signal to their compatriot captain, an underling Greek fisherman named Mikos, on his dinghy, that it was time to move in toward the target. They had chosen to work during the dusk hours so that they might slip away into the darkness of night toward the fishing vessel and then to San Francisco.

Warren had managed to set the whistle blowing—a ghastly malfunctioning contraption that often failed to blow when there was dense fog, but that instead necessitated only high tide to be triggered. That afternoon, the fog whistle reverberated its most unpleasant tone in stark sunshine. It was built over a natural blowhole in the rock, with a chimney to harness the breath of the island. Even on clear days, the whistle would sound for no apparent reason, as though the island were yelling at its occupants to leave it be. She considered the alarm as a sort of exhale, or sigh, by the island. In that sense, the whole rock was a living, breathing entity, with its most spectacular appendages those dwelling underwater. Standing up high on a peak of barren rock, she recalled the day at the abalone cave and how the brightly colored creatures living just under the water's surface had performed a sort of mesmerism on her, almost leading her to be swept off the rock and into the ocean forever. It wouldn't have been the great island animal's first capture of a pesky human into its underworld. She heard the whistle blow again from across the island and felt it in her chest as a cry to be left alone. The desperate sound helped her to justify their act of piracy. So often to Olive, it seemed this jagged landscape, littered with men and their need to take, take, take what little the island had to offer, begged to be left in peace.

When Olive heard the whistle blow another, third, constant, unending whistle, she knew that Warren had managed to rig the contraption to play its warning despite the unusually clear skies. She would have to work fast and signaled with a flash from a small mirror and the waving of her arms overhead toward the absconded dinghy. It began to come round with its empty crates toward the egg house. As the lighthouse men attended to the broken whistle and the egg men were busy eating dinner, the three thieves would meet at the egg house and gather as many of the eggs as the dinghy could carry and slip away unnoticed. That is, unless any tiny detail were to lay bare their plan. And on an island with no trees, where every living thing lived its life exposed to danger, there were certainly any number of angles from which the hammer of uncertainty might land.

Olive scrambled along the path toward the egg house, the rabbit bumping along at her hip. Inside, under the soft green leaves it had taken her all day to collect from different nooks of the island, tucked next to the rabbit, bounced the well-wrapped collection box. With each rise and fall of a veil of birds as she trundled past, she said her farewells. Goodbye murres, goodbye guillemots, goodbye gulls and cormorants. Goodbye puffin, oystercatcher, and auklet, alike. She had just started to learn their idiosyncrasies and habits. They had become friends, the many bird mothers tending to their young, keeping a slender thread attached to the memory of her own.

When she arrived at the fork in the path that led down to the egg house, her heart began to race. She could still turn back and return to the lighthouse barracks, to Richardson and the other lighthouse men. Perhaps she could finally befriend one of the two other women on the island who hid away in their small quarters with three or four children hanging in various weights from their skirt dresses. The women had turned up their noses when she offered to help them with their washing baskets one day. "Not necessary, young man," one said firmly, as though Olive might steal their babies and dash them on the rocks. *I'm a girl,* she longed to yell at them. *I'm just like you.* But she had taken their rejection in stride, as was necessary on this island where mankind held onto the most slippery of ropes when maintaining the sails of normalcy.

She paused and thought about poor Richardson and felt a twinge of regret at leaving the man alone with his delusions of grandeur and ailing eyesight. *What would become of that funny, half-blind man trying to run a lighthouse?* she wondered. He was one of four keepers, but so often it seemed as though he thought he was alone in the venture of keeping the light shining into the night. She would never be able to look back. There would be no carefully penned letters to Richardson with polite inquiries as to the functioning of the giant Fresnel lens, no recipes for meatless stew exchanged, no tender goodbyes. She felt that human twinge that exists, not quite in the heart or the head, but somewhere in between, that twinge that plucks all the strings of regret at once. The chord struck was not a tender or comforting tone. Across the island, the incessant fog whistle reminded her it was time for action.

As she made her way down the path, she looked out for anyone who might be waiting to ambush her during her incursion. It occurred to Olive that in stealing this shipment of eggs, they would be stealing from the thieves themselves. Her mother had loved to tell old Irish myths about thieving animals, many of which she took credit for crafting and embellishing herself. As Olive slid and skidded down the narrow trail, she recalled one particular story about a boy who stole eggs from wild birds and boiled them. He ate them down hungrily, but oddly found himself more hungry than before he had eaten the first round, and so he ate more and more. He stole from the songbirds and stole from the seabirds and even risked his life to steal from the eagle atop its giant precipice nest. But the boy just could not shake his hunger and grew weaker and leaner until one day, among the rocks of the Byrne, searching for a bird he had not yet stolen from that might satisfy his hunger, his life was suddenly and painfully seized from his very body by a lightning flash of talons. The bird flew off with his beating heart still tapping out a slow rhythm. As her mother told it, birds were prophets, so to steal from the birds, especially the raptors, was to steal the future right out from under one's own feet. Olive was eight at the time and she asked her mother, *Are not chickens birds, Mama?* To which her mother replied, *Not exactly, dear. Chickens are not wild, and they are certainly not prophets. They are in-between souls that give their bounty freely.* But a young Olive still wondered, as she paused with a forkful of omelet the next morning, if a large bird might swoop through the chimney to carry off her tiny beating heart once she took a bite.

Still wading through the boggy, bloody memory of myth and hearts being torn from chests, she ran almost headlong into Warren, who greeted her with open arms at the bottom of the path. After crashing right into his chest, he allowed himself to hold her only a few seconds extra, as they had urgent business to attend to. She could hear his heart beating fast and hard as a drum in the short moment he held her close.

"Are you ready to pull off this caper?" he said, holding her at arm's length.

"I'd call it more of a coup," said Olive, wild-eyed.

Their accomplice, Mikos, stayed in the dinghy as it rocked gently in the unusually serene ocean by the egg house. He had tied off with a long rope in order not to crash into the rocks and fashioned a smaller raft on which they floated the crates of eggs from the shore to the boat. Olive noted that the men had made quick work as she had made her way across the island from her signal post near the barracks. The egg house was open and over half empty already. The dinghy was almost full, with just enough room for a few more crates and perhaps three people to tuck into the spaces. As Warren floated over the last two crates full of eggs, they heard a loud shout from just beyond the crag behind them. It sounded like someone had called Warren by name with the kind of yell that usually begins a bloody first battle. It was the cry of war.

Warren pulled the rope of the dinghy with such force that two lines of red instantly burned into his palms. Olive remembered her stigmata from the first day she'd arrived at the island and felt a shudder in her bones as she was lifted and almost thrown between Warren and Mikos on the boat. She fell down into the crack between the egg crates and felt a sharp pain in her ankle as it twisted under her. By the time she had righted herself, Warren was in the boat and was pulling in the long rope from shore as Mikos pulled hard on the oars. The boat pulled sharply away from the shore and listed hard to one side with the burden of the weight aboard. A few gallons of water seeped over the edge, but they all leaned the other direction in ballast before the whole ocean was able to hop aboard.

Up on the rock, four armed men had just scaled to the top and were joined by a few more as they pulled themselves up from their mountain climber's ascent from basecamp. One of the men Olive recognized from the day on the beach as the one who had stolen her rabbits and questioned her gender. He loaded his coach gun with some effort and colorful language audible even at fifty feet and pointed his shotgun directly at the boat and yelled, "Halt! Warren. Do not dare take those eggs."

"Those don't belong to you," another man added.

The boat was some thirty feet off shore and moving quickly in the glassy water. In only another thirty feet, they would be hidden from view and the men would have to scramble up and down another peak, by which time the trio of egg thieves would be gone.

"And nor do they belong to you," Warren boomed back, cupping his hands to allow the message proper trajectory. And just as soon as his words had stopped resonating, the sound of a shot rang in the direction of the boat. Olive felt the world slow with the boom of the shot, her body only registering pain after her mind had already allowed itself to wonder at what kind of purpose these guns served to men on islands such as the Farallones. Did they shoot fish in the water? Shoot birds out of the sky? It seemed to her, before the pain began to tear into her side, that men used guns to gather by force that which didn't belong to them. These eggs, they didn't belong to anyone but the birds. But these eggs would never become young; they had been off the nest far too long. They couldn't put them back even if they wanted to. The damages had been wrought. She felt the pain rip through her body as though it were some penance for all the misdeeds of man. Then she fell into the hull of the boat and disappeared into darkness.

Warren uncupped his hands and checked his chest before noticing that Olive was slumped in a new way in the crevasse between crates. Her body lay limp, perfectly filling in the space between two crates as though it were trying to putty a drip, or caulk two bricks. He pulled up her shirt just as the dinghy rounded the corner out of view of the eggers and into the safety of smooth, quiet waters. Even if the men scrambled at full speed over the rock, their boat would be out of rifle range by the time the men caught up. The vessel moved swiftly over the darkening sea.

Under her shirt, there was hardly any blood at all, but Olive's breathing was slow and she still hadn't opened her eyes. Warren searched her soft skin desperate to find some scratch or wound that would explain how she had been hit. It wasn't until he turned her on her front that he saw the small hole, probably made by a single bead of shot as it entered her body, just above her angular, wide hip bones. No blood seeped out, but clearly something had gone in. A low moan emerged from Olive as he shifted her onto her back again.

"They belong to the birds," she said, and then slipped into a sort of quiet sleep with deep breathing as Warren watched in helpless terror.

In the cover of night, it took the dinghy only an hour before they reached the Greek fishing vessel, whereas they had planned for closer to two. It was fully dark, with an almost full moon lighting the path as the boat left a silver rippling wake behind. The men shouted greetings at Warren and congratulations until the dinghy pulled close enough to reveal the unconscious boy and the two pallid men's grave faces. Both Mikos and Warren were drenched through with sweat from pulling as hard as they could at the oars for an hour. The fishermen helped hoist the dinghy up onto the side with cantilevers and pulled Olive out first. The captain came to pat Warren on the back and ordered the ship's doctor to come and take a look at the still breathing boy. It wasn't until the doctor had Olive on the table that he discovered that she was bleeding not from her back, but from between her legs. The shot had found its way directly into her womb, where it ricocheted a few times before landing like a fishing weight on the bottom of a lake, just above the internal opening to the outside.

The doctor recovered as quickly as expected from the surprise and reconsidered the prognosis. He guessed he could get the shot out without performing the kind of surgery that would probably take her life. He reached up with a sort of thin plier to enter through the opening and retrieve the shot from inside. Warren stroked the finally conscious Olive and poured shots of ouzo down her throat to dull the pain. She gritted and railed at the procedure and anyone on the upper deck might easily have mistaken the event for the birth of a child. But it was to be the opposite. Olive would live, but her reproductive apparatus would be rendered useless from then on. Warren stayed by her side as she drifted into a fitful sleep troubled by nightmares of being carried off into the skies by winged creatures. She murmured and purred, then jolted half awake before settling down.

As the ship pulled into the port of San Francisco just before the morning broke, the atmosphere on the ship was that of celebration. The fishermen had received their two cartons of eggs as payment and were enjoying omelets and eggs over easy, sopping the yolks with dry crusts of bread. The payment was minimal compared to the risk they'd taken transporting known thieves—known pirates, as Warren preferred. But the fishermen had long been resentful of the Pacific Egg Company and the brutal way they enforced their "ownership" of collecting rights. They congratulated their once-protégé Warren on a job well done and celebrated the defeat of the eggers, with whom they had so long been in conflict, with the clinking of morning beers and the sliding of eggs down greased gullets.

"That'll change the meaning of 'taking the egg' now, won't it?" a small, bookish deckhand said to Warren.

"What a bricky girl you have there," said another to Warren. "She's lucky to be alive."

Warren sat quietly and finished his eggs unceremoniously, receiving each hard slap of approval on the back with a wan countenance the men mistook for fortitude, before heading below deck to check on Olive. He brought her an omelet and sat gingerly next to her small, hard cot.

"Are you hungry?" he asked. Olive eyed the plate of eggs and started to make a sort of gurgle from her diaphragm. She was thinking about her mother's story and the poor boy's body turned to dust on the Cliffs of Dover. She thought about how silly the whole thing was.

"Don't make me laugh," she said. "Not until tomorrow. Maybe the day after." And with that she pushed the tin plate away and curled her small hand into a ball inside Warren's warm paw. She wished she could curl up her whole aching body and stay in his mouth, maybe his chest, hibernate in the very chambers of his heart until the pain went away. As if he knew what she longed for, he told her, "I love you, little bird. It's going to be okay."

Heavenly Brass

Mojave Desert, California, 1941

ITCHING AN EARLY MORNING ride heading east toward Arizona in the back of a pickup with a chicken farmer, Victor settled among the crates of chatty hens. He looked through the slats in the wood into their eyes and watched as they closed their lizard-like lids with each bump of the truck. *Do they understand their fate?* he wondered as he took out the present from the old man, looked at the eggs nestled in their velvet corrals, and rewrapped the collection in an extra layer, an old wool shirt that was getting too many holes to wear any more, even for a tramp. He adjusted the old glass case carefully in the bottom of the bag as they bumped along an unpaved portion of road, then let himself doze in and out of sleep as the hens clucked away, forgetting completely about the envelope the old man had given him the day before. Crystal and velvet trumps paper—the flashy egg collection had managed to eclipse the memory of the envelope.

After catching a couple more rides and a short sleep in the dark of night on a park bench in a small town on the east side of the Sierras, Victor was finally heading into the desert for the first time in his life. He could feel the dry air drawing the sogginess from his bones. He thought about what he'd left back in Washington and imagined he would hardly be missed. His wealthy Seattle banking family had always tried to sweep their sensitive and strange youngest son's penchant for poetry and music under the rug. They grimaced when he broke into song at a fancy restaurant or in line at the movies, pulling him aside and threatening a beating if he didn't stop all his grandstanding. "He's a strange bird," they used to say to important, buttoned-up visitors invited into their beautiful home. "Don't mind him," they demurred when their young son came to dinner wearing a cape clasped by butterfly clips around his throat. When he was a teen he wore ascots, pillbox hats, or T-shirts with so many holes his nipples peeked through. But his parents *did* mind him and he knew it more than anyone. His leaving town of his own accord had simply taken the burden off his family of ever cleaning up another of his social messes again. He had done everyone a favor, he figured, by hitting the road the first chance he got.

The constant rain of Southwest Oregon was a distant memory by the time he braced himself against the hot desert wind in the back of a hay trailer barreling through the Mojave. It was still morning when they arrived in Needles, Arizona. Victor got off, gave the driver a tip of his hat in the rearview, and looked up and down the dusty street for a place he might get a cup of coffee. The rejuvenating effects of the one full night of sleep on the old man's couch had long evaporated into the desert air, and after the last couple days of bouncing around in various vehicles, he felt he might collapse without a cup of joe. The desert didn't quite make him feel like breaking into song, but he hoped more than anything that eventually it just might. He did a little happy shuffle with his feet as he walked up to the Oasis Diner. Standing just outside the entrance, he counted the coins in his stained leather satchel. Seventy-two cents. A scrawny bronzed kid of twelve or thirteen wearing only shorts and sandals approached him and said:

"You want coffee?"

"Yeah, kid, I sure do."

"Well, I've got something better than coffee." The kid held out a hand with a little shriveled brown button of some plant matter, maybe a cactus.

"No, thanks."

"You sure? This will change your whole world."

"And how do you know that?"

"I'm a shaman."

"Ha!" Victor laughed. "The world's tiniest shaman."

"Well, that just shows what you know." The boy recoiled his hand and looked away. "I'm a road man in training."

"Okay, kid. That's more like it. I'm a road man, too." He patted the kid on the arm, realizing he'd offended him. "How much for one of those buttons? What is it like? Will it wake me up? Slow me down?"

"All of the above. How much do you have?"

"I'm not giving you all my coin, but, seventy-two cents. That's *en total*, jellybean."

"Then give me one cent and we're good. I'll give you this if you want." He held out one button and paused before dropping it in Victor's hand. "But you'll have to come with me to take it. I'll show you a real shaman. I'm only inviting you because I was watching you and I get the feeling it will do you good."

"Okay, then. What do we do with this one-cent not-coffee miracle turd?"

"Don't make me regret inviting you."

"I'm sorry, little man. Really."

"We will eat it to clear your mind." The kid narrowed his eyes at Victor as if to make sure he was worthy of his efforts. "Follow me."

Victor looked back wistfully at the coffee shop with its inviting blue-and-white rounded booths and coffee percolating behind the counter. A girl in a crisp uniform walked briskly to a table with plates of steaming eggs, sausage, and buttered toast. Victor looked back at the boy and said, "Will there be something to eat at this shindig? Because there's a plate of eggs in there calling my name."

"There will be many things calling your name. Better not to eat now, though. But there will be a meal after, yes."

It didn't take more than a few seconds for Victor to decide that the adventure of following a tiny shaman trumped a hot breakfast. His stomach had grown accustomed to the raking and gurgling of hunger. No need to confuse the poor organ. He followed the boy past one stop sign and out of town. As they marched along the road, the growing heat of the afternoon filled up the wide-open spaces of the desert with the weight of an anvil, the oppressive sun making any meaningful communication completely impossible. Walking through that kind of heat can make the mind churn—thoughts become irascible, then quiet. Victor cursed his blistered feet and heavy boots, lamenting his decision to follow the kid, and then, just as quickly, forgot his aches and pains as one moment melted into the next. *There's no turning back,* he figured, as the road shimmered ahead like a black-and-silver lake. Back home they had always called him too soft to survive, but he liked to think he simply forgave the discomforts of the world. He rolled with the flow. He squinted his eyes at the shimmering vanishing point of the earth in the distance. It seemed to him that the boy was leading him to an expansive waterway somewhere far away. But the lake never seemed to get any closer as the two walked along the highway shoulder for a good hour. The illusion was untouchable.

As the heat unlocked the memory from his brain, Victor suddenly remembered the letter the old man Warren had given him. How had he forgotten to open it? He must be more exhausted than he even knew. He made a mental note to open the letter when he and the boy reached their destination. Despite the heat, they were moving at a good clip along the desert highway, rivers of sweat running down their backs. They walked past rubber rabbit bush and blooming orange globe mallow, the boy pointing out the names of the plants as they passed by, punctuating the silence to point: *desert star, monkey flower, lupine, penstemon, ghost flower.* Victor thought that "ghost flower" had all the makings of a cautionary children's tale about what might happen when a fool traveler wanders off into the desert with a stranger. He tried to let the poem form in his head, but as soon as it began, the heat wiped its heavy hand over the words and they were gone.

When they finally left the highway, it was to climb up into an arroyo with a wide sandy bottom and short cliffs on either side. Floods had marked where the water wore a clear path from the top of the mesa down the arroyo and into the wash, but it was hard to imagine any large volume of water in the hot, dry, spring landscape.

Alluvial fans of brightly colored eroded sand lay with impermanence in semicircles emanating from the middle of the mesa like a dancer's skirt fluttering in waves. At the mere idea of rushing water, Victor stopped and meted out a few, precious sips from his canteen.

"Watch for snakes," the boy said, not asking to share in the water. It was the first the two had spoken in a half hour.

"Duly noted," Victor said, taking a look around as though there might be a gang of rattlers already underfoot.

"They don't want to bite you," the boy said. "But if you are careless, they might just be forced to let you know they care."

As they walked up the canyon, the pink-and-yellow streaked cliffs grew higher on either side of them, closing them off from the creosote flats. It would take quite a scramble to get up one side or another. *There's something strange about that boy,* thought Victor as he followed the spritely kid in a zigzagging pattern up the arroyo. The young man's skin was such a deep golden brown it was as though he had spent his entire short life naked under the sun. The sun had worn in his forehead the even lines of a much, much older man. They pressed on and Victor considered the boy some more. He looked like a child, but he had the confidence of an old man. Almost the certainty of a grandfather. They traveled uphill until the canyon narrowed and they came to a place where the sandy ground gave way to a mass of loose boulders. The sun was starting to get low and Victor wondered briefly if he was being drawn into some sort of trap.

"It's not dangerous," the boy reassured him as if reading his mind. "Unless you make it."

"Okay, boss," Victor said, pulling himself up awkwardly onto the top of the first boulder. They scrambled up for another half hour through the slot canyon as it became steeper and harder to navigate, until finally the boulders seemed to be stacked right on top of one another. The boy stood above on a mysterious ledge out of Victor's field of vision.

"Almost there," the boy said. "This way." He waved him up.

Victor was muttering to himself something about the kid having said that an hour ago as he struggled to pull himself upright onto the boulder. Finally he stood up, pulling his sweat-soaked backpack up behind him, his knees cracking with the effort. He had a line of salt showing through his shirt where he'd been sweating profusely for the last two hours. As he straightened up on the boulder, what he saw up there was a surprise, to say the least. The slot canyon opened up into perfectly flat ground to either side and in front of the boulder. The even ground was protected by a red earth cirque that sheltered the area from the winds that blew strong along the top of the mesa some 150 feet higher. He could hear the wind rattle through the sparse vegetation up above but could not feel it from where he stood. All around him was stillness.

On the lower level, the calm air was cooling rapidly as the sun dipped close to the horizon in the distance. A giant mass of beavertail cactus bloomed in bunches of papery hot-pink flowers near his feet. The cactus and plants spotting the pebbled sand were evenly spaced in such a way they appeared as though a tended garden. Victor walked slowly in a snail's trail among the plants, pausing to look up at the pastel pinks, purples, yellows, and blues swathed across the sky, marked by thin clouds glowing in hues as bright as the cactus blooms in color, as bright as a fire. As he gazed down the arroyo and out over the creosote flats punctuated by the outline of the inscrutable Joshua trees, the serenity of the place caught his breath in his throat in a way he had never before experienced. He exhaled long and deep.

"Glad you like it," the boy said, looking up at him with his bizarre sense of grandfatherly approval. "I'd like you to meet my family."

The boy led Victor over to a small cave at the base of the cirque. A man in a linen robe tied at the waist with a cord arranged objects in front of him on a blanket. He didn't seem to notice the two approaching until they were very close. He sat back on his heels, his back still to the two.

"Well, what do we have here, son?"

"You told me to choose someone to bring to the ceremony this evening."

The man turned around to face the two sweaty travelers.

"And I thought you might bring one of your cousins from town. But I see you have chosen instead this blue-eyed stranger." He looked at his son with what could only be interpreted as judgment.

"I think you'll see he is a good choice." The little boy stood tall against the stare of his father. The man sighed and stood up with some effort. He was barely taller than his son, bent with age. He picked up a small gourd rattle off the blanket and shook it in the direction of the stranger.

"*Hatchoq*, traveler," the man said. "We will see."

The man walked away and over to the cave to talk to a woman raking the sand with a flat stick. He bent down to whisper to her and she looked back toward the blue-eyed stranger without expression before returning to her raking.

"White people have not always been kind to us," the boy said. "So you can imagine why they are suspicious of you."

"Don't blame 'em," Victor said, setting down his backpack gently in the sand. "White people haven't always been kind to me either."

"Good."

"I can leave if you think it's best," Victor said, looking uneasily back down the wash. "But I'm dog-tired from that little stroll you took me on."

"Don't go," the boy said. "Stay here." And he went over to the woman and whispered to her. She motioned into the cave and the boy went in and came out with a few hard cases that looked like they housed some sort of instruments. He opened a smallish case and took out a trumpet. He played a few notes and the sound made its way around the cirque as though it were rolling along touching each side, echoing over and over like a softer, further away version of the first note. Then the woman took out a tuba, and Victor smiled the smile of the delighted madman at his first circus.

More and more people, some of them carrying brass instrument cases, clambered up onto the topmost boulder and filtered in toward the raked sand, making their way across the flats and toward the cave. Not everyone in attendance looked like they belonged to a tribe. There was a large-boned woman with long blonde hair and a redheaded older man, his ginger hair and beard speckled with bright white. The robed father of the boy had started a diminutive fire and stoked it while waving a fan made entirely of feathers. Victor looked at the faces of the people as they arrived and clocked their distrust of his grimy, tattered clothes and his baked-blue hitchhiker's eyes. He made himself small as he squatted near the fire with his feet still on the ground, long legs tucked up under his body like a roosting heron. His bleached blue eyes flecked with gold as they glowed in the firelight. The group of fifteen or so collected around the fire naturally and without any prompting. Some picked up an item from the blanket, a gourd rattle, a feather fan, while others took out their brass instruments and laid them quietly in their laps.

"Thank you for coming to church this Saturday evening," the robed father started, placing an arrow onto the cloth with the other items from the box. "Any fool knows none of us will live forever. But as soon as we die we live on through our children." The man looked at his son as he said this. "My son has chosen to bring a guest tonight to our ceremony. And so we must welcome him as one of our own."

All eyes fixed on Victor as he shifted his heron legs beneath him and raised his hand tentatively in a wave. The woman who had been raking the sand spoke up to pick up where the robed man left off.

"We are here to experience time and eternity," she said. "There are many names for the spirits we bring forth, but today we will call it 'twelavelem' and hope to bridge the divide between the dead and the living."

"We do things a little differently here," the redheaded old man joined in, looking straight at Victor as he did. "We are from different tribes, and so we have different traditions. Me? I'm Irish. My wife is Mojave. Our child is a daughter of the sun." He held the hand of the woman next to him who had earlier been raking the sand and nodded toward a young girl sitting near the boy. "But together, from our different tribes, we have found common ground by incorporating the great tradition of John Sousa into the peyote ritual, by including songs as played on brass instruments. It is a way of making old traditions new and unified." Victor's eyes opened wide but he maintained his quiet. The sound of "The Stars and Stripes Forever" started up in his brain.

"There was a time not long ago," the robed man picked up where the redheaded man left off, "when we welcomed the great trains of white men who arrived in Needles as they passed through to the west to make their fortunes. We sold our wares on blankets and welcomed the travelers into town. But many were vile toward us, kicking our pottery and our women. They tried to assimilate us and erase our traditions. But the brass band came in as a new tradition, bridging the gap, and we have taken in the instruments to our church and made them ours. It is a symbol not of our defeat, but of our triumph."

There were murmurings of agreement among the people gathered. Someone shook a little rattle. The big-boned blonde woman shook her long mane like a beautiful pony.

"Here is the tea. Drink each cup slowly over the next hour." The robed man poured a dark brown tea into small silver cups and passed them around. The crowd was quiet as he began to sing a wordless song. After a while, more voices joined in, and someone started a slow beat on a drum. The sound of each note raced along the wall above them, back and forth along the cirque, the smooth curve of earth, echoing back. Victor rejoiced that he had finally found a group of people who enjoyed breaking into song.

The songs worked in thirds and fifths, Victor noted, suddenly aware of the tile-type melodic movement and remembering his piano lessons as a child. His parents had abruptly stopped them when he started learning ragtime and filling their austere house with the sounds of the saloon. He let the music weave in and out of his ears and imagined it as actual threads of light, moving with the precision of a needle through the night. How did he recall that the style was called a tile-type? It felt as though something were opening up in his brain and deep buried memories were flying forth like bits of paper on the wind. Information seemed to be channeling itself out of the stars and straight into his head. The song began to unlock and unwind memories so long buried they were dusted and vague. He was a kid on a pebbled Puget Sound beach quietly singing dirges to the dead birds washed up on the rocks. He was a young man hiding in the shed to play his forbidden ukulele. He was a slightly older young man writing poems in the bathroom despite the fear of corporal punishment if he were found out by his father. *Fairy,* his father hissed. *Weakling.* Each memory rose up and evaporated toward the stars. The almost full moon poured down cool, luminous light that hung on the surface of the smooth succulent cacti like mist. The ground and everything planted in it took on a glow in the near night. He watched the fire for a while as it made the form of a ghost, a bird, a beating heart. Each image appeared clear as day, then fell back under a new wave of yellow as the fire licked the slate clean. He leaned his head back and let the rock pour secrets in his ears as he listened to the beautiful sounds of the player's breath travel through brass and echo across the stone.

"I'd like to show you something," Victor said to the robed father after the song had ended. "It's a present from a friend on my journey." He started to rustle in his backpack, the inside of his pack seemingly huge and full of strangeness as he wound his hand to the bottom and clasped the tightly wrapped egg collection. He unwrapped and laid it on the corner of the blanket in front of the shaman, who looked at it for a long time before saying anything. Finally, he put his sun-baked hand above the collection.

"This is an old and powerful artifact," the shaman said, looking pleased with Victor for the first time. "There are many haly'a that have seen this little box. I can feel the force of its history."

"I'd like to give you this as a gift," Victor said.

"And I thank you. But I can tell that it is already tied to your story, so you should be the one to carry it on a bit farther on its journey. You will know when to pass it along."

Victor nodded, relieved a little. He suddenly longed to possess the stories from each egg, to keep the treasure a little longer.

"Please. Choose an instrument," the man said. Victor looked up at the sky just as the tuba began its first note. There was no melody to follow, only the layering of notes as the trumpet and euphonium joined in. Then a sackbut and serpent made their tones, like possessed, ancient versions of the trombone and cornet. He let the music fly into his brain and welcomed each bit of flack as it bounded around. He picked up a gourd rattle and shook it, listening to the sound of each seed inside and aware of each clink and curve of sound. The music was shaking loose in his chest the flak of being a strange kid, a freak, a worthless cur.

The cool night breezed as relief on his skin. All the troubles that had hung heavy since he'd run away from his life in Seattle began to lift out and into the darkness, as though leaping one by one from his very chest. The band played on in its drone song that morphed into a version of "The Invincible Eagle" and "Hands Across the Sea," two of Victor's favorite Sousa marches. The core band shrunk in size as some members dispersed to answer a message calling only them. Victor got up and walked the perimeter of the circle and out into the cactus garden, where he would continue the conversation about life and death with the plants under the woven sounds of the inimitable brass band until morning. Standing at the edge of the world under the moon and its new, visible fingers of light, he let go of some of the fear he'd been gathering like a dung beetle his whole life. He watched as all his anger and fear rolled down the arroyo and disappeared into the darkness, breaking apart into stars. His stomach heaved with the force of such an exodus, but as he had eaten nothing that day, nothing came up.

He peeled off his clothes piece by piece and folded them in a pile on a rock smooth as the very moon. Naked, he raised up his arms and let the world take over his skin. Everything he saw was new, which on some level was intensely frightening, but on another thrilling. He no longer knew what anything was, but allowed the strangeness and the unknowing to enter through his body like a ghost. The tuba sounded, louder than before, and the deep notes rattled his body and the cirque and the world shook a little for a moment, leaving traces of light in the air. He surrendered then and there to the desert, to the earth, and tendered his resignation to the prison of clothing. He would find a way to be new, to be free, and to never bend to the confines of a society that might dictate otherwise. He lay prone on the smooth rock, bathed in the baby blue of the desert moon, and lay for hours in a trance of the alive, until finally, just before morning light, sleep found him.

Victor awoke from his short, naked slumber on the flat of the topmost boulder. Someone had covered him with a thin wool blanket against the desert cool. His clothes were still in a neat pile at his feet. As he stretched his limbs and lay on the smooth rock, he felt as though he had finally found what he had left home looking for. He was free from the ties that bound him. He would find a way to remain naked from then on out. He kept the blanket around him for warmth as he rejoined the group and shared in a meal of corn cakes and stewed vegetables and beans that had been set up on the blanket near the smoldering fire. It was the most delicious meal he had ever eaten in his life, without a doubt. The memory of the hunger he had felt staring into the diner with its vinyl booths and black coffee seemed like a bad memory compared to the pure bliss delivered with each bite of food.

After the meal, he packed up his belongings and came upon the envelope. *The envelope!* He laughed out loud at how long ago that night eating peppered pasta with the old man felt. He hadn't noticed before how thick the letter felt. He opened it and inside was a stack of crinkled bills and a letter. He took out the letter and read its wavering handwriting.

Dear Wanderer,

Tomorrow is my last day on this earth, so I wanted you to have what is left of all I own. I trust I will not need it where I'm going. An incredible woman told me once that we could all use some kindness on this journey. I hope you find what you are looking for on the road. When you find something you love, trust me, hold tight to it and just let it be what it will.

Best,

Warren

Inside the envelope were thirteen worn fifty-dollar bills, two twenties, two fives, and four ones. He smoothed his fingers over the bills and the memory of his father's crisp, full billfold popped into his head. He had never been allowed to touch it as a child, though he longed to feel the mother-of-pearl clasp under his finger. It was the beauty, not the money that he was after. But that wad of dough was the apex of his father's power—his totem. His father's money was not alive, he realized, but a carcass of possibility. He wanted to do nothing with it but keep it in a moldering pile. There was no frivolity of spending allowed in his house. This money, Victor decided, as he filtered it through his fingers, would be different. He would dedicate its power to unlocking the secret voices of old things. He would collect all the world's amusements and curiosities, its antiques and literature, and celebrate each item's story by sharing it with the rest of the world. He would turn the money into an observance of all people and their curiosities. He would not let it become a symbol of greed. He also decided, looking up at the church members as they filed down the canyon, into the arroyo, and back into town, that he would wander no farther. Needles was his new home. He had finally found a place to be.

Monsters

ACH DAY WAS MELTING into the next as the temperatures rose high, higher, highest. Well before noon, as Sal loaded up her kayak, the thermometer that bounced off her backpack read 109 degrees Fahrenheit—that point marking discomfort, even for the seasoned desert dweller. It was her one day off from surveys that week, so Sal had decided to kayak down the Gila River a ways to find a nice place to swim and escape the heat under the shade of some riparian trees. The solo mission required some planning. She dropped her kayak off a mile up the road, then drove down and parked her truck by the side where she would be coming out with her boat after floating the river, then hiked the mile back to her boat to start the journey. She would have to gauge the distance just right and portage her way back up through the riparian brush to the truck after, but the whole process seemed more than worth it. She was not averse to a little struggle and planning. She dragged the nine-foot kayak down a sandy embankment toward the river, the center resting on her hip, bees buzzing around the bright red plastic as though it were some enormous nectar pot of gold.

She crouched in the cockpit, settled her legs in the hull, and pushed away from shore, feeling the floating freedom of a seal jumping into the ocean from land as the boat rocked and found its balance under her weight. She spun a neat little circle in the boat as she moved the paddles in and out of the muddy water to orient herself. The river felt cool, so she cupped the silty brown water over her well-covered arms and neck, the cool water turning warm almost immediately on contact but still providing some relief from the heat. She paddled upstream a bit just to get her muscles moving, then let the current take her lazily down, steering with the paddle as need be. The particular breeze that sometimes seems only to exist on the water's surface picked up and played with her wet, black curls, untucking one from behind her ear and flapping it in the breeze. She felt somehow less alone as the wind breezed up and over her wet clothes.

Rock canyon walls rose slowly out of shoreline's sandy beaches lined by arrowweed, cottonwood, mesquite, and willow. The cliff grew higher as she floated downstream around a bend until she entered a box canyon, the river flanked by tall yellow-and-red streaked sandstone. Bright veins of electric-yellow lichen streaked the gradation of colored rock. She paused as she found herself squarely between two forty-foot walls. Looking up, she noticed a couple flowering desert agaves reaching their long flowered stalks out over cliffs at an angle over the river, their spiky leaves and roots miraculously wedged into the rocky crevasses many feet above. She glanced up at the magnificent plants and aimed herself upstream, paddling against the easy current in order to stay in one spot and to better see their tall stalks rising toward the heavens. After decades of hard-won photosynthesis and growth, this was their one chance to show off and reproduce before they wilted under the harsh Sonoran sun and died. It was in these places that no human on foot could possibly access that Sal found herself breathing in what she considered true privilege. She exhaled deeply and pointed herself back downstream, feeling a part of the place.

Ocotillo clung to the cliffs and scrambled its spindly, thorny arms skyward. Bright bunches of red flowers dotted the shore. The rock walls became shorter and shorter until they gave way again to sandy shores dense with green. Sal rounded a bend and found a small beach with a huge native willow casting shade, so she shored her kayak, hopped out with some difficulty, and dragged it up out of the murky water onto shore. She guessed she'd floated only a half mile at that point, but was more than ready for a swim, a snack, and a siesta.

She stripped down to her underwear and jumped into the silted water, still muddied up by early monsoon rains.

After a good swim, she lay splayed on her towel, soaking wet from her curls down to her boy shorts. She pulled her requisite day-off gear out of the kayak's hatch (mini-cooler of water and beers, towels, books, binoculars) and stacked them in the shade, cracking a miraculously still-cold Tecate. Aware she would be dry in a matter of minutes, she enjoyed the brief reprieve from the heat and let the week evaporate off her form. Even in the shade, the heat had a brain-melting effect. She lay supine with all her strong muscles relaxed and thought of nothing at all.

She had only a moment to be quiet and enjoy the stillness before she found herself distracted by a chorus of begging calls as they bounced around above her in the willows. Against her will, as if possessed by her training, her eyes darted from bird to bird, measuring their tail length by sight. Two full-grown willow flycatchers were trailed by three juveniles with little stub tails less than half the length of their parents' tails. They were excellent beggars, these little birds with their still-wide gapes, and were making the most of the only time in their lives when they would be given sustenance for free. These food deliveries—fat insects dropped right into their open-gaped faces by a mother or father bird on hyperdrive—were their one leg up on a brutally difficult road to survival. Sal wondered if being a human parent was like that. Did it feel like you were running around trying to grab all the resources in a sort of desperate way to feed the mouths of your progeny? Her thoughts instantly turned to Alice. It had been almost a year since she'd written to or heard from her. The thought of her brought tightness into her chest, as though longing for a cool climate in the midday desert heat.

Wrested from her cool daydream of Alice, Sal sat up as something caught her eye in the water on the far shore. What she saw emerging out of the very same swimming hole she'd just spent a half hour splashing around in was, to say the least, surprising. A Gila monster, a huge pink-and-black mottled lizard, emerged from the water with some difficulty, heaving itself up the bank and holding on with long claws as it scrambled to right itself. She watched it rest a moment in the sun as the water rolled off its chain-mail skin in round droplets. The lizard, about a foot-and-a-half long, moved its fat tail back and forth slowly. Its beaded, armored skin looked slick and fresh after the swim. Above, the parent flycatchers raised alarm calls to the juveniles who had been flitting in a bush near where the Gila monster emerged from the water. The juveniles stayed put but continued their manic, begging calls, seemingly unsure how to respond. The youngest hatch, with hardly a tail to speak of, jumped around on the ground, attracting the attention of the lizard. The lizard moved slowly over toward the bush the young birds were in and paused not far from the youngest. The adult birds came in making a racket and darted directly at the Gila monster to draw its attention away, flying in and out of the lizard's striking range. The monster showed the parent birds its long fangs and opened its black gaping mouth with a hiss to warn them off, then moved slowly closer to the juvenile.

In a flash, the lizard caught the baby bird in its jaws. Sal felt stunned and numb as she watched, as though the venom were coursing through her own blood. The lizard devoured the bird in only a few swallows, not even a trace of blood spilled, swallowed and flicked its black forked tongue as it walked slowly off toward the rock shelf, its dotted pink-and-black skin wrinkling at its neck with each slow step, its very fat, rounded tail wagging slowly behind. Sal had been crouching on the other side of the creek as she watched the hunt unfold and sat back on her heels in a sort of relief when it was over. She looked around for someone to share in the strangeness that witnessing predation in the wild creates in the chest. Her heart raced a little faster, her brain moved a little slower. Her eyes darted around, but there was no one to talk to but the trees. One of the flycatcher parents called over and over for the rest of the time Sal stayed by the river, a sound as steady as a car alarm. If there were such a thing as mourning in the bird world, this surely had to be it. Sal cracked her neck, her muscles sore from always straining her posture upward. The breeze would just not do as a conversation partner this time, and seeing as there was no one to talk to, she decided to write Alice a letter. She took a data sheet out of her watertight clipboard, the only paper she had with her, and flipped it over.

Dear Alice,

My dear one! I just witnessed one of the wildest and most thrilling things. I think you would have totally hated/loved it. I'm still trying to make sense of it. Well, you know how you were afraid of Gila monsters so long ago when I first told you about them? Without knowing it, I just swam with one! And then, from shore, I watched it eat a baby bird. The whole thing took only a matter of minutes, but it's the kind of vision that I imagine will be with me for a long time to come. And I know this will sound sort of callous, but it was one of the most natural and beautiful things in the world. There's a part of me that feels so pleased when I watch energy transfer hands like that in the wild. I mean, the survival rate of songbird offspring into adulthood is less than one in two, anyhow, and the odds get even worse after that, so I guess in that sense it was a sort of commonplace occurrence. But to see the rare and secretive Gila monster killing to live another day? Incredible.

It's dastardly hot today at 110 degrees, but I've got a cooler of cold beer and water and I wish for nothing else than you here on this towel with me right now under this willow. I know you can't just pick up and come visit, but I really wish I could show you all the things in this country that so many people don't even know exist. They say the desert is barren. But, baby, it's the most full kind of landscape I've ever known. Drop me a line sometime, maybe one of your amazing postcards? I miss you.

Love,

Sal

She folded up the letter and put it back in the clipboard case, but she didn't feel satisfied. Why was she always dancing around everything she truly wanted to tell Alice? Was it the fear of rejection holding her back? Why could she not tell her about breathing in a landscape and allowing it to be part of her heart? Why could she not tell Alice that the smell of her strawberry blonde hair at the end of the day after a hike, the salty pungent scent of her oils and sweat, had been a part of Sal's heart for years? She took the letter back out, read it over, ripped it to shreds, and threw the shreds into the muddy water. *Back to the earth, cowardice.*

~

THAT VERY AFTERNOON IN Burning Woods, Alice stood at the mailbox a few extra seconds in her raincoat, staring into the empty cavernous space, and wondered why it had been so long since she'd heard from Sal. She couldn't remember whose turn it was in the long chain of correspondence, but she felt a little pissed off about the whole thing. *I guess she's moved on to another adventure that's more important than me,* she sighed, closing the mailbox against the drizzling rain. She felt very much alone as she walked the road back to her truck with the rain ticking away on the hood of her jacket. She sat in the old aqua Chevy and watched the water run in rivulets on the windshield as the truck warmed up a few minutes. Once purring, she would go pick up Lily from the bus stop. There had been some disturbing developments at Lily's grade school and she wanted to minimize the moments when kids might pick on her daughter. She'd heard from the teacher that the other fourth graders had started calling her "brainiac" and "wordy weirdo." Someone had also thrown many little pieces of shaved metal, lord only knows where they came from, into her fluffy white hair during class. Alice had spent a good hour plucking the metal bits out like a mother gorilla when she came home. Lily didn't want to talk about any of the cruelties to her mom, but instead just stuck her nose directly into a book the instant she came home.

At the bus stop, Alice saw Lily get off the bus and watched as a little boy pushed her off the last step. Lily stumbled but didn't fall all the way to the muddy ground. The bus driver ate a sandwich and looked the other way, as if on purpose. Alice felt a sort of beast take her over, the blood rising in her body, white lightning in her brain. She jumped down from the truck and clomped over to the boy in her galoshes and raincoat. She squatted directly in front of the boy—one of the Dickersons, she figured—held his shoulders in her hands, and looked lasers into his eyes.

"Look, kid," she said keeping her eyes locked on his. "If you touch my daughter again, I'll send all the evil ghost succubi vampire demons into your room at night and they will suck your soul right out of your mouth." The kid wiggled his shoulders a little and his brother laughed.

"Watch out, Dempsey. She's a super scaaaaaary witch."

"And you, too," she said, pointing a finger in the face of the older one. "You won't even know it has happened but you'll just find yourself wandering around like a zombie. No soul. Nothing." Little bits of spit flew from her mouth as she overannunciated.

The two brothers put their arms up and made like they were the walking dead, groaning and eating pretend brains.

"Nice job, Mom," Lily said as they climbed up into the truck. "You just bought me some more special attention from those boys."

"You'll see. That will teach them," Alice said.

"That will teach them to make sure my life sucks," Lily said, looking out the window.

On the drive back up the long gravel driveway, Alice glanced at her brooding little girl and felt like a failure. She had failed to defend her daughter, failed to keep the written affections of her beloved Sal flowing, failed to keep the monsters at bay. She parked the car and they ran inside under a sheet of rain. As the girls peeled their soggy layers in the silence of the foyer, she thought of only one thing she was good at. And so she went to the kitchen as her little daughter went straight for her book to escape the day and pulled out a bottle of whiskey from the cabinet. She poured the rest of the bottle into a highball glass, right up to the rim, and watched as the rain came down in sheets outside. The drink blazed a trail down her throat and into her belly. *Where warmth is lacking*, a foreign voice sounded in her brain, *there you must start a fire.*

Sheep vs. Goat

San Francisco, California, 1874

OLIVE RECUPERATED HIDDEN AWAY in a small apartment in the Marina District belonging to the Greek fishing boat captain, his mother, his wife, and their six children. The scent of charcoal, citrus, and bay leaf floated on the air, filling the space with a sense of sharp newness as she rested. There was distinct relief from the unrelenting winds of the islands as she lay in the still, warm air that floated from room to room. While the constant flow of screaming children and bickering was not the most ideal place to rest, Olive didn't mind. The babies were a welcome distraction after months on the Farallones without any contact with the young or old of the human variety. Olive's rabbit hopped around the apartment and delighted the children. The grandmother fed Olive magical lemon soup with rice, fried squid, and a hard sharp cheese called feta, layered with strong grassy oil. Olive had never tasted such glorious flavors and the tang revived her body, starting with her taste buds. The grandmother laughed when they told her the new guest's name.

"Olive," she scoffed. "Like zee oil."

"Yes, ma'am."

"We name our children after gods, emperors, or muses," she clucked, "not food."

"Can you imagine?" her daughter roared, "My little baby Myzithra?" She mimed kissing a baby loaf of cheese.

Olive knew they were poking fun at her, but she was floating in a happy fog of big-bosomed women bringing her plates of delicious, fortifying food and shots of ouzo to numb the pain of the wound. She was, though still in pain, a happy clam.

Warren spent the week in San Francisco making deals with various black market vendors. He unloaded the shipment of eggs bit by bit, so as not to arouse suspicion on the street. The fishermen had told him that the next ship wasn't scheduled to go out to the Farallones until the following week for deliveries, so he had to work fast before word could travel back from the island about the pirate egger and the lighthouse assistant boy who'd helped him pull the job.

He stopped at the door to a Chinese restaurant and regarded the naked plucked fowl hanging in the front window. Flies buzzed around and feasted on the goose-fleshed naked skin. Below, a tank with two live fish filled up the small space with their fatted bodies, watching and waiting for the flies to make the deadly mistake of landing on the surface of the water. Warren's mind began drawing circles and arrows from being to being, as though to illustrate the cycle of life. He took out his notebook but put it back in his pocket without documenting his thoughts, as he was late for his scheduled meeting with the restaurant owner.

He had an appointment to sell three crates of eggs but was surprised to find the place empty and dark. The tables were set apart by thin wooden screens elaborately carved with serpents, birds, and the gnarled limbs of a foreign species of tree. He started to think he had arrived at the wrong time and turned to go when an old man emerged from the back holding an armload of oranges and a large knife.

"What?" the proprietor said, as if quite ready to use the knife.

"Warren, here." He placed a hand delicately to his chest. "With fresh eggs. As per our appointment."

"Aaaaah." The man looked relieved as he let the armful of oranges fall into a crate. "Lots of men coming in here lately talking Chinese corruption. Prostitution. Many threats made on our lives. They make raids on some others, I hear."

"Yes," Warren nodded. "Men are distrustful of what they don't understand. The celestial culture is foreign, therefore threatening. It's their own ignorance at play."

"It is." The old man stood taller but still eyed Warren distrustfully as he twirled the end of his mustache. "You brought samples for me?"

Warren took out a murre egg hidden away in his inside breast pocket and handed it over to the proprietor. The old man held the egg up to the light and inspected the beautiful shape and brown-speckled bluish surface.

"They are fresh," Warren said. "But you must not tell anyone where you got them."

The man brought out a glass of water from behind the bar and let the egg drop into the water. It stayed on its side on the bottom, the sharp end just raised up enough to look like some pointer toward the divine.

"Good. How many crates can you give?"

"How about six?"

"Okay. Our secret," the old man said. "We can have egg flower soup again. All the neighbors have been missing it. Bring them tonight to the back door."

The men settled on a price agreeable to each and Warren left with half the agreed-upon sum, a stack of bills tucked away in his breast pocket where the egg had been. Outside in the sun, he watched the fish again, feeling the promise of a new life outstretched before him. The fish tried to move in a circle but was too large for the container and doubled back, folded in on itself. He was feeling the urge to free the fish, so that it might swim away as he was about to, when a man walked past on the street and hissed *traitor* in his ear as he passed. Warren watched the man as he retreated in the distance but did not turn his head to look back. He felt suddenly unsafe, unsure, and revealed on the city streets. The man was probably a run-of-the-mill bigot like the owner had mentioned, one of the increasing number of hooligans who had been storming Chinese businesses and looting, even killing, owners and patrons. He had been warned that the recession was causing outbursts of anger and desperation across the city. Citizen groups were forming on both sides. There were whispers of laws being drawn up to curb Chinese rights as contract workers and owners of land. Their rights to housing and employment had already been minimized five years prior. The vise of the white economy was clamping down, and hard. The man's hissed *traitor* was probably nothing more than a commonplace assertion of judgment on Warren after he saw him leave the restaurant.

But Warren couldn't be sure that the man wasn't referring to his heist. What if he was someone from the Pacific Egg Company? What if somehow word had traveled back? What if the Greeks had betrayed him? There would be a mob of angry eggers who would surely hunt him down and dismantle him limb from limb. His traitor body would be thrown into the sea to be taken by the sharks. He hurried along the sidewalk, his feet kicking up dust as he hustled back to the Greeks' apartment. He would hide out there for the rest of the day until it was time to deliver the eggs unseen. At least back at the Greeks', he could be by the side of the one human he trusted as she convalesced.

Under the cover of night, he sold the rest of the eggs over the next two days—to a baker, another Chinese restaurant at the opposite end of Chinatown, and the last crate he gifted to an orphanage at Olive's behest. After the fishermen's cut of the profits, there was enough money left for two passages north and for a small parcel of land, possibly even a cabin. Warren had heard that they were practically giving away land in the copper belt in southern Oregon and northern California. But they would have to leave town soon, before the Egg Company learned of their whereabouts and sent the police, or worse, to their door.

Olive was still weak, but able to stand, so she and Warren made plans to take passage at night on a freight train. They needed to leave no trace of their path and so finagled a deal with a rancher Warren knew who was planning to move some sheep north. On the evening of their departure, he ushered her out into the cool, foggy San Francisco night and through the streets as the ladies of the evening replaced the daytime throngs on the planked sidewalks of downtown. Olive held tight to the wicker basket containing the Russian Blue. Every corner held a potential threat, so they made as though a newlywed couple, kissing and engaging with one another in conversation. The ruse did not require great acting skills from the two. As they passed a tall braided prostitute who smelled strongly of roses and smoke, Olive grabbed his arm and asked to stop.

"There's no time to stop," Warren urged.

"Just a few seconds," Olive said.

Hazel looked confused by Olive's short cropped hair, but held a glimmer of recognition in her opium-laden gaze.

"Can I help you, dear?" she asked with lidded eyes as Olive approached.

"It's me. Ducky," Olive said.

Warren watched from a few feet away as the two embraced and Olive put something in the woman's hand, holding it tight with both of hers. The woman gave her a warm smile and whispered something in her ear before Olive walked slowly back to Warren.

"Who was that?" Warren asked.

"A lesson I learned early," Olive said, "was that hardships befall us all, and that all people deserve kindness. That woman helped me learn that." Warren smoothed her short hair back out of her eyes and decided not to inquire further. They just had to reach the train platform, find the right freight car, and they would be free. They hurried along the street, Olive clinging to Warren's side, and past a group of rowdy drunks arguing about a gamble gone wrong. One pushed the other just as Olive and Warren tried to pass close by and the man's shoulder hit Olive hard in the side. She winced and doubled over in pain. Warren's brain flashed to the fish in the tank and her limp body laid among the crates of eggs, then it flooded red. A fire burned in his brain and he was suddenly on the man, pinning him to the wooden ground, spit flying from his mouth like foam as he growled in an ur-language. He slammed the man's head into the sidewalk hard, grunting as he twisted the man's arm in a position the arm is not meant to ever go. A trickle of blood grew to a stream, headwaters behind the drunk's ear. The men pulled Warren off and skulked back into a doorway with their unconscious, bloodied, drunk friend like a pack of cur. They retreated en masse, nary a soul choosing to face off with Warren and his raging eyes, beard mottled with spittle, hair wild and unruly. His black eyes were open wide and invited anyone to dare step up. The men retreated down the street carrying their friend and he trapped their one small piece of luggage under his arm and picked Olive up carefully in his arms, sailing her the rest of the few blocks to the train station where he carefully set her down on a bench.

"Stay here," he said, as though nothing horrifying had just happened. "I'm to find the switchman." And with that he ran off across the empty tracks and disappeared behind a brick building. Olive sat with her hand on her abdomen, considering what had just occurred. This was her last chance to disappear. The drunk could potentially die from those wounds. Warren's outburst had scared into her the feeling that she was lumbering off with a wild bear as his wounded prey, being led into a dark, tunneled forest. She could be stuck on a train for days with him, lying with a murderer. Or she could take the money she had from their exchange, as Warren had thought it best to split the money into both of their coat linings in case they should be mugged or separated along the journey. She could continue to live as Oliver, she thought. There was a certain amount of freedom she had truly enjoyed as a male that she wasn't entirely ready to give up. There were conspiratorial whispers from other men. Richardson had called her a "brick" and one time even "boss." It felt good to be part of the secret fraternity and she saw the portal to that world closing. She could go back to the island and tell Richardson she'd been kidnapped or drugged. Or she could go back to find Hazel and live a new life. She could save her. The taste of salt rose on her tongue, the lemon of possibility. She considered her options, but remembered the kind soul she'd found in the cave and the feeling he'd unlocked in her chest like bubbles rising in the sea toward the surface to join with the beloved air of the sky. She would stay and allow herself to slip back into Olive's skin, she decided. She would stay and inhabit her old flesh, but on her own terms.

Warren arrived back and picked her up once again, completely ignorant to her struggle, and took her down the platform toward a still freight train in the distance. They paused before an open cargo car and he checked the number in his notebook before helping her up onto the hay-covered floor.

"Warren," she said. "If I'm to go with you and this is to be our life together, I will not tolerate fighting and bloodshed. Promise me that."

"I see," Warren said, looking confounded and for the first time remorseful of his actions toward the drunk. "I can promise that." He helped her up into the boxcar and followed awkwardly, his shoulders hunched like a sad giant or a dog that had just been shackled to a tree.

Once safely boarded, they inspected their surroundings. They shared the train car with an enclosure of goats and sheep, animals that despite their similarity in size and shape didn't seem to get along swimmingly. The animals' heads butted one another and pushed each other up against the walls of the train car. Olive inspected the profile of this burly man as he watched them without emotion, this man who seemed not to notice Olive's concern at his earlier brutish outburst. He blinked the innocent lashes of a babe as he inspected the car and set down the rabbit gingerly in the corner.

The racket of the sheep and goats' braying made getting sleep almost impossible. Warren arranged a comfortable corner for Olive with hay, blankets, and a very small down pillow he had purchased at a specialty store in downtown San Francisco and produced from his breast pocket. She thanked him, but still she tossed and turned. He adjusted her hair on the pillow and petted her forehead with his warm hand as she dozed in and out of sleep, minutely adjusting her position with each waking to minimize the pain. The wheels clicked and the car swayed back and forth like an impatient mother rocking a child to sleep. The little blue rabbit hopped around in a brand new basket twice the size of his last one, munching happily on his first-ever apple.

Warren held in his pocket a secret thing that he hoped to find just the right moment to reveal to Olive. She moaned a little and shifted in new sleep. She had become an annul of a woman, never able to reproduce. As the train rounded a bend she winced. The clacking marked the slow passage of time. She just wished to make it through each moment, hoping the next might hurt less than the last.

The early morning sun-streaked rays through the slats of the train car, a bright finger of light landing on Olive's face. She sat up with some difficulty, the pain of waking a harsh reality of countenance first thing in the morning. Warren lay curled around her like a baby but snored like a hog. The sheep and goats seemed to have worked out some basic truce and lay snoozing in segregated piles on opposite ends of the pen. Olive sat up against the wall and stretched her short legs out in the hay. It was these quiet moments when she wanted nothing more than to be waking to the sounds of china and cutlery clinking in her mother's tiny kitchen as she started the day. She longed to hear her say just once more, "Good morning, my fawn," as though they were simply two little forest creatures waking into the wildness. Instead she found herself clacking and chattering in a train car smelling of animal dung, with a man capable of great kindness and great brutality curled around her. She wondered if perhaps life was predicated on this kind of paradox— the tenderness all wound up in a knot with the threatening.

After two full days of travel, the train came to a stop and stayed that way for over an hour. She had been asleep as the train pulled up to the station but she woke at the sound of the boxcar door opening. Warren slipped out and talked with someone on the platform. The scent of sagebrush drifted in through the slats in the car. Olive put her nose up to one of the cracks and breathed deep. It reminded her of back in the Rockies, when her mother was well and they would leave the city for a few days to stay in a little cabin in the sagelands. The smell had always seemed to her the freshest scent on the planet. It came in through the nostrils and wove a path through the body like some careful, cleansing ghost. Sitting there in the hay, the smell revived her to boldness. The pain had just that morning subsided to the point of being tolerable enough to rise on her own, so she carefully stood and peeked out through the slats at the forms of the men talking on the platform.

Warren had his hands folded and his hat pulled down over his face as if to hide his identity from passers by. He spoke to a cattleman who gestured back at the train car where Olive sat watching. She couldn't quite tell if they were arguing or greeting one another, but arms began to fly in the air, gestures of some form of excitement or another. She scanned the faces of everyone passing by on the station to see if she recognized danger lurking in their eyes, but recognized no one. Finally, the crowd dispersed in wagons or on horseback, off to their destinations. When the two men were alone on the platform, Warren took out some bills from his pocket and handed them over to the cattleman who walked toward Olive and the bleating, increasingly impatient animals.

Once all the animals had been deboarded, Olive and Warren shuffled their belongings off the car. A pang of paranoia grabbed at them both once the sunlight hit their skin for the first time in days. Warren looked around nervously to see if he recognized any egg men who might have trailed them on their journey north. A painted wooden sign hung over the bench reading "Y R E K A." Olive stood with her hand shading her eyes, looking at the sign for a long time before breaking out into laughter.

"What's so funny?" Warren asked.

"Isn't it obvious?" Olive put her hand over her mouth and whispered, "Eureka, I think we've found it." She put her hand in Warren's warm hand. "It seems we may have found our home."

Rooster Riots

VICTOR HAD COME DOWN out of the slot canyon after the peyote ceremony feeling sleep-deprived but alive and full of veneration for the common. Colors hummed on the still cool morning air and lifted off the surface of all living things in lingering hues. He made a mouth trumpet and hummed a little Sousa tune as he hopped down into the wash at the bottom of the canyon and headed back toward the highway. The sounds of the desert waking up filled him with a sense of wonderment at how a place that one might think of as desolate could come alive in such tremulous chorus—birdsong, the rustle of wind through hearty stems and branches, and the sound of the very earth waking up danced in his ears. The sun rose hard and fast and with it spread an urgent heat over the crusted earth. Victor had never felt like he belonged anywhere, but he thought perhaps he had finally found a place he could settle down with these strangers, the fringe folk of Needles. His first duty was to find a place to rent, then he could begin mapping out what staying in one place for longer than a day might look like.

On his way back into town, he hugged the side of the highway until he noticed some wide circular cement tubes sticking up from the ground some 150 feet off the side of the highway. Curious, he wandered toward them and climbed a short set of steps to the top of the cement tube, sat down, and looked inside the rim. Inside, there was a sort of dusty floor some twenty feet across, sunk about ten feet below ground. Pecking around on opposite sides of the tube, two roosters scratched in the dirt. They looked scrawny and were missing tail feathers. The sun was already starting to heat up and Victor felt bad for the two beasts. He rifled through his backpack for some small morsel to give them to eat and found a half-eaten apple. Without further thought, he tossed the apple down onto the dusty tube floor.

The first rooster to notice the apple pecked at it with nonchalance. He threw it up in the air using his beak and ripped little pieces of apple flesh off the core. Once the second rooster noticed the first playing with the apple, the atmosphere shifted steeply. The second rooster flew over from its far side of the tube and landed hard on top of the first rooster. He pecked aggressively and the other rooster responded in kind. They tumbled over one another and stole the apple core back and forth, neither creature getting a chance to actually enjoy any of the fruit.

After a few minutes of the two roosters pouncing and posturing, spreading their wings and viciously attacking one another, the apple core flung up and down, up and down, blood began to fly. Little droplets speckled the dusty floor and both roosters' feathers began to grow matted with one another's blood. The second rooster ripped a little piece off the first's coxcomb, leaving the once proud appendage drooping and dripping with blood. Victor's heart beat faster and faster in his chest as he realized that he had started this bloody battle with his apple core. These must be fighting cocks. And he had just unintentionally started them fighting.

How to end a battle such as this, once it is begun? He couldn't think how he might subdue the fury between the two roosters unless he managed to separate them. So he jumped down into the pit with the two cocks and set about capturing one. First, with some difficulty, he was able to recapture the apple and fling it up over the edge of the tube. But this did nothing to calm the fight between the roosters. They continued to fight, as the one with the intact coxcomb pinned the other to the ground like a dog would a rabbit. It looked like the death grip for the pinned rooster. He grabbed the rooster on top and flung it over to the other side, the flapping of its wings spraying a fine mist of blood onto Victor's cheek. He picked up the rooster on the ground, now quiet and perhaps even dead, and put the bird under his arm. He looked for a way back up and out of the tube but could see no ladder. Finally, after running around in a circle with the other rooster hot on his trail, still mad as hell, he found some indentations in the cement that must be used to climb in and out of the tube.

He tucked the bloodied, apoplectic rooster into his shirt and started to climb. The other rooster jumped up and pecked at his legs as he climbed out. The warm bird's blood seeped out on his belly as he climbed up the cement wall using the hand and footholds. When he reached the top, he looked down to see the first rooster lazily picking out pieces of apple, or whatever it could find in the dirt, as though nothing had happened.

He pulled the rooster out of his shirt and inspected its wounds. His eye opened, which at least meant that he was still alive. It watched and flinched as Victor inspected the largest wound on its side. Rustling for a first aid kit inside his backpack, he looked back at the rooster and said, "What a strange way to start the day, huh?"

The rooster did not make a noise, but blinked its second eyelid, the thin sheath covering closed as he wrapped its body in gauze. When the bandaging was done, he ruffled his neck feathers as if settling into a new shirt.

"You should see the other guy," Victor said, winking at the rooster as he secured him in the top of his rucksack, pulling the string closed gently around its neck so it wouldn't try to fly away. He adjusted the torn coxcomb gently and tried to prop it back up, but it kept flopping back down and seemed like it might be a permanent alteration to the rooster's aesthetic. The rooster made a little *cruuu-cuuu-ruu* noise as Victor started on the road toward town, its head sticking out from the top of the pack bumping up and down like a baby on its mother's back.

"Let's go find ourselves a place to call home," he said as they headed back into town.

The town seemed more bustling in the morning than it had the day before when he'd first arrived and been led out into the desert by the boy. People set about on their errands, determined to get the bulk of their activity done before midday, when the desert heat would cast everything through a febrile, wavy lens. He walked toward a line of palm trees he guessed might be planted to lure travelers to stay at a motel. It seemed hard for Victor to believe that he'd only been gone up in the slot canyon a day. There seemed to be so much more time between the boy who disembarked from the back of a chicken truck to the person he was today. He had traveled the arc of a rainbow and through the ground as water, traveled the back of a single note along the rock face in echo. And here it wasn't even twenty-four hours later, yet he felt like an altered being. He stood in front of the iron gates surrounding an unnaturally blue swimming pool and sensed that when he went through the threshold he would be starting his life anew.

Secured in the cool of the motel room, he lay back on the bed and let the springs creak in lessening increments until the room was completely quiet. He let himself be completely still, relaxed and prostrate, for the first time since leaving Seattle, entire seasons, lifetimes ago. A little chirrup of a noise came from his backpack and he sat up slowly and took out the poorly bandaged, but still breathing, rooster and brought it into the cramped bathroom with him. He unwrapped the bird and set him carefully in the tub. The bird stood up briefly, demonstrating that both his legs still worked, but sat back down again, tired by the mere act of standing. He ruffled his blood-encrusted feathers and shook his waddle a little, peering up as if waiting for a command from his master.

"Well, champ," he cocked his head like the rooster. "What say you? Let's assess the damages."

The rooster was resigned to patience as Victor poured cups of warm water over his wings and torso to wash the dried blood off. The bathtub ran in rivulets of hot red. Anyone peering in through the crack in the window or a chink in the curtains might think there had been a motel massacre. Once the water ran clearer, he checked the wounds to see which ones needed attention. Only one gash truly needed a bandage, a two-inch-deep cut in the rooster's side where its opponent must have sunk a claw in good. Victor fished out a butterfly bandage and managed to make it stick to the bumpy fowl skin below the feathers. He nestled the rooster in a towel and set out some water and little bits of saltine, then closed the door to let the creature find its footing.

He lay back on the bed and let the exhaustion of everything he'd been through over the last few months, days, and hours, wash over him as a tender tsunami. He slipped fast into sleep and woke up after what felt like only a matter of seconds, but was probably hours, and heard the rooster crowing a strong *cockadoo-dle-doo* from the bathroom. This, he guessed, was a good sign.

In the shower, rivers of grime washed off Victor's body in little brown streaks, finding their way toward the drain like snowmelt toward the ocean. He let the warm water wash over him in a kind of ecstasy of leaving. He let the rides in truck beds and nights spent on the hard ground wash down and into the drain like an exodus of filth and hardship. As he showered, the rooster pecked around after a trail of saltines and peanuts in the room. While toweling off, a harsh knock sounded at the door. A large woman in pin rollers and a hair net stood with her hands on fleshy hips.

"Boy, I'm not sure what kind of establishment you think you're in," she started, "but we do not allow farm animals in our rooms."

"He's not from a farm, ma'am." He glanced behind him at the rooster, holding the towel closed with one hand. "Found him half dead in the desert."

"Even worse," she clucked. "There have been complaints. Please pack your bag at once." The woman accented the singular *bag* and glanced at the boy's single, dirty rucksack behind him, letting her eyes linger only briefly on his toned half-naked body, unable to keep a blush from rising in her neck and thus unable to maintain the purity of her superior tone. She turned in a huff and padded back to the office, adjusting the apron around her middle.

Back in the room, the rooster settled back in on the top of Victor's rucksack as if he knew it as home, allowing the rope to tighten the canvas around his winged shoulders. After dressing, the two set back out into the town through the gates, Victor giving the glowing blue pool one, last sidelong glance as they walked back to the street. He had missed his chance to let his body glide through the rippled, electric blue water. It had been one of his favorite things as a child to slide under the water in the community pool as if he were a porpoise. He would open his eyes and watch the blurred forms kick awkwardly under the water, pitying the poor humans who didn't understand how to channel their inner cetacean. The surface was smooth, undisturbed, as he stood and watched the light bend and dapple the bottom of the pool, the late afternoon sunlight painting the floor with slow, reaching fingers. He closed the heavy gate and let the brief chapter of comfort and shelter close, a motion he was more than accustomed to performing.

Man and rooster walked along Main Street until they stood in front of the Oasis Diner with the large picture windows and curved blue booths. The same waitress as the day before, a lifetime ago, set up the round tables for dinner. She wore fatigue in her shoulders and neck, the way she slowed as she leaned down to land the fork next to the knife. Victor settled the rooster down deeper into the pack and put the top flap gently over its head. He would not have his new companion erase all chance at being allowed in the establishment. His freshly washed hair he smoothed over his ears and he headed in to take the corner booth. A hunger as large as a continent raked at him from within.

He managed to secure the corner booth and the waitress brought him a hot cup of coffee and took his order: steak and eggs. Victor chuckled to himself that he would eat the flesh of a cow, the eggs from a chicken, but couldn't bear to watch the rooster *churr*ing softly at his feet meet his end in the ring. He took out the crumpled envelope the old man had given him and counted the bills again. It hardly seemed possible that he was now in possession of such funds. He remembered the way his wealthy, estranged father used to slip crisp bills off his thick billfold with a face like wrought iron. Each dollar that ran away from him was another dollar not in his hand and it was as simple as that.

Victor brought out the egg collection, careful not to disturb the rooster too much, and unwrapped it from its cloth. There were still two spots left to make the collection complete. He admired the object from all angles, as the beveled glass cast a tight little rainbow of color onto the Formica table. It delighted Victor to think of where this object had traveled from and where it might travel to in the future. As he inhaled his dinner, he wondered about spirits and how they inhabit objects. Did they live inside the very silver and silk threads of velvet? He had written a poem about the idea of spirits in objects and his dad had found it and burned it in the fireplace, holding the shoulders of his young son to make him watch. "That is what becomes of nonsense," he said. "I'll have no more of it." And so the young boy began hatching a plan to seek out and relish the nonsense of the world, to study it and make sense.

It was in this reaching back into childhood that Victor came to the idea of opening a curio shop. He would collect and share as much beautiful nonsense as he could lay his hands on. It seemed like Warren, the old stranger, would be proud. The waitress came back and asked if he was interested in pie.

"Apple or Coconut," she said.

"One of each." He smiled up at her.

"I like your spirit," she smiled. "What's your name? Haven't seen you 'round."

"My name is Victor," he said, just as the rooster chirruped a half crow from under the table.

"And who's your friend?" she whispered, darting a look back at the kitchen.

"His name is Champ."

"Victor and Champ," she said. "A match made in heaven."

"I suppose you're right." Victor felt the sound of his own name, spoken out loud for the first time in months, and thought that maybe he, after years of doubt, finally matched it. He was going to welcome the strange and curious objects of this world and he would be victorious over the boring, turgid life that others had meant for him to live. He was unshackled and tender as a new shoot of green in the desert, ready to make his way. He hoped he would make Warren proud in his path.

Cryptobiotic

Dear Alice,

   In your last letter you asked me to tell you about something especially fascinating that's found in the desert. I've been thinking about it a lot. Of course people are always gushing over the desert's charismatic megafauna—the cougar, desert ram, or condor. And they all certainly have their stories and caché. But what I've decided to tell you about, my dear one, well, it's cryptobiotic soils. Dirt, you say?! But oh, this is not your average dirt. Without a doubt these cryptobiotic soil crusts are some of the coolest things I've ever encountered. They are a combination of cyanobacteria, lichens, mosses, fungi, and algae. But it's the cyanobacteria that are the dominant and most amazing part. Most of the year, the cyanobacteria lies dormant. But when the summer rains come, when exposed to water, they become active, secreting a trail of mucilaginous sheath material as they grow. Microcoleus vaginatus is the name of one of the most important species found locally. Ha! I fuck with you not. It really is microcoleus vaginatus! Some taxonomist out there had as bizarre a sense of humor as you and I do, my dear.

   So, the important function of these cyanobacteria as they forge their way slowly and slickly across the desert floor is that they hold the soil together, making it less prone to wind and water erosion. It's like a thin layer of slow-spreading glue holding all that topsoil down. The cool thing is that they don't have to be alive to hold the earth together. Even the abandoned sheaths, the trails of the dead if you will, help hold down sandy soils. It is this expansive network of growing filaments and abandoned sheaths, like snakes and their shed skins all joined as one, that make up the enormous organism know as cryptobiotic soil. It is the pulling and threading of millennia of time into a highly nutritive blanket that benefits all desert life. I know the romantic poet in you has perked up her ears. Do with that what you will. There is literally a sheath of nutrients covering the desert floor.

Now here's where the story turns sad. These soils are very easily destroyed. Even a footfall can break the brittle soil up in the dry season. Add an off-road vehicle to the equation, or grazing cows, or a hundred trucks on a construction site, and you've got erosion disaster. Since the soil only grows when conditions are wet, the slow process of building a soil can be five thousand to ten thousand years in arid areas. That means if it is destroyed by human traffic and development it is pretty much considered a lost cause. A thriving desert area with a blanket of microscopic life that helps fix carbon and nitrogen for all other plant life can become a wandering sand dune in months. That magical time tapestry can be unraveled in a matter of moments.

This soil saga got me thinking. Some things are so slow to grow, but so incredibly important. What took centuries and millennia to grow can just be destroyed and washed away in a matter of minutes. How is it that in my thirty-two years I have not yet seized the day and asked you (and Lily) to come stay with me? What if I've spent my whole life like a tiny filament winding my way to forge an understanding of the natural world, but forgot to bind with you, my soil? Will you consider coming out to stay for six months or a year and see if you like it

out here? After the harvest someone can take over the orchards
if you promise them the yield. Maybe one of your workers
wants to give it a go? Or maybe one of those vanity farmers
moving out from the cities and into those pressboard-housing
complexes will jump at the chance. It will be a win-win affair.
Someone can learn to farm filberts and could potentially help
you should you choose to return, or you can pass the baton and
sell the damn place. Just give it a good think and let me know
what you decide. I've tried to write this same letter to you in
a hundred ways over the years, but was always held back by
my own fear. Those other letters ended up confetti in the wind.
Well, not this time. This sucker is going out across the wires to
you, my love. Write me back at my Globe PO Box. You have
the address.

Your lonely little filly-ment,

Sal

As if to demonstrate her point about soil erosion, wind picked
up and whipped through the mesa, bearing on it the gasoline smell
creosote leaves let off after a rain. It was the trail end of monsoon
season, most would say it was over, and the rain had been only brief,
not enough to tamp down the dust as it whipped up from the topsoil
and sailed into the town of Globe, Arizona, in gusts. Sal huddled with
her back against the brutal sandy wind as she stood in front of the blue
mailbox. The letter made a little metronomic *fwap fwap fwap* sound as
it sputtered and flapped against the metal in the wind. The sound bore
resemblance to a cartoon bomb counting down to detonation. She
pushed the envelope through the slot fast, before she could change
her mind. It was done. And with that, she put her handkerchief over
her mouth to avoid inhaling the sediment wind. She coughed and
hopped up into the driver's seat of her old Nissan 4x4, rolling up the
windows as fast as she could, and headed out to find a windbreak to
camp in for the night. The field season had just ended and she was free
to roam in whatever direction she chose. Virga clouds loitered in the

evening sky and caught the sun's last rays, reflecting them in bursts of golden orange. The fingers of condensation trailed down from the virga like fringe evaporating into the air before the water could even reach the ground. She had sent the message and there was no going back. All she could do was lose herself in the freedom of wandering and wait for an answer.

~

THAT VERY SAME NIGHT in Burning Woods, Alice sat alone in her house drinking a tall glass of bourbon and drawing a picture of Zombie Cat on a postcard-sized piece of thick paper. She hadn't heard from Lily all summer, but received regular updates from Boomer on her daughter's well-being. She finished strong in her junior year, of course. Honor roll, yet again. She was doing well in the first few weeks of her senior year, too. According to Boomer, Lily had joined Max in a craft class and was learning the ancient art of basket weaving from a woman named Yolanda, known to friends as "Mama Pepper." Alice felt a twinge of jealousy at the idea of anyone being any sort of Mama to her daughter, even if she was a pepper. Boomer also reported that Lily had stopped sticking out her tongue in disgust every time he mentioned her mother, which Alice could only take as a sign of progress.

All summer long Alice had been sending postcards every few days to her daughter with little snippets of information about the farm—updates on the battle with the fungus, the filbert yield, Donnie Jr. and her triumphant return to laying eggs. With each postcard she added one line of cryptic apology or a veiled appeal to come home. "Dougie sends his regards and says sorry he was such an ass," or "Zombie Cat seems a little down. I think she misses her partner in crime." She signed each card with LOVE YOU, triple underlined for emphasis, just in case Lily didn't notice the all caps.

Alice finished the postcard and downed the last finger of brown alcohol in one gulp. She had been consumed with the business of harvest time, and after paying the seasonal workers, thought there was a slim chance she might still come out on top. The harvest season was rising to a climax, a time that normally would have been exciting, but without Lily, she found herself knocking around the quiet, empty place like an agitated squirrel in the final days before hibernation. Never especially good at being alone, she felt restless. She called up Darla and made a date to meet at the Re-Bar and proposed that they get into some trouble. *I need to escape harvest madness, so let's party,* she said. *Let's make Randy jealous. And find some guys to flirt with.*

Pulling on her tightest jeans, she lay back on her bed and lifted her legs and pelvis skyward so she might zip the pants closed. She lay there with the tight pants hugging her insides like a vice, with nothing else on top, like some sort of encased creature trying to free itself from a too-tight chrysalis. She danced around the room to Dolly Parton's "Jolene," singing like a madwoman, letting the freedom of dance move and jiggle her top half wherever it wanted to go. She would let the night find a random path for her and would not feel bad that she was a wild woman. For years people had called her a slut or a heathen. So be it. She would give the people what they wanted. They didn't know how bad bad could be.

It was the first time Alice had been to the Re-Bar since she and Randy split. Inside, the bar glowed red, blue, and green from the neon Bud and Rolling Rock signs on the wall, the colors highlighting the hair of a packed Friday night crowd as they wandered among the ribbons of light.

"They're unintentional punks," Alice leaned in to whisper to Darla. "Manic Panic on the streets of Philomath."

"Maybe we should just stick to beer tonight," said Darla, raising her eyebrows, not a clue as to what her friend was talking about.

It was not Randy tending bar but some young, tattooed girl, probably his new girlfriend. Alice was disappointed he wasn't around to make jealous. She sighed and morosely stuck her tongue in and out of the top of her beer bottle. Darla requested they duet on the karaoke stage, something old country. The women pulled on their beers, perched up on two of the vinyl covered swivel bar seats, and faced out to survey the room. Two young men were playing shuffleboard and one leaned down in concentration before he let his puck sail down the long, salted field. He knocked his opponent's puck off the end as his settled just a third of the way off the end of the board garnering double points.

"Get schooled," he stood up and pointed at his friend, "in the realm of the master."

There was something very familiar about the guy. Alice could swear she knew him from somewhere. The curly, black hair, the way the planes of his face lined up like a perfect geometric puzzle. Darla said she'd never seen him before. But Alice couldn't stop staring at him, and then realized—he looked like Sal's male doppelgänger.

"Let's go play." She pulled at Darla's arm like a toddler.

"But what about karaoke?" Darla whined.

"Later," Alice said, adjusting her pants on her waist. "We have more important things to do."

The women introduced themselves to the two men and they played the next game in pairs. Darla and Alice planned a strategy and took their turn. Alice stood on her toes and raised her ass up as she bent down and grazed the puck back and forth over the grains of sand, taking aim. She waggled her butt slowly before the Sal lookalike. He watched her every move and grinned, gripping his beer with sweaty hands. Darla glanced back toward the karaoke stage and fiddled with her cuticles like someone watching a scary movie, looking for something to distract them from the plot at hand. Alice took aim and way overshot, the puck rebounding off the back board with an alarmingly loud noise that made people from all the way across the bar look over.

"Whoops," she said. "Looks like I don't know my own strength."

"You are freakishly strong," Darla giggled nervously. "Like a cougar, this one."

The other guy laughed. Alice narrowed her eyes at Darla, getting the message.

"How old are you two, now?" Alice asked, nonchalantly.

"Twenty-five." The Sal lookalike pointed at himself. "And twenty-eight, for that old man."

"How old are you two?" the friend asked suspiciously.

"Don't you know you never ask a lady's age?" Darla said.

"Young enough," Alice said.

"I'm Zev," the lookalike said. "And that's boring old Trevor over there."

Zev, Zev, Zev. Alice tried to remember hearing about a Zev. It rang a faraway bell drowned out by a long, whiskeyed distance. He excused himself after the first game to go to the restroom. From the back of the bar he motioned for Alice to meet him by tipping his head sideways, bending at the knee, and putting out one hand toward the back hallway as if to welcome a princess out of a carriage. Alice waited until he disappeared then excused herself as well, ignoring Darla's look of warning. Zev was waiting in the dark hallway and smiled when she joined him, then walked behind her as she trailed a hand along the graffiti-littered walls, past the bathrooms, and out through the back screen door into the parking lot. He followed her silently as she led him to the edge of the parking lot and slipped through a hole in the chain link and into a field of exotic waist-high grasses. She paused for a moment at the threshold like a runner in the blocks and looked back at him. And with that, they were off into the field under the rust-colored moon.

They chased each other around taking off one item of clothing at a time. Alice unlatched the button of Zev's jeans then ran away, quickly hidden by the grass. He found her and pulled her thin sweater off and tossed it up in the air with a whoop. They danced around each other like this, taunting and chasing until they were both down to their underwear. Zev grabbed Alice's hips and pulled her close to let her feel him hard against her as he grabbed her ass. The two fell to the ground, entwined, and rolled over one another with the particular passion that comes from feeling another person's skin for the first time. Zev took down his underwear and felt his way inside her as she closed her eyes. She saw Sal behind her closed lids, and imagined her lying naked across her kayak, sunning herself after a swim, arching her back. She imagined Sal with her head upturned to the heavens, beset by some sort of trance at the magic of the stars. As Zev groaned and she flipped him over and rode and arched, she imagined she was a falling star, just waiting to be caught. They shuddered as if the light fell from the sky and shot right through them.

"And that's how crop circles are actually made," Zev said, rolling over in the grass to trace the outline of her behind with his hand.

"And all this time we thought it was such a mystery." Alice shrugged, getting up and picking up her items of clothing one by one, plucking the grass and sticks off one by one. "We should probably get back before we are considered our own unsolved mystery."

"You're a truly beautiful woman," he said, lying on the ground pulling on his pants and looking up at her. "Not sure if I mentioned that."

"I'll take it," Alice said, giving him a hand to help him up.

～

SAL DROVE A HALF hour outside of Globe and found the most wind-protected spot she could to camp that night. The wind rattled the windshield wipers on her truck, threatening to rip one right off and fling it into the desert. About a mile off the highway, she pulled up to the bottom of a slot canyon with a sandy wash between one high wall and one shorter wall. The sand had clearly been run over by the monsoon rivulets, washed and rewashed by the intense summer rains. It looked like the footprint of a river that had recently been there but had disappeared through some sort of sorcery, simply lifted into the air. One could almost hear the rush of the water over the sand. Sal knew where the water had gone. It went straight down into the sand and the rest evaporated in the desert sun. It had sprouted bright green leaves on plants that months before looked dead to the untrained eyed. But Sal reassured herself that the monsoon time was over. It was fall, and the cool nights would bring a particular brand of quiet over the land. She just needed shelter from the intense wind, and quickly, as the moonless night was drawing in close and fast.

The winds and her recent declaration of love had driven a sort of exhausted madness into her mind. Sal, against all her training, set up her tent in the arroyo. She muttered something to herself about the heavy rains being gone for the season as she set up her tent and rolled her sleeping pad out inside. She cursed the new, giant inflatable mattress pad she'd splurged and bought for herself at the end of the season. It took so many breaths to fill she nearly passed out by the end of inflating it. But she was getting old and she had told herself the extra inches of cushioned air would help rest her tired bones. She inflated the mattress and flopped down on it. The wind still whipped and grabbed at the top of the tent, rocking it back and forth a little. Before falling asleep, she briefly considered getting up and sleeping in the bed of the truck up on the road, but knew the wind would keep her awake all night if she did. Finally, she let go of her anxieties and let the wind pick them up one by one like pollen in the wind. *Let someone else worry about everything for a while,* she thought. She was too tired to do it.

KRACK THA-KOW BA-BOOM. She woke in complete darkness to the sound of bone-crunching thunder close and loud as a detonating mine. One second later and the tent lit up orange and white with the complete illumination of a nearby lightning bolt. No rain accompanied the lightning and thunder, but she didn't need to wait for the pattering on her tent. She felt an urgent need to pack up and leave. She gathered up her things inside the tent as fast as she could and tucked them under her arm to head out of the arroyo, scramble up the cliff, and back to her truck.

But before she could even fully unzip the door flap to step out, a rumbling brought a swath of reddish water roiling down from above through the canyon. Dust kicked up in the dry area as the water from the rain that had fallen miles away swelled its way through the cracks and fissures, growing with force as it found its way toward Sal. Before she could stand up, the tent lifted up on a cushion of water and started to move downhill with the fury of a growing red-silted river flowing all around. As the tent bobbed more and more quickly in the current, Sal managed to keep the tent partially afloat by lying in starfish position across the bottom with one foot raised to keep the top of the tent up, stretched, and filled with air. Her instincts told her to stay as buoyant as possible, so she kept the thick air mattress beneath her like a lifeboat. Lightning continued to illuminate the caving walls of the tiny shelter as it bobbed and rolled down the arroyo with Sal inside.

All science fled her mind. All poetry fled her mind. Ideas were jumping ship as instinct took over. It was simply the moment of being and surviving. If she could keep the water under her and not over her head, turning her in circles and tossing her into the wall of the wash, she might have a chance of survival. As she was carried along in the current, the water began to swamp the tent, splashing in through the zipper and seeping through the nylon. She wondered if this was what people meant when they called it a watershed moment. She laughed the hoot of a madman and lay as a fallen star from the heaven, spread eagle inside the tent, letting the red river carry her along.

She had been part of the deluge for only a few minutes when the flow abruptly slowed. She floated on and the cushion of water seemed to be getting thinner underneath the tent as the pace of movement slowed. Sal clung to the only thing keeping her afloat, her ridiculously thick air mattress crumpled and folded below her, and managed to peek outside just as the tent was flung onto a silty shore and twirled in a violent pirouette toward the arroyo wall. The last thing she saw before the world went dark was a large boulder and drooping saguaro alternating in flashes like a slowing zoetrope, the movements caught into still frames. *The path of least resistance,* she thought, her muscles going slack. She caught her breath and held it as the tent whirled with great energy across the slick sand toward the wall of rock. It is the landing, not the flight, that hurts the flung thing.

Fruiting Bodies

Burning Woods, Oregon, 1994

LILY WOVE THE STRANDS of light brown grass one over the other, lost for a moment in the monotony of busy fingers. Max sat near her trying to get her attention, but she was completely immersed in the emerging geometric pattern, the triangles and hexagons. Over, under, under, over. Repeat.

"Hey, you," Max said, dipping his fingers in the grass soaking water and flicking it her way.

"What do you want?" she looked up, annoyed. "Dork."

"Want to go for a hike tomorrow?"

"We have school, numbnuts."

"Do we?" he asked. "What else is senior year for except to take a few days off now and then? I think your precious GPA is safe."

"I guess we could." She returned to her weaving. "Where did you want to go hiking?"

"I hear the first chanterelles are just coming up at the higher elevations. I thought we might go find some."

"Huh," Lily said. In all her years living in the valley, she had never actually looked for mushrooms. But she had heard about the hippies on Aunt Sal's commune cooking them up with pasta and butter. Alice always tried to get her to come along when she joined the commune's outings, but Lily had never been interested. They came back from their fall hunts with big sisal baskets overflowing with golden-trumpeted mushrooms, their gators hooked on over their hiking boots sopping wet. They posed in various silly ways with the mushrooms for pictures, with the mushrooms as horns, or beards, or eyes.

"What do you say?"

"All right then. Mr. Janowicz is getting on my nerves lately anyway. He's all, practice your equations, learn the life cycle of the shit fly."

"All right, grumpy dwarf," Max said. "Seems someone needs a little relaxation anyhow."

≈

THE NEXT DAY THE two loaded up the truck with mushroom baskets, knives, rain gear, snacks, and water. They drove up the ridge through a rain so fine it might more properly be categorized as a mist. There had been a strong rain a few days earlier, but the day promised to hold back its autumnal tears. They pulled off the road and onto a dirt, logging road and wound their way among the Doug fir, vine maple, and ash up toward the low pass of the coast range. Max pulled over on the side of the road.

"I think this is the spot, if I remember," he said. "Top secret. Don't tell all the white hippie folk."

"But I guess technically I am said white hippie folk," she said. "Plus or minus the hippie part. Jury's out on that one."

"It's nice to see a girl who has such a strong sense of identity," Max said, creaking open the heavy driver's side door and hopping down.

"You're really making me so glad I came today," she said, jumping from up high and skittering into the ditch. She could hardly believe she had ever had a crush on him.

The two walked along single file not talking for a while, letting the narrow trail provide a buffer for their irritation toward one another. They walked along a little creek filled mostly with ash and alder, the moody gray bark mottled with spots of black. Lily saw all manner of little mushrooms poking their umbrellas up from the ground.

Some were smooth and some ridged and pointed. Little white shelf mushrooms with clear edges grew out from a downed alder log.

"Angel Wings," Max said, pointing. "Some people might think those were oyster mushrooms. But those people would be wrong."

"Hmm," Lily said. "I wouldn't know anoyster from an angel's ass."

"This one," Max bent down to put his finger on a bright red mushroom with white spots, "is the first one you teach a toddler not to eat."

"Oh yeah?"

"So don't eat them." He smiled up at her mischievously.

"Asshole." She rolled her eyes.

The trail turned up away from the creek and into a stand of Doug firs. They headed straight up in a steep curve toward the top of the hill where Max stopped.

"If you want we can split up on this aspect and look for the golden trumpets here. Good vine maple and Dougie action."

"Trying to get rid of me, huh?"

"Nah." He punched her on the arm. "Let's just stay within earshot of one another. *Cr-r-ruuk*," he drew a very convincing raven call out from his throat. "That will be our signal."

"*Crraw Crraw*," she said with a cowgirl twang. "Roger that."

They made their way ducking under the vine maple and trudging through thick Oregon grape groundcover. Lily wondered how on earth anyone could ever find anything under all the prickly undergrowth. As she walked along she flashed back to her day in the forest when she'd first left home months before. She jumped over a mossy nurse log and landed hard on the other side, her boot breaking through the loamy soil and her leg falling up to her thigh into some sort of cavern below. *Shit,* she hissed. She remembered how she'd gotten hung up in the vine maple after running away, and how in that moment she had wished she could go back home and sit sullenly across from her mom and eat bread and eggs and sip hot coffee. She had almost turned back for the comforts of home, but something in her urged her forward and so she had made it out of that forest and finally to the ocean.

Whether the outcome of her decision was positive or negative was still up for deliberation. Of late she had been feeling pretty cruddy about the whole thing.

She looked up to see if Max was nearby and able to help her out of the hole. She did a poor, sick raven call but heard nothing in response. She managed to lift her leg out from the hole and fished for her boot down in the blackness. The memory of the spider bite tingled in the scar on her chest as she wondered what else might be down there in the depths besides her shoe. Her hand felt something and she grabbed ahold and pulled it out. It was a lichen-covered stick, the smooth plane of the lichen mimicking leather to the touch. She flung the stick away and put her hand back in and kept fishing around. Finally, she grabbed a lace and retrieved the boot full of loam and moss. She sat up on the nurse log and put her shoe back on and cawed one more time. This time she heard Max's perfect raven response, gathered her basket, and headed downhill toward the call.

She was looking down as she followed the slight ravine downhill when she saw the first seductive yellow curve sticking out from under some leaves like the petticoat of a can-can girl starting the show. She squatted down and lifted the green undergrowth covering the rest of the mushroom. The thrill of finding her first chanterelle filled her with the kind of adrenaline rush she hadn't felt in a while. She let a little whoop out and fished in her pocket for her knife. She flicked open the blade and pulled it across her skin, thinking briefly of her mom. This was just the kind of thing Alice would love. She cut the mushroom at the base and held it up to the light to see it better. The gills ran in jagged paths, uneven lines down the stalk of the fruit. She sniffed the cap and it reminded her of dried apricots and dirt. She put it in her basket and looked around to see if there were any more mushrooms, as Max had said they often grew in groups. She looked down and out of the shadows began to notice, one by one, a long golden trail leading as far as she could see downhill.

She was overtaken by a sort of hunter mind, the desire to collect more and more. With each fruit plucked from the fragrant earth she filled some great void she'd been feeling in her life, stuffing it full with little yellow mushrooms. The process of collecting felt like a small success. Her voluminous basket almost halfway full, she lifted herself out from the hunt. *Some people stuff mushrooms, but I mushroom stuff,* she thought. *Max would like that.* Feeling like she had eyes on her, she called out for Max one more time. Surely he was close. She'd heard his call not five minutes ago down this very hill. Just as she was looking around for Max, a raven lifted off from the branch above her and the pieces of the puzzle started to fall into place. She'd followed the call of an *actual* raven. She was lost. Yet again.

She tried using human language, yelling for Max in every way she knew how, but there was no response. *Maaax.* Nothing. *Maximus Asshooooleum.* Her voice rang out pinched and small. *Helloooooo.* The curious raven called again and landed in a tree to watch her. At least someone was concerned about her whereabouts. Trying to retrace her steps in her mind she looked up the hill and realized she had sort of blindly zigzagged down the hill toward the sound of the raven call and then further lost herself with the line of mushrooms. Max could be anywhere at that point. She wandered for another fifteen minutes looking and calling but heard nothing but the babbling of the creek. She finally decided the only way to go was up. She started scaling the steep hill, holding on to the sword fern for support as she pulled herself ridge-ward.

Her heart was racing and she was covered in a thin film of sweat as she raised herself up onto a flat, mossy area with little ferns growing from the cracks. There was a cut stump at least ten feet across, a long ago felled giant. She set down her half-full basket of chanterelles and lay down on the mossy, eternally moist top, and listened hard to see if she could hear Max shuffling through the underbrush. She listened for his whistle and imagined he must have been a bit frantic to find her at that point. It had been over an hour since she'd seen him.

The sound of her heart reverberated in her ears was backed up with a chorus of branches and leaves moving with the wind. A sound like a tiny helicopter taking off rang out somewhere close by. If it was hunters, their guns didn't sound like any she'd ever heard. Then came the boom. She heard her own heartbeat meld with another louder, stronger booming. It wasn't exactly alarming as much as it was foreign. She wondered if it wasn't the giant mycelium under ground, the curling networks of michorhizal fibers twined in and among every other plant rooted there. *Boom.* As she lay and listened her nerve pathways were wide open and she could feel a sort of soft electricity coming off her fingertips and toes, out the top of her head like a beacon. Her vision grew blurred, like it did each time before she fainted. But she stayed conscious this time, one foot out of the dark tunnel. It felt as though she were being protected by some life force against falling down into the dark tunnel that had taken her away from living into blackness so many times before. She heard the ocean and the sky and the wind in the beating drone of the sound booming out from below the earth. It wasn't an earthquake, but more like the earth waking after a long slumber. Lily felt herself falling, passing into some recombinant realm where beings merged. There were giant nerves made entirely of light coursing unseen underground in an intricate pattern of pathways, and they welcomed her to taste from the fountain. Landscapes flitted through her brain; images of sea cliffs, sagebrush, desert mesas, and forests melted into each other in a blur. The blind harrier's face loomed large as Lily felt herself growing closer and closer to the cavern of the bird's sightless eyes, until she finally disappeared into the cave and the visions went dark. She heard a sound like a huge wave crashing onto shore and her eyes opened and slowly focused on the shadow hanging over her. Standing above her breathing hard as a horse after a race, Max smiled. A drop of sweat dripped off his nose onto her forehead and he leaned down and kissed her square on the mouth.

"I was so worried," he said, straightening up. "I've been running all over trying to find you. Thought the forest hobgoblins had made you one of their own."

"Not totally sure they didn't," Lily said, rising up slowly and sitting with wide eyes. "I just had the weirdest dream, or, vision, or something."

"Ha! Another sex dream about a—"

"No."

Something in the seriousness of Lily's face made Max cut his teasing short. She looked sallow and pale, like she'd just experienced the paranormal, or vomited. She put her hand on her chest, feeling for the same huge beat she'd felt earlier, the enormous, yearning sound of mycorrhizal fibers clinging and roots growing, of fern fronds unfurling toward the light. It had all been right there, under her hand—inside her. But all she felt under her hand was the gentle *pum-pum, pum-pum*, of a single little organ pumping nutrients, hormones, cells, and oxygen along their merry way. The community within whistled while it worked as though nothing had happened.

"Did you faint?" Max asked.

"Not exactly. No."

"Good haul," Max said as he peeked in her basket. "You found a vein, I see."

"I did," she said, getting up slowly and putting her arms around her friend. "I really, really did."

The two walked back to the trail together, sticking close and chatting about the science of mushrooms. Lily tried to shake the strangeness of what she'd experienced—the out-of-body feeling of floating into and out of other living objects—as she listened to Max. Her mom had mentioned astral projection once. Maybe that was it. Max talked about mushrooms as they walked and mentioned that one of the largest known living organism was an underground micorrhizal structure over a mile squared that weighed over a hundred tons and was over 1,500 years old. He said Jancowicz had told him they were finding new and even larger species of these massive creatures all the time. Max talked about the filaments all matting together and fruiting little mushrooms up through the forest floor. As she stepped along the narrow trail, Lily countenanced the idea that she'd somehow been part of the mushroom as she laid there on the log, as though the wild beast of her soul had been unleashed to run around underground before returning to her body. She'd hitched a ride with the mushroom for one wild, crashing wave.

"Makes you think twice about the human definition of 'community' now," Max said, interrupting her thoughts.

"Like," Lily finished, returning to the conversation, "if a fungus can figure out how to make it work with all the other living creatures around them, why can't we?"

"Exactly," Max said. "You're the only person who gets me." He turned around to give her a high five.

They found the trail and walked back down the hill out of the chanterelle zone and back toward the slender rocky pathway flanked by creek alders. Lily felt a sadness leaving the giant fungus under the soil and thought about her mom for the first time with a sort of longing. She could almost sense her all the way across the coast range sitting like an old mushroom in her library, her nose in a book, hand on an overfilled glass of wine. It occurred to her that she and her mom were just two parts of the same huge organism, fruits from the same tree. The forest closed behind Max and Lily in a dappled tunnel of quaking ash as they walked the last half-mile single file. The subsonic booms had shaken something loose in her. Under the protected canopy, among the living, breathing world, Lily left behind something dark that had been clinging to her, letting it slide off her and return to the earth, to mingle and settle with the ages. Let it be taken up by the forest floor and allowed to bloom however it could find a way.

In the truck waiting to turn onto the highway Max turned to Lily.

"You know what I just realized? Lily of the Valley. Your mom must have named you after the flower, right?"

"Hmm. Not exactly." Her face grew dark.

"But she must have, like, on some level. She's such a nature girl." He poked Lily. "Like you. Birds of a feather." There was a long pause.

"Would you mind taking me home?" she asked.

"You mean to the orchard?"

"Yeah. I think I'm ready."

"Sure. I think that's a great idea." He gave her the smug smile of someone who had just gotten his way.

As the truck pulled up the driveway to her mom's house, Lily sensed that something was different about the place. The harvest workers were just leaving for the day but her mom's truck was not there. She waved at the men in their dirty coveralls as they pulled the big orange harvester to the side of the barn for the night and covered it with the old tarp. They waved back exhausted, polite waves. Lily and Max went to the front door and she was almost surprised to find that her key still worked. Calling for her mom she ducked in the library, the kitchen, and the bathroom on the main floor, but they were all empty. Dishes sat on the table with what looked like at least two-day-old food crusted to them. *Gross, Mom*, she muttered to herself as she climbed the stairs. All the bedrooms were empty, so she ducked into the upstairs bathroom because the light was on. No one was in the room, but she glanced around at the disarray. Clothes lay strewn pell-mell like someone packing for a trip in ten minutes. Shorn leg hair clung to the sink in little clumps, her mom's toiletries basket upturned and rifled through. Sitting on the edge of the counter was a used pregnancy test. Lily picked it up and in a state of disbelief saw two pink lines running parallel like train tracks into the unknown. She checked the box to confirm the pink lines meant exactly what she thought they did.

Lily pocketed the pregnancy test on instinct, like an investigator, or judge. It was proof. But who, exactly, besides her mother, linked to the proof was still in question. She went back downstairs and found Max on tiptoe in the library reaching for an old tin half hidden behind some books. He took it down and handed it over to Lily when he saw her in the doorway.

"I've always been good at snooping," he said, a little embarrassed.

Lily opened the tin and laid out the contents on the coffee table. A little notebook caught her eye, a small, worn blue-leather bound thing with an elastic closure. She flipped through the pages. It was some sort of calendar of days, lots of things scratched out beyond recognition or legibility. She flipped back and forth until she started to make some sense of what was inside. There were a few entries on days that hadn't been scratched out. *No drinking today* was underlined on February 3 and then again on March 20 through 25. *Only one drink today* was crossed out several times on March 26. *Smoked a little green today* was written on April 1. And under that, *thought a lot about the significance of rain.* The little notebook struck her as funny at first, all the details laid out about drinking or abstaining. She looked up at Max with a laugh and then as quickly as it had made her laugh the smile drained off her face.

"It's a vice notebook," she said. "Like a diary of all the drinking and smoking my mom did."

"Well," Max said, letting his full weight flop down on the old couch beside Lily, "at least she's aware of her vices. That's a lot more than I could say for a lot of people."

"Don't defend her, please," Lily said. "Not right now." She put her hand on the outside of her pocket, the secret evidence of the pregnancy test inside.

"Hey, look," Max said as he sifted through the other items in the tin. "There's a letter for you here."

The envelope had been folded several times and the penned *Lily* on the front had a stained mark where a drop of water, or perhaps a tear, had fallen on the ink. Lily turned the envelope over several times in her hand before opening it up and unfolding the one-page letter inside.

Dear Lily,

My dear, inquisitive daughter. Let me just start by saying I am so incredibly proud of who you are—a bright, funny, independent spirit. I know you get frustrated by not knowing about your father, and I wish more than anything that I could answer all the questions you have. But the truth is that he was simply a blip on your timeline. He was not a nice man, and his contribution to your genetic self is probably the best thing he ever did in his life. Life is full of these kind of quandaries, and some of the answers we seek are truly better left undiscovered. You left me two months ago to live with Boomer and Max, and I don't blame you for the decision. But all I can ask is that you accept me for who I am—your flawed, fiery mother who loves you unconditionally, forever. Please consider coming back to me my fawn, my deer, dear.

I love you,

Momma

Lily folded the letter back up in its envelope, stood up, and walked over to the mantle where the egg collection sat, patiently waiting, as always. She peered in through one of the portals and for the first time thought about how each of those eggs had been the promise of life at some point. They were the baby birds that never were, and they were beautiful and still and perfect in their frozen state. Their life had been drained leaving behind only the specter of possibility. She opened the lid and felt a trembling in the house, her fingers shaking like she had drunk too much coffee. She thought for a moment she might faint, and then as quickly as it began, it stopped.

"Did you feel that?" she whirled around and asked Max.

"Feel what?" he said, looking up from the contents of the box.

Just then a loud *thwack* rattled the old, wavy glass of the library's picture window. The two looked up and saw a flash as if something had been thrown at the window.

"Now that, I heard," Max said, getting up.

Outside they looked around and saw no one. Then Lily noticed a brightly colored form lying still below the window. She ran outside to get a better look. It was a robin-sized, orange and slate-blue bird lying motionless on the ground. Lily put her hand on its chest to see if she could feel its heartbeat, but felt nothing but the soft, warm feathers under her hand. Stillness. She admired the orange of its breast feathers with the black band like a broad necklace around its neck. The bird had broken its neck on impact, so when she picked up its form the head rolled to the side as though no longer connected. It occurred to Lily in that moment, as she held the still warm body of the bird, that life was here and gone as quickly as that. She or anyone she loved could be gone tomorrow and there was nothing she could do about it. She set the bird down and started digging a hole over at the base of the white oak across the driveway. As she dug, the dirt under her nails filling in under the paint, she decided that she would give her mother another chance. There were just too many uncertainties in life to not accept the imperfect, flawed love she was offered. The pregnancy test shifted in her pocket and she felt suddenly protective of her mother. Across the field she saw the blind harrier flying low along the fences, dropping into the grass for a successful kill. If that creature could make it work for so long, it seemed to Lily that both she and her mother could find their way in this new darkness of uncertainty. She wiped the dirt off on her pants and brushed the rest from her palms. The next order of business was to find out where Alice, pregnant with a stranger's child yet again, had found herself flung off to.

Road Women

Tucson, Arizona, 1994

S AL WOKE TO THE layered sounds of alarms and beeps. Her eyes focused slowly on the hanging tubes and machines littering the hospital room. There was the sound of a robot breathing nearby her head, the strange, even, compression of air in and out in a plastic bladder. She tried to move but her body was tethered in many places— her ankles were cuffed by inflating and deflating sock-like things, her arms tacked down by multiple tubes attached to the arteries in her upper arms. She felt no pain, but in a way that made her think that she had been delivered so many drugs there had to be a walloping amount of pain underneath the numbness. She looked down and noted all her arms and legs were intact.

A nurse came in and gave her a weak, tired smile. She looked at Sal as a specimen, making eye contact but at the same time checking the movement and size of her pupils in both eyes.

"Welcome back," she said. "You took quite a ride down that canyon, I heard."

Sal tried to make an affirmative noise, but the sound got caught up in a gravely sludge in her throat. She tried clearing her throat to say, "I feel so stupid," but all that came out was a little "ugh."

"No need to answer me," the nurse said, patting the side of the bed but not actually touching Sal, as though she might damage her if she were to make contact. "We're used to one-sided conversations here in the ICU."

Sal moved her head a little to the side and blinked slowly. Lines of green, red, and blue lights lit up switchboards like a Lite-Brite, an echo of light trailing off each in a blur. She remembered Alice writing her and telling her about the Lite-Brite she'd purchased for Lily when she was five and how Lily immediately made a series of glowing insects. Alice had been so proud of her little naturalist, she'd said in the letter. She was in awe of what magic resided in her daughter's brain. She wondered where they were, if someone had miraculously been able to contact them about her accident. How long had she been in the ICU? Was Alice listed as an emergency contact? She doubted it, but the idea that Alice and Lily might be outside in the lobby waiting for her made her feel better. The thought lingered and she pictured them sitting side by side, reading books, as the lights faded on the machines and the sounds of the constant little alarms faded back into dark silence.

A hallway of fading souls away, Alice stood before the vending machine, wiping at tired, sore eyes. None of the brightly colored packages appealed to her. She put her hands on her hips, letting her palms slide forward onto her belly in secret acknowledgement over her uterus. *Don't get attached,* she told herself. The smells of stringent cleaners mingling with any and all odors produced by hundreds of sick bodies in the hospital were not helping to assuage her nausea.

"Alice Treeble?" A nurse asked in front of the front counter.

"Yes, that's me."

"You can come see your friend, now. She's been transferred up from the ICU and is resting."

"Great, thanks." Alice wiped her hands nervously on the front of her dress as though she'd been caught doing something bad.

"Let's keep this visit brief, as she's had a rough twenty-four hours, okay?"

"Of course."

Alice walked into the room and Sal raised an arm a few inches as though to wave. Her tanned skin looked jaundiced under the lights, drained of the vibrant pink that buoyed the color in her cheeks when she was well. She looked a lot older than Alice remembered. The immensity of sickness incited her flight instinct. Pausing just past the threshold of the door, she felt the urge to back out slowly from the room, to run back to the airport, board, and be gone. Instead, she took a deep breath, paused, and took a few careful steps into the room.

"I saw you on the news," Alice said. "You're a local legend. The 'storm rider,' they called you."

"My fifteen minutes," Sal eeked out the words. "Always wondered when I'd get them. Too bad I'm famous for being an idiot."

"But the thing is," Alice stopped, unsure how to proceed, "by the time I heard about you on the news I was already here in Tucson."

"You were?" Sal's eyebrows rose.

"I got your letter and came straight here."

"Well, don't we just have perfect timing," Sal said.

"A regular Larry and Moe," Alice said, taking a step forward.

Alice put her hand on Sal's arm and her sallow skin felt cold to the touch. She looked into her eyes and tried to keep the tears from welling up, but couldn't stem the flood. All the tears she'd never cried for her parents, for her runaway daughter, they came out one by one and formed a front line, brimming on her lower lids before falling all at once onto the sheets, splashing onto Sal's cold skin.

"Well, we should be celebrating, not crying," Sal said. "I'm told I'm not dead."

"You lost a lot of blood from the head trauma," Alice said. "They gave you a transfusion."

"They gave me the extra good blood, I hear." The gravel in her voice was smoothing out. "It's gotta be from a triathlete, or something. I'm gearing up for a bike ride, right now."

"I'm sorry," Alice said, wiping her tears. "You're the one recovering, and here I am crying. I'm just really emotional right now."

"Why?" Sal said, doing her best to wink, "Are you mysteriously pregnant again or something?"

The silence after the joking question hung for a long time in the air, interrupted only by the door of the room whooshing open on its oiled hinges.

"Time to go, Alice," the nurse smiled. "Our patient needs her rest."

"Come home with me to Oregon and I'll take care of you," Alice said. "I'll do all the driving, I promise."

~

IT TOOK ANOTHER FIVE days before Sal could be released from the hospital. The doctors commended her recovery, said she healed faster after a full transfusion than anyone they'd ever had through their doors. She left with presents from the nurses themselves, people happy to celebrate a recovery from a floor where many people left under a sheet. When Alice helped her out to the car and the front sliding doors opened, the rush of the late summer heat blasted her face, the familiar sensation welcoming her return to the living.

After a full day of driving, the two women stopped in Lake Havasu City for the night, dropped their bags off at a cheap motel room, and took a short stroll over the London Bridge before dinner.

"Too fast?" Alice asked, slowing her already slow pace.

"No, just fine."

"So, this is the real deal London Bridge, right?"

"That's what they say. Brought over brick by brick by some chainsaw magnate who just had to have it." Sal ran her fingers along the stone blocks.

"It's so strange how Americans long for the castoffs—the antiquity and realness of artifacts from more ancient cultures—but then we turn them into some sort of carnival."

"You know what they say. You can take the American out of the carnival—"

"—But you can't take the carnie out of the American."

The two women stood surrounded by things interfered with by man—the dammed waters of the Colorado, the banished bridge, and the neon promenade lights twinkling on the water. Everything was incongruous and disconnected, out of time, yet when they put their hands together and strolled along watching the water and the stars, it felt like something had finally settled into place. Amongst the rubble and flooded banks, the tourists in fluorescent bikinis and backward baseball hats, the two women took slow steps in synch as counterweight to the bizarre. Their union felt ancient and real.

Back at the motel room, Sal remarked that it never even occurred to her to stay in a motel room the night of the flood.

"You know," she said, "I think I may have lost my mind a little that night."

"Well, you had just sent something very brave and frightening," Alice said.

"You have no idea how many letters I didn't send," Sal said. "Before you go giving me too many bravery points."

"Huh," Alice cocked her head and laughed. "Me too."

"But with all that wind I knew there was a storm brewing. I should have known better." Sal said, rifling through her luggage for answers. "It's my job to be smarter than the weather."

"Every storm rider needs a storm, I guess." Alice slipped out of her dress, pausing naked for a brief moment before stepping into some cotton pajama pants as Sal watched her.

"I'm not sure I'm strong enough for that just yet." Sal sat down slowly on the bed and raised her eyebrows. "Hot stuff, woman."

"Well, thank you." Alice blushed and spread out in the starched sheets reeking of bleach to her pregnant, superhuman nose. She arched her back toward the ceiling, reveling in the silent torture she so clearly inflicted on Sal. Breathing deep, she was able to smell the ink on wallpaper, the old milk curdled on the neck of a baby that had stayed in the room a week ago. As Sal snorted and covered her eyes in mock terror at her naked supine form she wanted nothing more than to bring up the pregnancy to Sal, but didn't know how. And so she just lay with her hands behind her head waiting for an answer to fall from the popcorn ceiling.

The trip northwest back to Oregon over the next few days was a series of gas station snacks, frequent rest stops, and singing along to a series of seventies and eighties mixtapes stashed in Sal's truck.

242   E M I L Y   S T R E L O W

As promised, Alice did most of the driving, which allowed her the freedom to stop and pee whenever she felt the need. Sal had asked at the beginning of the trip about Lily, and when the answer was a curt, "She doesn't want to see me right now," she let the matter lie. There was plenty of time to uncover the details of the situation.

"Let's stop in Needles for a minute," Sal said. "I want to see if this one shop is still there."

"Sure," Alice said. "I have to find a bathroom anyway."

"Do you still have that antique glass case I sent you when you were pregnant with Lily?" Sal said as they pulled up the main street in town.

"Of course. It's my most prized possession."

The road had been paved since Sal had last been through and looked less like an old ghost town than it once had. Freshly painted signs hung over shops, swaying slightly with the breeze. Sal scanned them for NAKED ANTIQUES, but couldn't find the sign. In the location she thought she remembered the shop being, a pediatric dentist's sign with a toothy, grinning teddy bear swayed in the breeze. She decided to go inside and inquire.

When she came out Alice was scribbling on the back of a postcard. She looked up, a little manic.

"I forgot to tell Lily I was leaving town," she said. "I need to send this as soon as possible."

"Needles, Arizona," Sal laughed. "Where urgent communiqués from women to their loved ones happen all the time."

"Needles!" Alice looked up. "I had forgotten. I remember that postmark. You know how much I have treasured that gift over the years, right?"

"I'm glad to hear it." Sal looked sad. "I was going to introduce you to the man whom I got it from, but it sounds like he passed away last year. He was a real character. Owned a shop called NAKED ANTIQUES. Went around naked except for a little modesty cloth." She cupped where her balls would be. "Interesting guy. Kept a rooster as a pet in the store."

"Sounds like my kinda guy. Own drum, and all that."

"Yep. I really wanted you to meet him. Not really sure why, but I just always thought you would meet him someday."

"Well," Alice put her hand on her clearly fatigued friend's back. "I have a little part of him on my mantle at home. Sometimes the legacy of someone is even better than the real thing."

"I suppose so," Sal sighed. "Why don't we get on the road and back to the cool green of Oregon, huh? I'm looking forward to some of that really soft, misty rain. Not the kind that tries to flood you out and murder you."

Over the next two days the scenery changed from banana agave to creosote flats to sparse grassland leading into sagebrush. The treed mountains rose up from the sagebrush as they headed west toward the ocean in Northern California. They stopped in Weed for a minute to get a bite to eat. Sal said she was feeling better and didn't think she needed the pain pills anymore. But as they wore off, Alice could see the pain when Sal winced, sliding into the booth. A veil had been lifted and she sensed for the first time how close her friend had been to death. She held her hand across the table and the two held hands, garnering an unfriendly stare from the couple across the aisle with their cadre of redheaded children and overflowing waistlines.

"Maybe you should take the medication until we can get home and rest up properly," Alice said.

"Yeah. You're probably right."

They sat the rest of the lunch in silence, burdened by the weight of all the things they needed to say, the years of unspoken thoughts all shyly lingering in the dark until it was their turn to be spoken. Finally, Alice sighed.

"I guess I should just tell you that I'm pregnant."

Sal looked up expressionless.

"I'm not really sure what to do about it." Alice continued. "I mean. I'm still young."

"But the great thing is," Sal said cautiously, "you have a choice in the matter."

"You're right. And that makes this whole thing feel so much easier, to be honest."

"Was he at least charming and handsome?" Sal said, nudging a leaf of her salad across the plate.

"Both, unfortunately." Alice grimaced a little. "Reminded me a lot of you, to be honest. You don't have a little brother named Zev out there somewhere do you?"

"Not that I know of," Sal said. "But I wouldn't put it past Charles, king of free love, to have forgotten to tell me about one of his many progeny."

They kept holding hands and ignored the judgmental clucks and stares from provincial, closed-minded diners as they filed past. Alice paid the check and they settled back in the truck before getting back on the road. They drove a little while before passing a sign printed on the top of a metal barn roof on the side of road. YOU ARE ENTERING THE STATE OF JEFFERSON, it read. Underneath the sign a group of unhappy cows wandered around in a small, grassless pen reeking of manure. Sal switched the airflow on the dashboard to recycle the air already in the truck.

"I've heard of that movement. Whenever people think they can make money from the land," Sal sighed, "they'll find a way to justify their own madness."

"It's a big freak show, this country," Alice said. "Too many strange notions to find a consensus."

"It's why I'm mostly just friends with the birds. Honestly, they seem to have their act together more than we do," Sal said. Then she remembered who was driving. "And I'm friends, of course, with you."

"Well, some of my friends call me little bird," Alice smiled. She had been waiting to tell this to Sal for a long time.

"My big, little bird," Sal patted Alice's long leg, a shiver running up both their spines. An unearthly, loud noise, perhaps a hunter discharging a rifle on the side of the road, resounded in their bones. Both women's skin dotted with goose bumps despite the warm air blowing in from the vents. They looked at each other quizzically, raised their eyebrows, and let the feeling pass in and out of their bodies like a ghost.

"So, is the egg collection full?" Sal asked.

"Almost. There's just room for one more egg."

"Perfect," Sal said. "I know just the one."

"Perfect," Alice said, her hand resting gently on her abdomen. "Not all birds are meant to fly."

Sal and Alice both felt a certainty come over them that they were on exactly the right path, a sensation that had eluded both women for a long time. They drove the last six hours watching the land change and shift along the road as the tires rolled, heating with the tread of each mile. The light shifted and the sun hid and returned. As they rushed up into the lush Willamette Valley, greens swayed from the yellowed to the blued and back again in patches, in blankets of light and dark. Their minds wandered in and out of duty and consequence, family, and vice. Alice wanted a drink, but also enjoyed the feeling of depriving herself. It was time she took a good, long break from her habits, but she knew she needed help in doing so. Just sitting next to Sal filled her up with newness and possibility. Meanwhile, Sal felt the beating of her own heart in her ears and marveled at how everything still seemed to be working inside. In short glances she admired the curves on the jaw and cheek of the beautiful woman sitting next to her.

They pulled off the highway and stopped at a roadside turnout to look at a kettle of turkey vultures numbering in the hundreds overhead. The birds circled slowly and wobbly on their wings as though they might drop out of the sky at any moment. But still they hung and wobbled, the wind warm below them as they circled and circled looking for food.

"What would we do without the majestic vulture?" Sal remarked, her head tilted skyward.

"We'd be overrun by carrion," Alice said, her face lit up by the evening light. "Swimming in death."

"They are the arbiters of tender rot. Death isn't an end for those birds."

"Oh, it's definitely more of a beginning."

Once they got back in the car, questions still to be answered started to line up on both their lips, but waited to jump. They sat in silence as the truck rumbled back to life. The sun was setting and the vultures settled into the trees to roost with precision and speed, as though trusting the trees to catch their hefty bodies as they hurled their way toward the earth. Back on the highway, farmhouses, cities, and factories flew past. The two women drove by life upon life—human, animal, and plant— but could not possibly know what would become of every last one, as much as their difficult, scientific hearts might yearn to catalogue them all. The living world flew by in a rush of greens and browns—the hues of beginnings and ends. These things would live; these things would die. An intense, deep blue settled in the sky behind the dying light. As they moved north, there was an unspoken agreement that this movement they took together was that particular kind of migration that, while complicated by the buzz of uncertainty and danger, compelled a being to keep going, to stay in flight.

Acknowledgements:

I FEEL EXTRAORDINARILY LUCKY to have so many people who helped me in the process of writing this book. To every one who is listed here and to all the people who aren't but were involved in one way or another, a huge thank you for helping me take this journey one step at a time.

An enormous and emphatic thank you to Bill Clegg, my super agent, who, in the editing process, managed to maintain prodigious levels of intuition, acuity, insight, and humor. Without your eye for the details of structure and meaning, this book would not hum quite the same song.

To the incredible team at Rare Bird Books—Tyson Cornell, Julia Callahan, my editor, Andrew Hungate, and everyone else on the team, an enthusiastic and heart-felt thank you for everything you have done, the details of which are too many to enumerate without drastically altering the page count of this book.

And now to thank my family and friends, who together comprise a beautiful sea of love and support that I often feel overwhelmed by in the most wonderful way. To my mom, my first ever reader, who said, maybe this very, very, long short story should be a novel, honey; and to my dad, who I'm so thankful trickled down some of his humor and literary prowess through our DNA; and also to my sister, who I love dearly for being such a patient, loving ear. To Matthew Dickman, who has been a critical eye, a helpful hand, and a belly laugh along the way. To each and every one of the Tillinghasts. I'm so lucky to have married into such a wonderful, loving, and literary family.

To Melanie Nead, my brilliant studio mate, reader, and rosé-sipping friend, who workshopped our manuscripts and gazed out over the beautiful city lights of Portland with me. Without all your support and insights I might have just chucked the whole dang manuscript out onto the train tracks below our studio window.

A huge thank you to Lisa Mangum, my oldest and cherished friend, and Liza Rietz, Megan Kohl, Belle Chesler, more old and treasured friends, and Renee Jenkinson, Caroline Buchalter, and Julia Perry, who in our many ladies' nights and escapades together banded together to provide the most wonderful, supportive fabric of lady love along the way. You are my people, you believed in me, and I cherish you.

Thank you to my teachers. First, to Allyson Goldin for being one of the first to help me find and focus my passion for writing, to Maya Sonenberg, David Shields, David Bosworth, and Charles Johnson. Your gentle nipping at my grammar's heels, your stellar book recommendations and literary guidance all helped urge me toward finding my voice.

Thank you to the birds, who through their incredible feat of migration and breeding moved me to see beyond my own nose and write furiously in the bed of trucks, and in tents, inspired by the perseverance of such tiny, fragile creatures as you. And thank you to all the field biologist friends I worked with along the way. Your ways of seeing the world as a biological systems and beyond was truly inspiring.

Moon, thank you for shifting in me the tides of my mind and heart as I pieced together the mystery of human connectivity over the years.

Lastly, and most certainly not least, a thank you to my husband Andrew, who is my most beloved and treasured reader. You rescued my kayak when it flooded, bought me pens when I needed them, extracted cholla needles from my chest, and read my words and responded thoughtfully with that big, beautiful brain of yours.